KING OF HEARTS

Also by Susan Moody

Take-Out Double
Grand Slam

KING OF HEARTS

Susan Moody

HEADLINE

First published in Great Britain in 1995
by HEADLINE BOOK PUBLISHING

10 9 8 7 6 5 4 3 2 1

British Library Cataloguing in Publication Data

Moody, Susan
    King of Hearts
    I.   Title
    823.914 [F]

ISBN 0-7472-1160-4

Typeset by Keyboard Services, Luton, Beds

Printed and bound in Great Britain by
Mackays of Chatham PLC, Chatham, Kent

HEADLINE BOOK PUBLISHING
A division of Hodder Headline PLC
338 Euston Road
London NW1 3BH

--Dedication--
--still to--
--come--

1

Summer. Or so they'd have you believe. Official summer. Clocks gone forward, first cuckoos heard, baggy shorts and fishbelly legs already sighted in the supermarket. Nonetheless, this breakfast time, the sky was overcast and arctic winds howled in the rotting thatched roof of Honeysuckle Cottage. Beyond the front hedge, rain poured glumly into Back Lane, turning the unmade-up surface into swamp. Dressing-gowned and frumpish, Cassandra Swann looked out of the kitchen window and hankered to be elsewhere. In the damp heat of India, say, or on some tropic beach in the South seas. Though come to think of it ... As furious gusts of wind rattled rain against the cottage windows, it occurred to her that in actual fact she'd *hate* a tropic beach. All those lithe, tanned bodies, all that taut flesh on display. Besides, lying about in the sun was so ageing. And imagine the horror of having to stroll casually about with her stomach sucked in, pretending not to mind as hundreds of complete strangers tried to stop themselves throwing up at the sight of her hips encased in patterned Lycra. Opening the larder door, she removed the cake tin from one of the heavy slate shelves and stared into it with a mixture of dismay, astonishment and guilt. Two days ago it had contained a whole unwrapped Battenberg cake. Now, only a last thin slice remained. Which meant, did it not, that in the past forty-eight hours, someone had snuck into the larder and wolfed practically the entire thing?

No prizes for guessing who was responsible. Picking up the remaining slice, she wrapped it in a piece of paper towel and threw it virtuously into the garbage, on top of the dessicated remains of an *epiphyllum* which had finally cashed in its horticultural chips after hanging about for some weeks looking like a pot full of decaying apple parings. Such a dietary falling-off would never have happened if she hadn't been invited to two weddings later in the summer. Weddings meant frocks. Weddings meant diets. Weddings meant the bloody twins, neat as almonds, in miniature matching outfits, plus the carefully non-judgemental eyes of Rose, their elder sister, roaming the peaks and hollows of Cassie's figure. The peaks, mostly. Despite the fact that for an entire fortnight, Cassie had subsisted on powders out of packets and the occasional sliver of celery, there weren't too many hollows to be found. She looked again at the cake tin. Something must have snapped. The craving for carbohydrate had become too strong to control.

Dolefully, she put the kettle on and sat reading the papers over breakfast. There was an article about a woman who suffered from something called Sub-clinical Eating Disorder. '*Most nights I dreamed about food,*' she was quoted as saying. '*Most days, I thought of little else.*' Know the feeling, baby, Cassie thought. She reached for the second of the two cauliflower florets which, together with a carrot stick, made up her breakfast, and stumped upstairs to have a bath.

In fact, food was not the only thing occupying her mind. Business was definitely picking up. Once people heard about her existence, they seemed to feel that she could fulfil needs they had not until then been able to articulate.

At the moment, as well her established series of evening classes, she was currently considering offers from two other local authorities; a proposal that she join a cruise in the Indian Ocean as the bridge expert; a letter from the Headmaster of St Christopher's, a nearby private school, wondering if the two of them could work together for their mutual benefit, and three new hotels wanting her to set up Bridge Weekends in their establishments.

She got out of the bath and trailed into her bedroom to stand naked in front of the cheval glass which had once been her Gran's. This was not something she often did, and gazing at her reflection, she could see why. It seemed so unfair that while men had thighs like young oaks, women had cellulite. Not that Cassie did – be thankful for small mercies. While she was searching for signs of the missing Battenberg on her hips, the phone rang. Picking it up, she said: 'Cassandra Swann.'

'Hi, Cass,' replied an unknown voice. 'I'm Tony Farrar.'

'Who?'

'I write for the Bellington paper.'

'Have we met? I don't remember—'

'Not as far as I know,' Farrar said cheerfully.

In that case, Cassie wanted to say, where the hell do you get off calling me Cass? 'And how can I help you, Mr Farrar?' she said, frostily.

'I have this column in the *Bellington Times*,' explained Farrar, and I'd like to do an interview with you.'

'Column?'

'It's called "People & Places".'

Surveying the landscape or her body, its ridges and escarpments, its rounded contours, Cassie said: 'Which category am I?'

'Um ... I'm not quite sure what you – What we're

3

trying to do,' said Farrar, 'is highlight someone local each week, focus on anything unusual about them, anything out of the ordinary.'

'When you say "out of the ordinary" what exactly do you mean?'

'Anything, really, which will point up the fact that although we are a small community, we are, nonetheless an interesting and diverse one. Take yourself, for instance.'

'Yes,' Cassie said cautiously.

'You earn your living as a bridge player, don't you? That's unusual – not too many of *those* lying about on the ground, are there?' Farrar had a professional breeziness about him which Cassie could easily have done without, especially this early in the morning. 'You teach inside the local nick, too, and I understand that you'll soon be launching your own business.'

Cassie didn't want to be interviewed by the local paper, but it would be useful free publicity. She could mention her availability for bridge classes, explain that she was always ready for new ways to apply her particular brand of expertise, talk up the bridge supplies business which would be operating from the converted outbuildings in the garden – as soon as the builders pulled their collective fingers out and got moving. 'When do you want to come?'

'Would tomorrow morning be OK? I'm seeing some-one out your way at lunch-time, so it would suit me if you could fit me in.'

'How personal is this interview going to be? I mean, you're not going to ask me about the lurid details of my love life, are you, Mr Farrar?'

'Not unless you want to tell me, Cass.'

A new couple had joined the evening class. Indian,

possibly, or Pakistani. Cassie smiled at them warmly as they sat uncomfortably at the back of the room, wedged into the undersized seats provided by the Archbishop Cranmer Upper School.

'How nice to see new faces,' she said. 'Could you tell us your names?' and immediately felt like a patronising idiot. Of course they could – and undoubtedly would. 'I mean, we'd love to—'

'I am Dr Sammi Ray,' said the man, attempting to rise and finding himself wedged between seat and attached desk. 'We are new here.'

'Where are you living, Dr Ray?'

'We have bought a house at Larton Easewood,' Ray said. 'I have just taken up a three-year appointment as a consultant gynaecologist at the Bellington Memorial Hospital.' He beamed at Cassie. 'We very much wish to learn to play bridge.'

'Good,' said Cassie, beaming back. 'It's a—'

'For social reasons,' continued Dr Ray. His pure Oxford vowels were a quaint reminder of those vanished colonial days when God was still an Englishman. He gave a broad grin. 'We are anxious to mix with the right sort.'

With the exception of Charlie Quartermain, the rest of the class froze at this naïve statement. The English may live with the social system they have had nearly a thousand years of rampant snobbery to perfect, but they rarely refer to it. Even as a joke, which Cassie suspected this was meant to be.

'Well,' she said. Her voice had the false brightness of a kindergarten teacher with a particularly unruly group. 'Well, you've come to the right place. Bridge crosses all sorts of barriers and divisions. It appeals to all ages, all – uh – social groups – all occupations. I always think it's like

5

marriage: for better or worse, for richer or poorer, in sickness and in health, bridge is a game which remains...'
She moved into a routine she had used before, at the same time wondering how anyone would ever explain to Dr Ray that by the mere fact of saying, even, or perhaps especially, in that he wished to meet the right sort, he had almost irrevocably doomed himself to meeting either the wrong sort or no sort at all.

The class continued to keep its collective heads down, staring at the desks in front of them in order to avoid any involvement in Dr Ray's unseemly honesty.

Then Charlie, his huge haunches bulging over the edges of a seat designed for sixteen-year-old buttocks rather than middle-aged spread, shifted on his chair. 'Where're you from, mate?' he asked.

'We have just spent eight years in the United States,' Dr Ray said. 'At Johns Hopkins. But originally we are from Delhi.'

'Well, may I welcome you and your lovely lady to England,' said Charlie formally.

'Thank you, sir'

'Yes, indeed.' Cassie smiled again, thinking that if the new couple had been white-skinned rather than brown, she would not have felt obliged to make such ceremony. 'And we hope that you both very much enjoy your stay here.'

'Thank you,' Sammi Ray said again. He was in his late forties, good-looking, a little fleshy, his moustache showing the first signs of grey.

As the rest of the group, apart from Quartermain, sat without the slightest sign of welcome on their faces, Cassie found herself not only irritated but revolted. This island race, she thought, this bloody constipated island race. 'And your wife...?' she prompted.

'Dr Vida Ray,' Sammi said. His wife smiled vaguely at the room, then dropped her eyes again. She appeared to be some years younger than her husband, slim and elegant, with a stick-on heart-shaped mark in the middle of her forehead. She wore a long tunic of plain blue cotton over matching trousers, with a white scarf flung across one shoulder. Despite a severe pair of horn-rimmed spectacles, in the grey-painted shabbiness of the Archbishop Cranmer classroom, she was as exotic and out-of-place as a starfruit in a sack of potatoes.

Later, Cassie sat with Charlie Quartermain in the pub at Market Broughton, sipping a tomato juice. Not from choice, but because tomato juice was the most filling drink on offer. Each Thursday, she attempted to evade Quartermain's invitation to join him for a drink, and each Thursday she ended up with him at the Old Plough in front of the real log fire. Why? She was a strong woman of independent mind, wasn't she? And while she would not have said she disliked Charlie, she certainly did not want to spend any more time with him than was absolutely necessary. Yet week after week, that was what she did. Usually Kathryn Kurtz, her nearest neighbour, and Giles Laughton, local dairy farmer, joined them. But having become engaged within what, in retrospect, seemed a matter of seconds after meeting each other, they were both now in the States so that Giles could be introduced to Kathryn's family. Cassie would have to cope with Charlie alone. Not only did she find him irritating company, she was also oppressed by the fact that her irritation was based on nothing more worthy than an undemocratic shrinking, a completely snobbish fear, that people would assume they were a couple.

'I thought you were terrific this evening,' she said warmly.

'I'm always terrific, darlin'.'

Sure you are, Charlie, if what you're shopping for is a buffalo. 'All the others were so po-faced. You were the only one who tried to make the new couple feel welcome.' She swallowed tomato juice. 'What did you think of them?'

'Whorr!' said Charlie. 'She looks as though she'd go like a bunny.'

'For God's sake . . .'

'Notice how he spoke as if she didn't even exist?'

'I could hardly help it.'

'She's a sawbones too. Gawd. I'll take my trousers down any time she asks.'

'Why do you always have to come out with those stupid sexist—' Cassie could feel her mouth creasing up with distaste, just like Aunt Polly's. It was her worst nightmare that one morning she would look into the mirror and see her aunt's face looking back.

'Hasn't got a job yet, but she's hoping for a post at Oxford,' said Charlie. 'Or so she told me in the break.'

'And they're living just outside Larton Easewood?'

'On the edge of the village,' said Charlie. He burped, not discreetly. 'They bought the Old School House, apparently. I drove by there the other day: lovely window arches but they really need some work doing on them. Pollution's a real killer, far as that old stone's concerned.'

'I hope they get on all right.' But Cassie felt apprehensive. Small communities did not often welcome the incomprehensible. And she had a feeling that the Rays might find it difficult to fit into rural society.

Charlie went over to the bar and bought another pint and a double tomato juice. 'Why don't you have a proper drink, this time round?' he asked.

'Alcohol's full of empty calories, with absolutely no nutritional value.'

'Right. But it tastes bloody good.'

'Does it?' Cassie said, despondently. 'It's been so long, I've forgotten.'

'I don't know why you bother, girl. Gorgeous bird like you.'

Even coming from Charlie Quartermain, the words made Cassie feel better.

As she raised her second tomato juice to her mouth, Charlie nudged her hard. ''Ere, did I tell you I've decided to change the habits of a lifetime?'

'And do what? Stop breathing?' said Cassie crossly, mopping at the red stains on her skirt.

'Nah,' he said. He pulled on a cigar and blew out far more smoke than he could possibly have breathed in. 'Going to start betting on fast horses and slow women.'

Oh God. 'Why?' asked Cassie dutifully.

He grinned. 'Been doing it the wrong way round until now, haven't I?'

He waited for her laugh. In vain. Instead, Cassie made a Vicarage face. 'Have you?'

He dropped into pseudo-Runyonese. 'I'm layin' a C-note on a real dark horse doll, and I'm tellin' youse de guy's grandfather is no bum steer.' He began rasping out an approximation of the 'Fugue for Tin Horns', from *Guys And Dolls*, which had the other people in the Saloon Bar bewilderedly reaching for their cellular phones.

Cassie studied the contents of her glass, hoping that nobody she knew would come in. 'Charlie!' she hissed.

'Dontcha worry, doll.' The end of his cigar fell onto the top of his shirt and lodged near the place where a missing button revealed hairy flesh. 'Betting on the gee-gees is a mug's game. I only have a wager when it's something like the National, when it's anybody's guess who's going to make it to the finish. Are you having a bet?'

'I don't gamble,' Cassie said, prim as Mary Poppins.

'Oh, yuss? What about...?' He made card-dealing motions.

'Bridge? That's not gambling.'

'Don't you sometimes play for money?'

'Yes, but not *my* money.'

As so often with Charlie Quartermain, Cassie was aware of being on shaky moral ground. After all, what was she but a bridge player and, at its lowest level, what was bridge but a game of chance? Skill came into it, of course it did, but even the cleverest bridge player was only as good as the cards allowed her to be. And even if someone else put up the stake, wasn't it a gamble of sorts? Sensing that if she were to argue this out to its logical conclusion, she would be forced to concede that Charlie was right, she asked quickly: 'So who are you going to back on Saturday?'

'Thought about Any Old Iron, who's down at 66–1,' Charlie said. 'But then this mate of mine bells me from Ireland, so I decides the gods is trying to tell me something.'

'Why would you think that?'

'Don't you know anything, girl?'

'Not about racing.'

'So you don't know who's running in the National?'

'Uh...' A name popped into Cassie's head. 'Red Rum?' Her dad and Gran often used to have a flutter on the horses, but after the move to the Vicarage, there hadn't been much reading of the sports pages, though Uncle Sam followed the cricket and even turned out on occasion for the village team.

'Leave it out,' Charlie said. A great rumbling laugh began to billow somewhere under his shirt and the wedge of cigar ash started rolling slowly down the massive curve of a belly which even Nicely Nicely Johnson might have disowned. 'Red bleedin' Rum? Blimey, he's having trouble finding his nosebag these days, let alone legging it to the finishing post.'

'What's this got to do with your friend from Ireland?' Cassie said repressively, as half the ash hit the floor and the other half landed in Charlie's drink, to spread itself palely across the surface of his beer before drifting to the bottom of the glass.

'My mate lives in Londonderry, see. Got a little business out there. I reckon it must have been a bit of celestial intervention, him calling me like that out of the blue, so I stuck a pony on Derry Boy.'

'Is he the favourite or something?'

'Gawd, no. Derry Boy's a no-hoper, down at 66–1.'

'A pony means fifty pounds, doesn't it?'

'Twenty-five, darlin'.'

'What's the point of betting on a no-hoper?'

'It's anybody's race, isn't it?' Quartermain said. 'Especially with the weather we've been having. The grounds be like treacle and the forecast for the weekend said there're going be snow showers. Under conditions like that, ninety per cent of the runners probably won't even make it once round the course. Matter of fact, I wouldn't be surprised if they called the whole thing off.'

'You seem to know a lot about racing.'

'I used to work Saturdays as a bookie's bagman – I was always a big chap, even in those days – used to go to all the race meetings. I was still serving my time as an apprentice mason then, needed the cash.'

Cassie nodded, covertly eyeing her watch. How much

longer would she have to stay before she could suggest leaving without seeming overly impolite? Another tomato juice, at least. Oh, Lord. She tried not to sigh.

'And how long have you been earning a living by playing bridge?' Farrar said. He spoke in the direction of a small tape recorder which sat on a low table between Cassie and himself.

'Nearly six years.'

'What prompted you to leave a – um – more orthodox career in teaching?' Farrar wore baggy chinos, the kind of boating shoes which have leather laces all round the rim, and a pair of outsize spectacles with red plastic frames. There was a wedding ring on his left hand.

Cassie chewed her lower lip, considering this. Which reason would sound the least insulting, were there to be a stampede of her former pupils or colleagues for copies of the paper? The fact that her fellow members of staff at the exclusive girls' school where she taught biology had been without exception the most cynical, boring, bitter group of people she had ever come across? Her fear that she too, might end up with the same cramped aspirations, the same joyless perspectives? The daily challenge of spending most of her time with young women who could scarcely have mustered a decent boob between them, let alone a pair? The pervasive cling of alien smells, from formaldehyde to armpits? Her inability to maintain life in even the hardiest of houseplants? The—

'I wanted to work for myself,' she said, 'rather than for someone else.'

'Wouldn't it be true to say that you've chosen a precarious way to earn a living?'

'Yes.'

Farrar waited, as though expecting her to add to this.

When she did not, he raised his eyebrows, leaned forward, clicked off the recorder and said: 'Would you care to elaborate on that?'

'A simple affirmative says it all,' said Cassie. 'What more can I add?'

He sighed, as though she were being obstructive, and clicked on the recorder again. 'You told me earlier that you teach bridge, as well as play it. I believe you've actually taught inside Her Majesty's Prison at Bellington.'

'Yes.' She would have left it at that, but seeing his face, added: 'Two ten-week sessions during the academic year. I start again in September – if there haven't been more cutbacks in the educational department by then.'

'Apart from the nick, is there a lot of call round here for bridge lessons?'

'A reasonable amount, yes. Bridge is one of those democratic games which cross class barriers and social divisions, which appeal to all ages, which need a challenging amount of concentration without requiring a university degree. It's the mixture of skill and chance which make it such an enjoyable and fascinating game and since I would rather play bridge than do anything else in the world –' she thought of Paul Walsh and faltered slightly, '– *almost* anything else in the world, I've never for a single moment regretted giving up the security of a teaching job to branch out on my own. I always think it's like marriage –' Smoothly, she completed her spiel and then smiled at Farrar. 'How many people are lucky enough to be paid for doing what they like best?'

'And presumably paid reasonably well,' Farrar said. 'You're obviously not starving.'

Was that a sizeist comment or what? 'How do you mean?' she said coldly. Think Big, she told herself. Think

Beautiful. If this creep with his Buddy Holly specs and dirty fingernails thought he could get away with veiled insults – though this one was not so much veiled as full-frontal—

'. . . pretty cottage close to the county borders,' he was saying. 'You run a car, building works going on, obviously you're managing to make a living wage . . .'

Perhaps she was being overly sensitive. 'The cottage is rented,' she said. 'The car's an old banger, and the building works are largely financed by a grant from the local council. Apart from that, yes, I just about make ends meet, most of the time. But then I didn't go into it in order to get rich.' Again she smiled, at the same time thinking of tomorrow night when Paul Walsh was taking her out to dinner and coming back here afterwards.

As though reading her thoughts, he dropped his voice. 'You mentioned earlier that you had a lurid sex life, Miss Swann.'

'I most certainly did not.'

'Would you care to elaborate for our readers? Leather gear, crotchless panties, that sort of thing, is it?'

'*What* did you say?'

Farrar leaned forward and switched off his recorder.

'Just kidding,' he said, with a grin. 'I like winding people up.'

'You want to watch that. Could get you into trouble.'

'No, seriously, I'm not a bit interested in your sex life.' He put his head on one side and looked at her over the tops of his specs. Dead boyish. 'Should I be?'

'Ever heard of the clip-and-flip syndrome?'

'Uh . . .'

'Remember Lorena Bobbitt.' Cassie rose. 'I assume you'll send me a proof of your article before you print it, just so I can correct any glaring errors.'

'I don't make errors.'

'Even God made errors, Mr Farrar.' She didn't add that she was looking right at one. 'Since bridge is the way I earn my living, I can't afford to have mistakes made about me and my – if you can call it that – profession. So before you came, I took the trouble to read one of your columns. It contained at least four inaccuracies.'

He blushed slightly, his grubby fingers pulling at the long cotton scarf knotted trendily around his neck. 'Was that the one on Jennifer Daubeny? Yeah, I admit I got a bit carried away there.'

'As a matter of fact, it was the one about some man who'd just come back from working as an ecologist in the Brazilian jungle.'

He frowned. 'Mmmm. Yeah. Take your point. OK, I'll let you have a proof.'

'Good.'

2

Cassie spent Saturday morning curled up in bed, reading a book which someone had once left in her car. As crime stories went, *Killing Me Softly* wasn't bad, but she had read better. At lunch-time she got up, thinking she would do some work on her vegetable garden, but by mid-afternoon, the weather had worsened so she put on the television set instead. God: whoever was responsible for the English summer should be publicly burned at the stake. Although she seldom watched daytime TV, in view of the fact that it was Grand National Day and that Charlie Quartermain had placed a bet on Derry Boy – a pony on a pony, as he had said at least three times last Thursday evening – she decided, for want of anything better to do, to watch the big race at three-fifty. Ten minutes to four. Tea-time.

In the sitting-room, a plummy voice discussed the state of the Aintree course and the possibility of the race being disrupted by animal rights protesters. Cassie made a pot of tea, put it on the tray along with a cup and saucer and added the milk jug. Goodness, how bare it looked. How inhospitable. How unfriendly. She carried the tray in from the kitchen and set it down on a table in front of the hearth. The TV voice was going through the betting on the runners: the odds on Charlie Quartermain's outsider, Derry Boy, had lengthened and it now stood at 100–1.

In the event, although snow had fallen on the hills some ten miles from the course, the race had not been cancelled. Pouring tea, Cassie watched as, on the television screen, horses milled about in a purposeful way, being shown the first jump by their riders, walking in tightly nervous circles, while the commentator spoke of blinkers and girths, weights and colours. A man in a brown trilby said something unintelligible to a man in a flat tweed cap. Another man in a British Warm climbed some steps and looked at his watch, horses danced delicately behind a tape, a red flag was waved and then suddenly, they were off.

'And it's Any Old Iron the first to show, followed by Duty Free and, on the inside, Prince Charming,' droned the commentator. 'Behind them come Baby Blue and The Chancer with ... blah blah ... And as they come up to the first fence, let me hand you over to ...'

'... Duty Free travelling well with Gay Cavalier – in second and Captain Hook behind him, My Way has fallen, Haven't A Clue is down, and as they thunder towards the fifth, it's ... blah...'

'... Becher's Brook ... Captain Hook has unseated his rider and who's that? It looks like, yes it's The Chancer, down at Valentine's ... blah blah ... but now back to...'

The voices carried smoothly over from each other, like a well-organised relay race, while a lot of small men were carried at high speed on the backs of horses who either negotiated or failed to negotiate various obstacles placed in their way. Cassie drank her tea, trying not to imagine how much nicer it would have been with a slice, a single slice, of Battenberg cake. She struggled with herself. If a slut was a woman who went to the laundry basket and found the cleanest dirty bra, what did you call a woman

who fished cake out of the trash? Especially cake which
had been in the trash for a day and a half.

It was an unequal contest and one she knew she was
bound to lose even before she began. Jacob didn't have
nearly as hard a time wrestling with the Angel as Cassie
Swann did with herself. In the end, beaten vanquished,
she was about to head for the swing bin when something
caught her attention.

'...it's Derry Boy at the Chair, followed by Gay
Cavalier and now coming up on the inside is Handsome
Harry, and as they head into the second circuit Handsome
Harry is edging up on Gay Cavalier and now...'

Cassie sat up. Handsome Harry? Her face felt hot.
Unlike Charlie Quartermain, she did not believe that the
gods passed on racing tips via telephone calls from Ulster.
Nonetheless, if not a tip, this was surely at least a hint, a
nod, a nudge. Feeling her heart bump, she reached for the
morning's paper and found the list of runners – in the
three-fifty at Aintree. Handsome Harry III, she saw, was
priced at 100–1, owned and trained by someone called B.
Fraser.

If this was a divine whisper of some sort, what exactly
was it trying to tell her?

She got up and went over to the escritoire which stood
between the two deep-set windows. Beyond them, the
garden swayed like an evangelical choir, first this way and
then that. Rain battered the rusty concrete mixer which
stood beside the stone outbuildings half-way down one
side. From one of the cluttered pigeon-holes of the desk,
she collected a handful of photographs and sorted through
them until she found the one she was looking for. It
showed a man wearing a grey topper and morning dress, a
good-looking man with binoculars hanging from his
neck., his arm around the shoulders of a woman in a

black-and-white spotted dress. Her features were hidden
for the most part beneath the brim of a big straw hat, the
crown sheathed in a matching scarf. Although Cassie
knew that the woman was not her mother, the man was
definitely her father, Harry Swann. Handsome Harry
Swann.

'... and now it's Handsome Harry travelling well,
ahead of Derry Boy and Duty Free as they come towards
the last fence,' shrieked the course commentator. Rain
was slanting across the camera lens as the horses galloped
down the course, divots of turf flying from their heels.
'Handsome Harry neck and neck with Derry Boy, with
Duty Free keeping with them as they turn into the home
straight, and it's Derry Boy from Handsome Harry, with
Gay Cavalier half a neck behind and it's – at the elbow,
Derry Boy has broken through, Derry Boy has taken the
lead, Derry Boy with Gay Cavalier behind him and
Handsome Harry half a length behind – it's Derry Boy,
Derry Boy has won the Grand National with Gay
Cavalier second and Handsome Harry in third place, and
it's back to Gerry in the...'

Microphones were being thrust into faces as owners
and trainers, even jockeys, were asked for their views.
The owner of the winning horse, a former television
personality renowned for having done something fairly
unsavoury with a gerbil, spoke at jubilant length, punching the air from time to time and flashing yards of
expensive teeth. Cassie waited. The owner of the second
horse, a smooth-faced Saudi princeling, was interviewed
and talked in impeccable Etonian English about all the
people who had made today's triumph possible. Finally,
the owner and trainer of Handsome Harry III stood in
front of the mike.

'Brigid Fraser, owner and trainer of the third place in

this year's historic race,' the man from the TV said, in case Ms Fraser hadn't yet cottoned on. He turned and confided to the six-million-strong audience: 'Handsome Harry III was bought as a two-year-old, on a...' he turned back to the owner, '...no more than a whim, wasn't it?'

'More or less.'

'Just liked the cut of his jib, did you?'

'Yes.' Ms Fraser was evidently a woman of few words, all of them terse.

'And how do you feel about your horse this afternoon?'

'How would you feel?'

The TV interviewer opened his mouth and clutched at his brown trilby. Uh...'

Ms Fraser relented. 'Always knew he had it in him,' she said. 'Plucky old chap ... just kept going ... jumped brilliantly ... more than satisfied...'

She was wearing a caped riding man and a green tam-o'-shanter pulled jauntily to one side. It was obvious that if she no longer was, then at some time she had been, something of a beauty. In spite of her unflattering garments, her boyish figure and slim hips were just beginning to raise a fermenting envy in Cassie's buxom breast when the telephone rang.

'Why don't I take you out to dinner tonight, darlin?' A wheezy voice asked.

'That's very kind of you, Charles,' said Cassie. 'But—'

'It's you or some other lucky lady, and I'd much rather it was you. I want to celebrate.'

'Your horse just won, didn't it?' Cassie said, deflectively.

'Yuss. Earned me a nice heap of sovs. What a little star,' Quartermain said. 'Did you see the way he sailed over that loose horse? Did you see the way he took the nineteenth?'

'I did indeed.' Cassie was abstracted, staring at the screen where Ms Fraser's green tam-o'-shanter could still be seen among a bunch of waxed jackets and flat tweed caps, and the occasional grey of morning dress.

'So much for playing your hunches, eh? Was I right or was I right?'

'I hadn't realised it was a hunch,' said Cassie. 'I thought you'd been given a tip straight from the gods.'

'In a manner of—'

'So, instead of taking women out to dinner, shouldn't you be showing your gratitude with a large donation to the charity of your choice?'

'Listen, darling the charity of my choice is called Charlie Quartermain's pension fund,' Charlie said. 'So how about it tonight?'

'I can't.' In spite of herself, Cassie felt compelled to add: 'Truly.'

'Why not?'

Repressing the annoyance this question engendered – what, after all, did her comings and goings have to do with Charles Quartermain, master mason, master slob? – Cassie said: 'Because I'm going out.'

There was a moment's silence. Then Quartermain said quietly: 'I won't wait for ever, Cass.'

'Charles, I never asked you to join the queue.'

'It's that policeman friend of yours, isn't it?'

'Who the hell do you think you are, my mother?'

'Just asking.'

'I'm glad you won,' Cassie said coldly. 'Now, if you'll excuse me...'

'When are you going out?'

'That's my business.'

'If I can't take you out for dinner, could I drop in for a cuppa? I'm not far from your place.'

Cassie sighed heavily. This was the point at which, were she a fully paid-up member of the Society for the Advancement of Feisty Independent Women she would tell him to bug off. Unfortunately, she had mislaid her subscription form. 'All right, come,' she grudged. 'But you can't stay long. I've got to—'

The phone was slammed down.

Perhaps ninety seconds later, someone knocked at the front door. Knocked was something of an understatement. Pounded would be more accurate. Thwacked. With some kind of offensive weapon. When Cassie wrenched the door open, Charlie Quartermain stood outside, a large umbrella in one hand, a wired and gold-topped bottle in the other.

'What on earth do you think you're doing?' she screeched, aware of unflattering shrewishness. 'This door's been here for centuries and you're trying to break it down in—'

'Gotta mate with a door shop,' Charlie said. 'Says these centuries-old jobs are harder than welded steel. Look...' He peered at the carved oak, '...Not a mark on it.'

'How did you get here so quickly?'

'I was watching on the portable. Got the motor down the lane.'

'You should have come in and—' The sentence drooped as Cassie recognised that had Charlie Quartermain turned up demanding to watch the race with her, she would have given him short shrift.

With a faint smile on his big face, he watched her recognising. Waving the bottle of champagne at her, he handed her the umbrella and shouldered his way into the sitting-room while she stood aside, feeling mean.

Sometimes her conscience smote her about Charlie. Why did she find him so difficult to come to terms with? He was kind. He was generous. He was an achiever. He repeatedly told her that he thought her beautiful. Even, that he loved her. He ought to have been the sort of man any sane mother would want for her daughter. Or, in Cassie's case, any aunt for her niece. But he wasn't. As far as Cassandra Swann was concerned, Charlie Quartermain, gross, unbuttoned, sphenisciform, might be St Francis of Assisi and the Angel Gabriel rolled into one, with a touch of Paul Newman on the one hand and a dollop of Socrates on the other, but that still wouldn't make up for the fact that basically she just didn't fancy him, simply could not imagine the circumstances in which she would ever share a bed with him. As for making love with him – oh, *please*...

There was also the added inconvenience of the fact that she was under some kind of moral obligation to him since, only a few weeks ago, he had undoubtedly saved her life.

'Glasses, woman!' Charlie suddenly roared. At the sound of his voice, the drooping spider plant on the mantelpiece jerked visibly, as though undergoing some vegetative form of ECT. Chlorophyll rushed into its etiolated leaves.

Cassie stopped. '*What* did you say?' She was prepared to take an in-your-face stand on this one. Woman, indeed. Her moment of complicated self-aversion evaporated like breath on a windowpane. 'Anyway, I've told you several times that I don't really like drinking at this time of—'

'I do. Get the glasses, girl: I want to celebrate.'

He stared at the television screen, where Ms Fraser in her green tammy was leading a blanket-covered horse towards the camera and grinning like a slice of Edam.

'Gawd,' he said. 'Old Biddy Fraser 's still a stunner, isn't she?'

'Do you know her, then?' The breadth of Quartermain's acquaintance never ceased to astonish Cassie.

'Did some restoration work for them, when I first started out on me own, for her and her hubby. The two of 'em was just setting up as trainers.' He shook his huge head. 'Doing all right, and then out of the blue, hubby did a runner. Word was, there were some dodgy goings on, but I don't think anything was ever proved.'

'What sort of goings on?'

'Doping, fixing that sort of thing.'

'Was the running connected to the dodginess?'

'You'd think so, wouldn't you? Someone probably got on to him, threatened to call in the Old Bill if he didn't cease and desist. After that I used to see her at the races from time to time – nobody ever thought she'd make a go of it without him around, but she carried on and now here she is, actually placed in the National.' He spoke as though Ms Fraser had personally leaped Becher's, Valentine's, the Canal Turn.

'Only because everyone else fell over or fell off.'

'Are you bringing those glasses or what?'

Forget in-your-face. Exhaling obtrusively, Cassie found a couple of glasses and gave them to him. It was easier, really. From experience, she knew that however hard she protested, she would end up sipping the best possible champagne – Roederer Cristal today – and drinking to his success in the National.

'I was thinking of the Wheatsheaf,' Charlie said, as he poured his third glass. The first two had gone down his enormous throat with, as he put it, no pain.

'What for?' The Wheatsheaf was one of the best restaurants for miles around.

'Tonight. Seemed the most fitting place to take you.'

Cassie ignored this. 'What else did you do besides work for a bookie?' she asked, making conversation. It was a fair old certainty that there'd been other disreputable jobs. Sometimes she even wondered if he'd been inside.

'I was in the merchant navy for a time,' Charlie said. 'Started out as cabin boy on some old rust-bucket, worked me way down to ship's cat.' He roared with laughter at this jest. He roared alone.

'Really?' said Cassie.

'Would've made captain, eventually, if I hadn't blotted my copybook.'

'And how did you do that?'

'It's a bit too dirty for your shell-likes, darlin'.'

'I've been around; try me.'

'What goes around, comes around,' Charlie said, enigmatically. 'Matter of fact, that's where *I* screwed up. So I came out of the service and took up wrestling for a couple of years.'

'Wrestling?'

'Yer.'

'Did you wear one of those one-piece men's bathing-suit things?'

'Mine was silver lamé,' said Charlie. He did not appear to be joking.

'Sounds tasteful.'

'I was known on the circuit as Quicksilver Quartermain, the Kid Who Never Quits. The outfit went with the name.'

The knowledge that he had once gone round with a silver lamé bathing-suit covering his huge belly rendered out of the question the already remote possibility that Cassie might one day be insane enough to take him to the

Vicarage to meet Aunt Polly. ('A *wrestler*, Cassandra? Is this some kind of cruel joke?')

Cassie knew that Quartermain had gone to an inner-city secondary mod and escaped at the earliest possible moment. He spoke with an accent which made Cassie wince, and which would have brought on terminal attack of class consciousness in Aunt Polly, yet sometimes she wondered why it was that a non-BBC voice and a lack of basic academic qualifications were enough to wipe out all Charlie's good points. For a more admirable woman than herself, they would not, of course. Why was she not strong, determined, independent-minded enough to look beyond such middle-class irrelevancies and value the man for what he was, instead of despising him for what he was not?

Rather than dwell on her own shortcomings in this particular field, she said: 'Tell me more about Brigid Fraser.'

He adopted the kind of loutish grin which instantly answered her question about why he was so intolerable and made her long to push his appalling dental work straight down his throat. 'Bit of a goer,' he said. 'Know what I mean?'

'I'm going to pretend that I don't,' Cassie said. Icicles of disapproval hung from every syllable. 'Where did she – uh ...' she coughed, suddenly sure that he would know exactly why she was asking, '...Uh ... get the name Handsome Harry?'

'The Third,' Charlie corrected. 'Dunno, luv. When I knew her, she owned a nag called Handsome Harry the Second. Perhaps this is his son. Never knew the first one though.'

On impulse, Cassie showed him the photograph of her father. 'Is that Brigid Fraser?'

27

'Why do you want to know?' he asked.

'Is it her, or isn't it?' she said, turning away from him.

He looked down at the black-and-white square. Between his fingers, it seemed the size of a postage stamp. 'Bit hard to tell,' he said. 'With her face hidden like that under her hat.' He was about to hand the photograph back when he stopped. 'Hang about. Got a glass?'

'There's one on the table beside you.'

'A magnifying glass, I meant.'

'Oh.' Cassie got up and searched through the escritoire again. She was pretty sure that in one of the drawers there was a heavy old thing through which Robin's nanny, long deceased, used to read the daily paper ... yes, here it was. She gave it to Charlie. With far more stertorous breathing than could possibly have been necessary, he focused it on the photograph. 'Thought so,' he said triumphantly. 'See this?'

She went over to stand beside him. 'What?'

'The dots on her dress?'

Cassie stared. Under magnification, the dots were no longer dots but something else. 'Don't. Do. That.' she said, through gritted teeth, grabbing the udder-like hand which he had just placed on her left buttock.

'Sorry, darling Can't help myself round you. Face like an angel. Bum like one, too.'

'Angels don't have bums. And if they did, God would have a word or two to say to anyone who attempted to touch them.'

'Don't fancy a quick nip upstairs, do you?'

'Charlie, I'd rather stick needles in my eyes.'

'Playing hard to get, are you?' He leered.

Cassie squinted down at the elongated dots of the dress. 'What am I supposed to be looking at?'

'See those dots?'

28

'What are they?'

'I'll tell you exactly what they are, darlin'.' Charlie said. He moved away from her. 'They're horse's heads. Tiny little buggers, navy blue. She always wears it on racing days. Told me once she was wearing it the day of her first major win – and she's got that good-luck charm round her neck.' He looked once again at the photograph. 'Yer. I'd say that's Biddy, all right.'

'Ah.'

'Who's the bloke with her?'

Cassie didn't answer. Couldn't.

Quartermain put his hand gently on Cassie's jaw and turned her face up to his. There was a softened look about him which ordinarily would have caused her to snatch the photograph away from him and say something acid. But for the moment, she felt too stricken to move. 'someone you know, girl?'

Cassie swallowed, throat dry, stomach churning. 'My father, actually.'

'And where does he hang out when he's not at the races?'

'He's dead,' said Cassie, with difficulty. 'Murdered. He was called Harry Swann. Handsome Harry Swann.'

3

'My socks,' Robin said.

'What?'

'My socks. My Leander socks.' There was a silence which Cassie, having located the clock on the table beside her bed and registered that it was six forty-eight on a Sunday morning, did not try to fill. 'For Henley.'

'Zzzz.'

'Cassie?'

'Mmm?'

'Have I woken you up?'

'Not yet.'

Robin blew out a gusty breath of exasperation. 'Really!'

'Do you know what time it is?' demanded Cassie.

'I like to get up early.'

'That doesn't mean *I* bloody have to. Besides you're an hour ahead or something over there.' If he had not been ringing her from France, Cassie would have replaced the receiver and tried to catch another couple of hours of sleep. Pain clung batlike to the underside of her skull: after a boozy evening the night before, she and Paul Walsh had not returned to the cottage until well after midnight and once in bed ... well, sleep had not been uppermost in their minds.

'Oh fie, we *are* in a pet, aren't we?'

31

'It's Sunday, for God's sake,' said Cassie. 'Normal people don't ring up other people this early on Sunday.'

'My dear, normality is something I've spent a lifetime striving strenuously to avoid.'

Cassie's head throbbed. She was alone in the bed, except for a note on the other pillow with three letters scrawled on it. Four, if you counted the Xes. 'What *about* your bloody socks, anyway?'

'Language, Cassandra. Surely your Aunt Polly brought you up better than that.'

'Bugger my Aunt Polly.'

'What a truly terrifying thought.'

'Anyway, she didn't bring me up, my father did. The damage had already been done by the time I was moved to the Vicarage.'

Robin dropped the campness. 'I know, my dear. Believe me, I know.' Both of them were silent for a few expensive trans-Manche seconds. Then he said briskly: 'My socks: did you find them?'

'No.'

'Did you look?'

'No.'

'Honestly, Cassandra. I asked you about this weeks ago I'd have thought you could have taken a few minutes to—'

'Robin, this may come as something of a surprise to you, but a pair of lobster-coloured socks has not actually figured very high on my recent agenda. I mean, people have been *murdered*, for heaven's sake. People have been attacked. Me, I'm talking about. *Me*.'

Just thinking about it brought Cassie out in a sweat of retrospective fear – even though it was some weeks since the hired killer had beaten her as she came home from a party at Kathryn's cottage.

'Yes,' said Robin. 'I'm sorry. I'd temporarily forgotten about poor Portia Wickham.'

'Not to mention poor Cassandra Swann.'

'Absolutely dreadful for you, I'm sure. But if you do come across those socks, you will let me know, won't you? Otherwise it'll mean ordering a new pair and with the postal service the way it is these—'

This time Cassie did replace the receiver in its cradle. She loved Robin, mainly for himself but also because he had loved Sarah, her long-dead mother. Sometimes it was hard to remember either reason.

She squinted at Walsh's note. It wasn't the first time he'd left it. TBJ, it said – the bloody job. And three Xes underneath. She smiled. Falling in love with a policeman still seemed such an unlikely thing for her to have done. Last night, under the restaurant table, when his foot pressed itself urgently into the space between her thighs, she had thought how amazing, how miraculous, it was that though their relationship was still budding, already the slender bones of his feet were as familiar as her own. Love, she had thought. How it galvanised, how it exhilarated. She had looked across at him and remembered the last time his mouth had touched hers; remembered too, although it would not happen until later, how he would come home with her when they had finished eating, would close her front door behind the two of them, would take her hand and lead her up the steep cottage stairs to her bedroom.

'Paul,' she murmured into his pillow, loving the sound of his name. 'Oh, Paul.'

Next time she awoke, she could see through the gap in the curtains the beginnings of an irritatingly indeterminate summer day. Mostly overcast so that sitting in the garden was not going to be an option, but with intermittent bursts of sunshine so that neither was snuggling up in front of a blazing fire and pigging out on crumpets.

Not that that was an option. Not with those weddings coming up.

The bat-claws of hangover were still hooked to the inside of her head. Never one to recoil from the sound of popping corks, Cassie suspected that she had probably somewhat overdone it last night. But then Walsh had been in ebullient mood.

'We had a sweepstake at the shop,' he said, 'and I drew Derry Boy.' He had smiled at her. 'I wonder what the third thing'll be?'

'How do you mean?'

'Three times lucky, isn't that what they say?'

'Not quite.' Cassie had squeezed her thighs together. 'Third time lucky is what they say, meaning that the first two times, you didn't quite make it.'

'I made it, all right. First, meeting you. Then drawing Derry Boy. Fortunes never come singly, so what's next for me?' He raised his glass < to her. 'For us.'

'Troubles,' Cassie had said. 'It's *troubles* that never come singly.'

Now, she lay in bed and thought about a man and a horse. Both of them called Handsome Harry. Twenty years ago, Harry Swann had intervened in a street brawl on the pavement outside his pub, and been stabbed to death. , No one had ever been charged with his murder and for years, Cassie had blocked it out, tried to pretend it had never happened. Recently, however, she had realised that however painful it might be, she owed it to the big, laughing man she increasingly could not remember, to look more closely at what had occurred that night.

34

Having made the decision, she had allowed other things to dominate her life, chief among them, her love affair with Detective Sergeant Paul Walsh.

No longer. Something must definitely be done.

Quartermain was right and the woman in the photograph with her father was indeed Brigid Fraser, was he the original Handsome Harry? If so, what was his relationship with her? Had they been having an affair? Did breeders name horses after their lovers? She thought again of the coincidence of a horse called Handsome Harry running on almost the only afternoon in the entire racing calendar that she happened to be watching. She thought of Charlie Quartermain's belief in a tip from the gods. If the heavenly turf accountants offered you such a sure thing, could you afford not to bet on it? *Should* you?

Tomorrow was Monday. She had better go up to London and start placing her wager.

Outside the Highbury & Islington tube station, traffic circled endlessly round Highbury Corner. Cassie stood on the pavement and watched it swirl. Rain fell from a dreary sky. Some of the lamp-posts, not sure whether it was night or day, glowed an intermittent orange. She drew in lethal lungfuls of the carcinogenic air; it'd be more fun to flirt with Walsh than with death, but Walsh wasn't there. This was familiar territory to her. She had spent the first thirteen years of her life more or less round the corner from here, gone to school just down the road. Coming back, she realised, as she had only a few weeks earlier, was never going to be easy. Any more than it was easy to return to Uncle Sam's house, to which, thirteen, awkward, plump and grieving she had been transplanted after Gran's death. After the warmth, the loving safety of the rooms above Harry Swann's pub, nothing could have been less congenial than the Vicarage. Except its tiny female inhabitants.

Cassie did not want to remember the indignities of those years before she was able to get away to university. She had been made to feel guilty about her own exuberant bloom and swell while her cousins cautiously produced pubic hair, anorexic bosoms, hips you could grate carrots on. It wasn't so much the physical differences between them and her which wounded, it was the implication of their superiority, that because they weighed less than she did, they were more worthy people. And thinking this, she wondered if some of her antipathy to Charlie Quartermain rested on the fact that until she moved to the Vicarage, she had spoken with exactly the same unruly vowels and glottalled consonants as he did.

This was not stuff she had come here to think about. Behind her, two girls in carefully ripped denim began a foulmouthed conversation about their boyfriends, larded with the crudest of obscenities. The F-word. The C-word. The C-Word. Words Cassie didn't even know. Neither of them was older than eleven. On a rush of diesel fumes, Cassie made her way to the public library. In the reference section, she found three Asian students poring over economics texts, an unkempt man who smelled of stale beer asleep on the *Financial Times* and a librarian reading a copy of *The Shining*. Stephen King might not have liked the evident relief with which she put it down when Cassie asked about the microfiche.

'How far back do you want to go?' she asked.

All the way, Cassie wanted to say. Back to before my mother died, before things started to go wrong. She explained what she was after.

'You might be lucky,' the librarian said doubtfully.

'Most of our records cover that length of time, but not much more.'

'I'll have a look, shall I?'

Seated in front of the microfiche gadget, Cassie told herself that at this distance in time it could hardly matter about the circumstances in which her father had died. The past was alien territory, over and done with. Nothing could change what had happened; what was the point in digging it all up? Yet vividly she remembered the last time she was here. Making what she hoped were discreet enquiries in her father's pub, she had spoken to two of the clientele – Old Ruby and her friend Bert – who had actually been around at the time, and both had grown distinctly twitchy at the possibility of someone looking into past events Cassie wanted to know why. Was there more to her father's death than she had been told?

As her eyes flicked through the jerking sheets of microfilm, she wondered again how she could have let so many questions remain unasked for so long about what was the major event of her life. The most traumatic. The most seminal. Dad, dead. Blood on the road outside the pub, pale faces of policemen, an arm on her shoulders, a quick sympathetic touch from people she did not know: men in work clothes or women with children and shopping in their hands. And the awful, awful sound of Gran's phlegmy sobs behind the closed door of her bedroom – the first time in her life that Cassie had known she would not be welcomed if she knocked.

If it had not been for the coincidence of meeting someone – an inmate at HMP Bellington – who had been in the pub the very night of her father's murder, would she have left the memories undisturbed? Or was it inevitable that one day, sooner or later, those semi-obliterated recollections would rise to the surface of her mind and demand that she examine them? Would the gods have gone on nudging her as they had nudged on Saturday, until eventually she had no choice?

The film jerked, and there it was. A headline, big letters fuzzy on celluloid newsprint. Death of Local Publican. The landlord of the Boilermakers' Arms in the Holloway Road, knifed as he tried to intervene in a street disturbance. Just the stark facts. Only Cassie's own specialised knowledge enabled her to add colour to the bare account. The young policewoman on the ground, the thugs facing each other across her body, snarled insults, the glint of a knifeblade, someone raising a window further down the street to yell at them to be quiet, a car passing, eyes and quickened breaths in the darkness. And then the door of the pub opening to spill light across the pavement, Harry Swann stepping outside, crossing the little street...

There was a picture of the policewoman in her hospital bed, with a young man sitting beside her. The photograph's caption explained that this was brave WPC Jill Lockhart, victim of a street brawl in which a man died, and PC Ivan Davis, her fiancé. Cassie closed her eyes. Gran had told her everything, just once. From then on, Cassie had blocked it out, gone into denial. But it was all there still. And always would be. She leaned her elbows on the table and rested her head in her hands, filled with grief and regret.

Someone put a hand on her shoulder. 'Are you all right, dear?'

She turned and looked up. Behind her stood the librarian, her face concerned. 'No,' Cassie said. 'I'm not.'

'Can I get you something? I'm sure there's some aspirin in the first aid box.'

'I'll manage.' Cassie tried to smile reassuringly but

instead found her eyes full of tears. The only thing that
saved her from unsightly gulps was the thought of how
utterly mortified Aunt Polly would have been at this
undignified lack of control in front of a stranger.

'Are you sure?'

'Really.'

'Well . . .' The woman went back to *The Shining*.

Wiping her eyes, Cassie trawled further. She read that
a verdict of murder by person or persons unknown was
returned at the inquest. There had been a suggestion from
the investigating officer of the possibility of the death
being the result of unsavoury happenings – organised
crime, drugs, prostitution – but it was not taken up or
referred to again after the initial mention. This was new to
Cassie and she did not for one moment believe her father
could have been involved in anything criminal. But
perhaps it explained why Aunt Polly had been so
unwelcoming and why she had treated her niece so very
differently from her own daughters. If it hadn't been for
Robin, her godfather, stepping in to send her to boarding
school . . . not that *that* had been much of a Sunday School
picnic, either, but at least there she had been judged on
her own merits rather than castigated for something over
which she had no control.

A stress headache was forming behind her eyes.
Leaving the library, she walked towards the Holloway
Road. She could have gone to the Boilermakers' on the
corner, braved the landlord and his eyebrows, questioning two old folk who'd been there last time, only a few
weeks ago. But she sensed that if she was seriously going
to resurrect the circumstances of Harry Swann's death,
then she ought not to go back to the pub again until she
had more concrete questions to ask. Both of them had
turned hostile as soon as she revealed her identity, though

she had assured them she was only there for the sake of auld lang syne. Were she to show up once more, they would probably clam up completely.

Or worse. Hadn't Kip Naughton, at the nick, said something about one of them – Old Ruby – being 'looked after', meaning being paid to keep quiet? And if she was, if what she was keeping quiet about was something to do with Harry Swann's murder, suppose whoever was looking after her came after Cassie? No thanks: she'd had enough of people trying to finish her off to last a lifetime. And she was still being harassed by Steve, a former inmate, who had been a member of her bridge classes while he was on the inside. Phone calls in the middle of the night, veiled insinuations, the definite information that he had been to Honeysuckle Cottage, that he knew where and how she lived – it was scary stuff, without her trying to add to it.

So, for the moment, it was best to keep away from the Boilermakers' until she had more information. Even if Old Ruby was the aunt of the man who might have struck the fatal blow.

Back at Honeysuckle Cottage, she defiantly poured herself a whisky slug. Her headache had more or less gone: with any luck, the alcohol would dispel the last lingering rags. Drink in hand, she picked up a spider plant by the hair and carried it out to the compost heat. Another one bites the dust. It wasn't her fault. She tried to look after her houseplants, she really tried, but all they did was grow ever more wan and sickly until they died. 'Death is the cure of all diseases,' she said aloud, though she had never determined exactly what disease afflicted the plants in her care, or for that matter, whether the disease was theirs or hers.

In the garden pond, goldfish lurked under flat lily-pads, and a cloud of small brown sticklebacks hovered among the flag stems, beneath a growth of weed which looked like lime jelly. She returned to the house and, picking up the telephone, dialled the number of her friend, Natasha Sinclair. For a few minutes they discussed the conversion of the outbuildings into display rooms and office. Once the work was complete, it was planned that the two of them would move in and set up their mail-order bridge supplies business.

'Though we'll be lucky to be ready by the millennium, the way the builders are moving,' Cassie said.

'Go and give them a bollocking.'

'I already did. Several times.'

'At least it gives me more time to build up our stock,' said Natasha. 'By the way, I met a girl last week who does fabulous appliqué work: I thought we might commission her to run up a few linen table-cloths with bridge motifs on. White on white, really elegant. What do you think?'

'You're the ideas woman. I'm leaving that to you – as long as I have the right of veto.'

'It's going to be so exciting, isn't it? We really ought to be thinking about what to call this enterprise. I've got all sorts of plans for expanding it.'

'Let's get started before we expand,' Cassie said. 'By the way, have you come across a couple called Ray who're living near you? A doctor and his wife: Sammi and Vida Ray?'

'Mmmm,' said Natasha.

'Call me obtuse, but I can't quite read that mmmm. Is it sceptical? Disapproving? Enthusiastic?'

'Puzzled, I'd say. They've been around for a few months now and I've met them both here and there. There's something slightly weird about them, but I can't decide exactly what it is. I had her to tea the other day, thought I'd introduce her to some of the locals. Why do you ask: have you met them?'

'Only once. They showed up at my bridge class last Thursday. She didn't speak the entire evening so it was difficult to assess her. He seemed all right, if a little domineering.'

'That's one way of putting it. He's had several shouting matches with the village cricket team – they use the paddock behind the Rays' house. Some fuss about balls landing in his garden or denting his car or something.'

'That can't have endeared him to the local community.'

'Too right. Tell you what: I'll invite them to dinner next week. You come too – and bring your policeman. You can tell me whether I'm just suffering from Bored Housewife Syndrome.'

'That's supposed to be lethal: have you seen someone about it?'

'Not yet.'

'Maybe you should. If you don't take care, you could end up with a nasty attack of dishpan hands.'

'Don't laugh, Cass. I'm getting worried about myself. It's a direct result of not having enough to do. You start looking at your neighbours and imagining the most ridiculous things about them. Last week I saw Canon Granger – the Rector – coming out of the ironmongers with some electric flex and a roll of dustbin liners, and I can't begin to tell you what I immediately suspected he must get up to on his kitchen table.'

'Did he have two pairs of silk stockings as well?'

'Now you come to mention it ... No, seriously, Cass. I'm taking an unhealthy interest in small-town affairs: the sooner the two of us can get this bridge show on the road, the better, as far as my sanity's concerned.'

'You could always go back to modelling.'

'Don't be ridiculous. These days you're past it by the time you're twelve.'

Her conversation with Natasha completed, Cassie dialled 192 and eventually an electronic voice gave the number of the police station at Highbury. When she got through, she asked to speak to WPC Lockhart. Jill Lockhart.

'There's nobody here by that name,' the duty sergeant said.

'I didn't think there would be,' said Cassie. 'But I know she was there twenty years ago.'

'Twenty years? Blimey, who're you – Mrs Rip van Winkle?'

'According to the newspaper reports, WPC Lockhart was engaged at the time to someone called Ivan Davis, who was also on the Force.' In the library archives, the photograph had showed her leaning against her fiancé's shoulder, her arm in plaster and bandages over one ear, a line of stitches crisscrossing one temple, her lip puffed out to three times its normal size. Her fiancé was holding a teddy bear. Both of them had managed to smile at the camera.

'Hang about,' the sergeant said. 'Davis rings a bell or two.'

'It's to do with a murder. A street brawl. The publican of the Boilermakers' Arms, Harry Swann, was knifed outside his pub,' said Cassie. Once again she explained the circumstances. The death of her father was taking on the distant, other-worldly qualities of a book once read, a film seen years ago, the details easily researched but the original feeling long since dissipated. Its relation to herself grew more and more fragile with every step she took back towards it.

'Harry Swann?' said the man. 'I've been here fourteen years myself and I can't say that I remember the case. But I'll tell you what I'll do. Leave me your number and I'll ask someone to have a quick shuftie through the files. And next time Jimmy Bright drops in, I'll have a word.'

'Who's he?'

'Retired now. Often pops in for a chat and a cuppa in the canteen. But he was based here twenty years ago and more. He might be able to help.'

'That's very kind of you.'

'Haven't done anything yet, dear. Can't promise anything, either, but I won't forget, all right?' He took down Cassie's telephone number. She imagined a scrap of paper being shoved to the back of a drawer or falling onto the floor to be swept away by the cleaners.

'Thanks anyway,' she said.

There was always the tip from above. Trouble was, she hadn't the faintest idea how she started to look for Brigid Fraser.

Unfortunately, she knew a man who did.

'Charlie,' she said.

''Ullo, darlin'.'

'Um ... how about meeting me for a drink this evening, if you're in the area.'

'Sorry, girl. I'm leaving like half an hour ago for Dresden. Got a cathedral to work on.'

'Oh yes. Look ... Charlie,' Cassie hoped she'd managed to hide her relief at not having the make the penultimate sacrifice after all.

'Yuss?'

'You know that woman, Brigid Fraser, the one who trained Handsome Harry the Third ... if I wanted to go and see her, where would I find her?'

There was a silence. Then he said: 'Is that the reason you rang me, Cass? Or did you really want to meet me for a drink?'

'A bit of both, actually.' Cassie had always found it extremely difficult to come right out and lie about things, though possessing a distressing tendency to elaborate once she'd crossed the initial barriers. 'I'd really like to hear more about what you're doing in Dresden. I was there about two years ago and—'

'Cass,' Charlie said. 'Sorry to interrupt but I have a plane to catch.'

'Sorry,' said Cassie. 'Sorry.' And, as she put down the telephone, wondered why she felt so chastened. It was a while before she realised Quartermain had not given her the information she required but when she rang back, nobody answered.

4

'So how many children do you have, Dr Ray?' Natasha asked, passing a cheeseboard round the table. Although the question was directed at the space which hung between the two Rays, Dr Sammi fielded it.

'Three,' he said.

There was a mew of protest from his wife and with a wide smile, he added: 'Plus, I should say, one black sheep.'

'A black sheep, eh?' said Chris, Natasha's husband, who had been fairly reckless with the wine bottle during the previous two courses and showed no signs of being less so over the Stilton. 'What's his name? Baa baa?' Unsurprisingly, this sally did not appear to go down well with his two guests. He offered them a pack of cigarettes. 'Smoke, anyone?'

'Neither I nor my wife smoke,' Sammi said 'It is a disgusting habit as well as an unhealthy one.'

'You're absolutely right,' said Chris. He tapped a cigarette on the table and lit it gustily, although Cassie knew that he never normally smoked.

'Are your children with you over here in England?' she asked hastily. She wished Detective Sergeant Walsh were there – but wishing that was becoming an almost permanent state. She accepted that the demands of his job with the CID meant that he was not his own man. For the moment, it was enough that he was hers. For the moment...

'One,' said Dr Sammi. 'is at Harvard, reading law. One is at Stanford and the third is a student at MIT.'

'Impressive,' said Cassie. 'You must be very proud of them.'

'I am.'

'And the fourth?' Chris rolled his eyes dramatically. 'The back sheep: what's he up to?'

'He is an actor,' said Sammi, clearly not sharing Chris's amusement. He spoke as one might about a child-molester. 'But not, so far, a very successful one.'

'Does he – uh – pursue his career in England?' asked Natasha.

'He pursues it wherever he can find a job,' Sammi said frostily. 'England, India, Australia, the States.'

'Acting's one of those professions where you need a lot of luck, isn't it?' said Cassie. She found it disturbing that Dr Vida, although presumably an intelligent woman – she was a doctor, after all – never spoke. Talk about the spectre at the feast. Tonight she was wearing a sari of dark-green silk edged with gold, over a cropped vest-type thing which left her midriff bare. On her forehead was a stick-on circle of matching green; her arms and fingers were heavy with gold and behind her glasses, her eyes were heavily made-up in translucent pearlised colours which went with her sari. It was difficult to tell her age: Cassie would have said she was in the early thirties but if she had grown-up children that was clearly impossible.

'These days, just to stay alive needs luck,' Natasha said.

Vida Ray opened her mouth to speak but before she could do so, her husband had forestalled her. 'Do you not think that we all make our own luck?' he asked.

Chris leaned forward across the table and waved his

forefinger about. 'Be honest, Dr Ray. You speak disparagingly of black sheep but–'

Dr Sammy frowned and plucked at his moustache. 'I have very good reason to do so.'

'– but aren't the black sheep often the most interesting? Isn't it the people who opt out of so-called...' he made heavily ironic inverted comma signs in the air, '...*conventional* careers who are, in the end, the most fulfilled as individuals?'

Familiar with him, Cassie knew that Chris raised the issue merely as a conversational focus from which the discussion would flow wide and free. He was a transplant from NW3 where this was the accepted convention of dinner parties whenever two or three of the chattering classes gathered together. Dr Ray did not know.

'This is not the case in my family,' he said, displeasure making him puff up like a thrush in winter; visibly he saw Chris's remarks as a criticism of some kind. 'My son—'

But before he could say any more, Dr Vida shook her gold bracelets down her arm and put a soft hand on his sleeve. He subsided. Turning to her, he adjusted the sari across her shoulder. Cassie frowned. Was that a bruise he was hiding there? He caught Cassie's eye and, after a pause that seemed a tad too long, added: 'My poor wife Vida is very clumsy, is that not so, Vida?' His wife nodded. 'Always walking into things, you see. Always forgetting her glasses because she is getting old; she forgets where she has left them and so she cannot see.' He laughed heartily. Dr Vida flicked one side of her mouth upwards, as though determined to share the joke.

'Old?' said Cassie. 'It's hard to imagine she has four children, let alone grown-up ones.' She caught Natasha's eye but strained to keep her expression absolutely neutral. Was this guy a pompous prick, or *what*?

'How do you like your new neighbours?' she asked.

'We have not met many, so far,' Sammi said. His face closed a little. 'They do not seem very friendly.'

'I'm sorry,' Natasha began fatuously, but Sammi went on: 'They do not seem very considerate, either. Already I have had problems with the cricketing fraternity. Balls have landed on my car and indeed, last Sunday, one very nearly hit my wife.'

'Oh dear,' said Natasha, frowning at Chris who sat sniggering quietly and blowing smoke about.

'And there is a dog,' Sammi continued. 'A large dog, incontinent in its habits. Several times it has come into my garden and has had to be expelled. I do not like dogs. Nor does my wife.' He smiled round at them. 'But I expect these are problems which can be overcome with a little goodwill, aren't they?'

'Exactly.' Cassie and Natasha spoke together.

'My Gaaaahd!' Natasha said, flinging herself onto one of the long sofas and collapsing against the cushions. 'Chris, pour me the largest strongest whisky you can find and forget the ice and soda. Jesus. Talk about heavy going.'

'Not a couple you'd rush to invite in for a wife-swap,' Chris said splashing whisky generously into a highball glass.

'Had you thought they might be?' asked Cassie.

'Chris lives in a constant state of hope,' said his wife. 'Though why he thinks I'd let anyone swap with me, I can't imagine.' She gazed fondly at him 'Plump, he may be. Diminutive he may be—'

'Don't forget trichologically disadvantaged,' said Cassie.

'Bald he may be,' agreed Natasha, 'but I love him.'

'Don't you think,' Chris asked, 'there's something odd about those two? The wife is obviously ferociously intelligent but –'

'How on earth can you tell? She never says a word,' said Cassie.

'I was watching her,' Chris said. 'And the reason she doesn't speak is because he doesn't give her a chance.' He pushed his glasses further back up his nose. 'Sammi strikes me as a typical sinker. Unlike me. He's never even heard of women's rights. Doesn't know the first thing about the New Man.'

'After living in the States for eight years, you'd think some of it would have seeped through,' said Cassie. 'If not to him, then to her.'

'I was picking up some very bad vibes about the relationship between the two of them.' Natasha screwed up her face. 'Did you – I hate to say this – but did you get any kind of a feeling that maybe he – uh – beats her up?'

'Funnily enough, I was wondering exactly the same thing,' Cassie said.

'For God's sake,' said Chris. 'How the hell do you work that out?'

'That bruise on her shoulder, for instance. And a mark on the back of her hand as though...' Cassie grimaced at the thought, '...as though it had been burned with a cigarette or something.'

'What is this, an example of female intuition? You see a woman with a bruised shoulder and you immediately assume she's a battered wife? Give me a break.'

'Shut up, Chris. Neither Cassie nor I are given to jumping to stupid conclusions. If we both get the same gut feeling about those two, it might well be because there *is* something rather nasty going on between them.' Natasha touched her mouth with her fingers. 'And if we're right, can we do anything about it?'

'Why don't you drop by tomorrow and ask her?' Chris said. 'Excuse me, Dr Ray, but I just had this womanly hunch that your husband beats you: would you care to confirm or deny?' He flung himself impatiently against the back of the sofa. 'Talk about unwarranted interference in the affairs of others.'

'For the moment, we do nothing,' said Cassie. 'Chris – though patronising and, I suspect, more than a little drunk –'

'I am not.'

'– is quite right. We've absolutely no proof at all and no right to intrude into someone's private problems.'

'It's the way she looks at him,' said Natasha.

'Anyway, aren't battered wives supposed to like it?' Chris asked innocently. 'Aren't they always coming back for more?'

'Don't dignify that with a reply,' said Natasha angrily. She looked at her friend and her husband. 'You're both so damned *English*. if that woman is in trouble, we ought to try and help her.'

'All we can do,' said Cassie, 'is to let her know that there are concerned people around if she needs them.'

'How are you going to do that?' demanded Chris. 'Hello, Dr Ray, I understand you're a battered wife and I want you to know I'm a concerned person if you should ever feel you need one? Ladies, *please*.'

'Shut up, Chris. You behaved very badly tonight.' Natasha nodded at Cassie. 'That might help.'

'And then again,' Chris said. 'It might not.'

Wednesdays were always quite heavy. In the morning, Cassie drove almost to Salisbury to coach a foursome of well-off farmers' wives who were determined to win some local championship, cost what it might. In between vicious rubbers and a host of complex local conventions, they talked in soft Cotswold burrs of government subsidies and set-aside schemes and the difficulties farmers were having in keeping their heads above financial water. Cassie found it hard to show sympathy: outside the expensively furnished, beautifully maintained farmhouse where they were gathered, there were two top-of-the-range four-wheel drives and a new BMW, while inside their hostess's garage waited a Bentley and a Land Rover. Poverty is relative, she knew that, but these women weren't even distant cousins. Since she hoped they would be future clients for the bridge supplies business, she said nothing.

At lunch-time, she travelled to the north of the county to partner Lolly Haden White at a charity bridge drive in aid of the Bosnian refugees. Lolly had been a champion player in her time; today, it was difficult to believe. Several times, her attention seemed to wander in the middle of a game. Three times she reneged or else played a card so hopelessly wrong that even their opponents raised their eyebrows. When the scores were added up, she and Cassie had come last. Afterwards, in a hurry, Cassie brushed aside her partner's apologies, pointing out that everyone was entitled to an off day.

By the middle of the afternoon, Cassie found herself on the side west of Oxford, playing with one of her regular foursomes, this time simply for love of the game.

Two of them – Lucinda Powys-Jones and Naomi Harris – she knew well; she had been playing with them for more than two years and though they rarely met except across the bridge table, Cassie would certainly have called Lucinda a friend. Naomi she was less sure about. In fact, if she was really honest, she would have said that she didn't like Naomi: the woman was too obviously discontented, too ready to criticise other people. The newest member of the quartet, Anne Norrington, she knew less well. Today they were in Naomi's house, Bridge End, a pretty seventeenth-century cottage built of pale Cotswold stone, with prospects from every window over an elaborately beautiful garden. It was all too easy, here, to make unwise assumptions about contemporary society, to presume that God was in his Heaven and Heaven was just at the end of the dog-rosed lane.

I wish, Cassie thought. Heaven was an elusive place. She could not forget the bruise on Dr Vida Ray's shoulder, nor the faces of the men she had taken for bridge classes in the prison at Bellington. She could not ignore the fact that many of the pupils at the big comprehensive in Bellington where she had been forced, by a temporary economic crisis, to teach biology for a couple of terms, would leave school unqualified and, in recession-hit Britain, without prospects. She could not dismiss the ugliness with which detective Sergeant Walsh spent his working life, some of which, by association, rubbed off on hers But what could you expect when for the past fifteen years the country had been ruled by complacent Haves whose only message to the unemployed, the single mothers, the homeless, the disadvantaged was: 'Hey, listen, *poor* people: fuck you, because we've never had it so good?'

Yet, to say that Naomi and Lucinda and Anne lived in a bubble of isolation, cut off from the real world, was patronising. Their world was real, too; they also had troubles, which were just as personally traumatic, even if they were of a different kind.

Naomi, for instance There was something seriously

wrong with Naomi. Was it the fact that she and her husband had Persian cats instead of children? Was a marital breakdown about to occur? Or ... Cassie remembered that recently they had had to cancel a bridge session because Naomi had gone into hospital for tests. Please, she thought, doubling Anne's tentative bid, *please* not cancer. Yet evidences of some major problem lay everywhere in Naomi's hitherto immaculate house: cobwebs linking the edges of the lampshades, dust on the fruit which sat in a bowl on the equally dusty sideboard, silver which needed polishing. Not that Cassie was in any way criticising Naomi's housekeeping abilities, her own being of the minimal kind: it was simply that in the past, tarnished silver and dirty windows at Bridge End would have been unthinkable.

In spite of her feelings about Naomi, she decided she would have to find out why she appeared to be under such stress. Perhaps later, when there were no other people around.

Totting up the final scores at the end of the second rubber, while Lucinda and Anne stepped out through the doors into the garden to admire the view across a flat piece of river past ancient tree and pastoral church spire to the mellow curves of the Cotswold landscape, she looked up and caught Naomi unawares. She was frowning, biting her lip, her face so miserably unhappy that Cassie leaned across the table to put a hand on her arm. 'Naomi,' she said quietly. 'What's wrong?'

'Is it that obvious?'

'You could have hired a sky-writing plane, I suppose,' Cassie said.

To her horror, Naomi's eyes filled with tears. 'I can't talk about it here, not with the others...' She nodded at the two women just outside the windows.

'I'll call you,' Cassie said. 'As soon as I can, all right? And whatever it is, do try not to worry, please.'

Finding herself so close to Oxford with time to kill, Cassie decided to drop into the Ashmolean and look at the still lifes. There was something so reassuring about those riotous bouquets and garlands, those bursting grapes and half-peeled lemons, the lovingly-painted Delft, the almost photographic drops of water. But walking along the Broad, she was deflected, unable to resist the lure of Blackwell's. Sun shone for once, honeying the carved heads outside the Sheldonian, glancing off cobblestones, illuminating the gloomy length of Holywell Street. She stepped inside the shop and began sniffing the air like a truffling pig. Books: new books. They had an almost aphrodisiac quality. Moving through the bustle of under-graduates and academics, she hovered with a dragonfly attention span over the tables, sipping the honey from a fragment of recently published poetry, a page of new-editioned Dickens, the opening paragraphs of the latest bestseller, full-bellied pictures from a book of naval history.

Her eye was caught by a handsome young man near the door into the street, who was pretending to look at guides to the Scottish Isles. He really was extraordinarily good-looking, in a flashy kind of way: dark-skinned, black-haired, wearing a faded blue denim shirt tucked into well-cut beige trousers. Too old to be an under-graduate, Cassie decided. And much too sharply dressed in a male model kind of ways. Not that tacky meant you couldn't at least chat with a guy. But was someone who looked like that going to give a thirty-three-year-old bridge teacher, who was not exactly fat but certainly had dense bones, a whirl?

Before she could get around to answering this question honestly, the outside door opened on a puff of wind and a woman looked around briefly, then joined him at the Travel section. She wore designer jeans and a T-shirt printed with a washed-out version of Van Gogh's Sunflowers. Even with large sunglasses obscuring most of her face, her beauty shone in the dusty motes slanting through the windows. Cassie tried not to feel like a hippopotamus at a gazelle convention.

'I am free,' she told herself, pulling back her shoulders. 'I am Woman. I stand outside the chains of convention. I do not need bathroom scales to reinforce my validity.'

Quite.

She could hear snatches of conversation from the couple by the guides. '*So* sorry,' the woman said? '...got held up ... been waiting for hours?'

'Not hours...' The young man kissed her cheek and then, ignoring her embarrassed look, hugged her, lifting her off the floor. The pair of them looked like the second leads in some Merchant–Ivory productions Even in this city of youth that, if not entirely gilded, was for the most part silver-plated, they stood out.

'Where shall ... go?' the man said.

'...to you.' The woman had one of those husky voices which lies somewhere between a sexual invitation and laryngitis.

'...the Randolph?' The pair of them began to drift towards the door into Broad Street.

The woman fiddled with the clasp of her soft leather shoulder-bag. 'Any luck ... job...?'

The young man shrugged. '...they'd let me know.'

'Don't call us...'

'Story of my life.'

'It'll ... one day ... it will.'

'Yes, but *which* day . . .'

The bell above the shop door tinkled as the young man held it open. Cassie moved after them as they stepped down onto the pavement. From behind the half-curtain which cut off the shop from the window display, she watched as they turned right and headed towards Cornmarket Street. When she came out, a few minutes later, they were peering through the big wrought-iron gates into the garden of Trinity. She followed them at a distance, past Balliol, past the Martyrs' Memorial and across Cornmarket Street but by the time they had turned into the Randolph and she herself had finally negotiated the thickets of traffic in Beaumont Street trying to head north, and reached the haven of the wide stone steps leading to the doors of the Ashmolean, she was too agitated to give further thought to either of them.

Completely knackered, she was home by eight forty-five. After a glass of chilled water and a nourishing supper of lettuce leaves, she went to bed.

The was fast asleep when the phone rang. Without opening her eyes, she groped for the handset beside the bed and brought it to her ear, realising her mistake too late to cut off the hateful voice.

'How's tricks, Cass? Is there some guy in bed with you or are you there all alone? Cuz if so, you've only to say the word, Cass, and I'll slip along and join you – that's if your *br-i-i-g* dog George, what you lied to me about, won't start barking and waking up the neighbours. Not that you've got a lot of them, have you, Cass, stuck out there in the fields, and the American lady gone away –'

She slammed the down the phone. Tomorrow she would do what Detective Sergeant Walsh had recommended she do ages ago, and arrange to have her calls

monitored. Trouble was, these particular calls just weren't
that frequent. And putting a monitor on the telephone
could be counter-productive, might frighten off potential
clients. There was a natural reluctance in people to do
business with someone who seemed to be mixed up with
something slightly dodgy, even if it was nothing; worse
than a persistent heavy breather.

She switched on the bedside lamp and sat up, hugging
her knees. She knew who the caller was, but Steve
Blackburn, a former inmate of HMP Bellington, a former
member of the bridge class she had conducted inside the
prison, was much too canny to call more than once every
few days. Steve was a weirdo, a pervert, a slasher of
women's faces, women's bodies. Steve was a time bomb
waiting to explode into murder. And however brave a
face Cassie put on it, she was terrified that she would end
up being the first victim he killed.

5

A large man in torn flannel trousers was sitting on the bench outside the kitchen window when Cassie came downstairs the following morning. Filling the kettle at the tap, she watched him reading the back page of the *Daily Mirror*, a cigarette in his hand, and a general air about him of someone comfortably settled in for the morning. Since what he was supposed to be comfortably settled in to was the conversion of the outbuildings in the garden, it was easy to believe the cliches about the British Workman. In fact, she was about to open the window and make this point when the telephone rang. She picked it up.

'Hello,' she said. Walsh had told her never to give her name or her number. He'd also advised her to go ex-directory, but that was difficult to arrange retrospectively.

'Miss Swann? It's Sergeant Wilkinson here. From the Highbury police station?'

'Oh, yes.'

'Funny you bringing up that old murder case.'

'Was it?' Outside, the builder, unaware of her presence only a pane of glass away, had risen to his feet and had thrust a hand down inside the waistband of his trousers in order to conduct a comprehensive scratching programme.

'Don't know if I mentioned Jimmy Bright, last time we

spoke? Used to be based here, along with WPC Lockhart – as she then was – the one you were asking after?'

He paused, to make sure she had followed him thus far. Cassie hated conversations where she was expected to confirm after every sentence that she hadn't fallen into a coma since the end of the last one. 'Yes,' she said.

'He came in the day before yesterday, asked to look through the files, because some local historian was interested in writing up the area? There've been some famous murder cases round here, you see, and he thinks – this is the historian bloke, not Jimmy Bright – that he might be able to interest a small publisher, or even do it himself? These days, with the desk-top printers and that, it's quite easy, apparently, to produce your own books without having to find one of the big commercial firms who's prepared to take you on?'

Cassie looked at her watch. She would like to have asked if it was a slow day at the cop shop, or was he always this garrulous. Reminding herself that he was doing her a favour – or might be, if he ever got round to it – she said: 'Really?'

'Your dad came into the conversation, naturally? Jimmy was saying there'd been this case, the Harry Swann murder, still unsolved, and he'd like to refresh his memory, look at the files?'

'Yes?'

'Turns out he *was* here at the time, though he wasn't actually on the case himself, knew Jill Lockhart quite well? Not that she *is* Lockhart any more, but Jimmy said he'd kept up with her over the years, exchanged Christmas letters, sent postcards when on holiday, that sort of thing, and he'd drop her telephone number in at the station for you next time he came in so I could pass it on?'

'Yes?' All these question marks were making Cassie feel very indeterminate. In case he thought she wasn't pleased, she added: 'That's wonderful.'

'Turns out she lives somewhere Bristol way,' said Wilkinson. 'Husband's got a sporting goods shop or something? Teaches PE at one of the local schools? Two kids, everything hunky dory.'

'Sounds great,' said Cassie. 'Look, I'm extremely grateful for all your help.'

'It's got a name, hasn't it?'

'What has?'

'That sort of thing. You asking about your dad, and then Jimmy Bright bringing it up himself before I'd even had a chance to mention it?'

'Coincidence, do you mean?' said Cassie. 'Synchronicity? Serendipity?'

'That's the one. Here, hang on,' Sergeant Wilkinson said. 'I can see him now, Jimmy Bright, coming up the stairs. I'll see if he's got that number for you. Takes him a while these days, with that leg of his, he has to take it careful and the polish they put on the lino, you wouldn't believe. He's at the top now, he's pushing the doors open, he's—'

It was like listening to a commentary on a Grand National being run in slow motion. While the man outside her window was joined by a couple of skinny mates, who also started to read the paper, Cassie was beginning to feel as though she had somehow wandered into one of those appalling television programmes where some Dachau-thin girl in skin-tight Lycra leaps out of helicopters or abseils down abandoned mine-shafts, all the time commenting breathlessly into a microphone for the benefit of the couch potatoes back home.

The big builder turned, shaded his eyes and peered in,

pressing his face against the kitchen window. Seeing Cassie only inches away from him, he nodded a couple of times and with a hopeful raise of his eyebrows, put up his two forefingers, one across the top of the other, in the shape of a T. Tea should come as a reward for hard labour, Cassie felt, rather than preceding it. Nonetheless, she made encouraging faces, while in her ear, Sergeant Wilkinson finally talked Jimmy Bright up to the desk and extracted – this meant another blow-by-blow account of Jimmy feeling in his breast pocket then his wallet, then remembering he'd put it in his trousers, no, come to think of it, in his shirt pocket so as not to lose it – a telephone number.

By the time Cassie had written it down, with the former WPC's address, she was vowing that if she ever got free of Wilkinson, she would mal e a drastic change in her life-style, publicly thank St Jude via a newspaper ad, join the Moonies, shave her head, anything to indicate her relief at having finally escaped from his telephonic clutches.

'I'm so grateful,' she kept saying, and had to force herself not to add a question mark.

Warnford, on the outskirts of Bristol. Twenty-seven Haines Crescent. Maybe tomorrow, or the day after, following the bridge session she had booked with four women living on the big housing estate at Frith, she would drive on down there and find Jill Lockhart. Or Mrs Ivor Davis, as she now was.

Having attended to the creature comforts of her builders and expressed the hope that they weren't run-ning behind schedule, especially as there were penalty clauses in the contract, Cassie rang Natasha to say she would be dropping in with various documents and important pieces of paper relating to the bridge goods enterprise. She would not have said that theirs was an equal partnership: Natasha was the one with the business head, the flair, the organisational skills; Cassie was the one with the body-image problem. It was hard to see why the two of them had decided on this venture in the first place. Or was it? With all her children at school for most of the day, Natasha was suffering from a serious crisis of confidence in herself and her future, while Cassie needed desperately to prove that Aunt Polly's unconcealed scepticism and Uncle Sam's concern at the cavalier fashion in which she had thrown away a good steady career as a biology teacher were ill-founded. So far, she had managed to make ends meet, though there were some months when it was a bit of a financial scramble. All she hoped for from the business was that it would eventually provide a year-round, if low-grade, economic basis from which she could operate.

The hedges were thick with whitethorn and may, the scent of summer so heavy in the air that it was almost visible. Moretyene Wood had greened over, so that only occasionally could she see the lines of tree trunks with bars of solid sunshine falling between. She slowed to admire a pair of Canadian geese which floated on the pond at Frith: if they had any sense, they'd wing it out of there before the kids from the housing estate caught sight of them.

When she arrived at Natasha's house, it was to find Dr Vida Ray also sitting in the big family kitchen. Cassie had already said: 'Hello: nice to see you again,' when she became aware that the atmosphere was full of tension. 'What's wrong?'

The two women stared at her, then Natasha said slowly: 'Something absolutely awful's happened, Cass.'

'What?'

'Tell her,' Natasha said to Vida and then, before the

65

other could do so, rushed in herself: 'It's just so dreadful, Vida and her husband have been the victims of racial attacks, I just can't believe it would happen here, I mean, I know everyone round here and no one – I can't imagine *anyone* would do this. Letters, Cassie, and the other night, a fire. A deliberately started fire. Can you *believe* it?'

'Someone pushed a petrol-soaked rag through the letter-box,' Vida said tonelessly. 'And a lighted match after it. Luckily I heard the sound of the letter-box snapping shut – it's rather stiff – and came out into the hall to investigate.' It was the first time Cassie had heard her speak. She used precise English, with a transatlantic intonation. Today, there was a fresh bruise on her upper arm, and a scratch near her right ear.

'Have you told the police?' Cassie said.

'Not yet,' said Natasha, answering for Vida. Was it something she'd unconsciously picked up from Sammi, or was Vida so placid, so lacking in character, that other people took her over? The former, Cassie suspected. 'She's had dog turds pushed through the door, too, Cassie. More than once.'

'I'm appalled. I don't know what to—'

'There's these, too. Look.' Natasha pushed over a small pile of notes scribbled on pieces of lined paper torn out of a cheap notepad.

Cassie glanced at the square black letters; although the writer had used capitals, it seemed an educated hand. It was only necessary to read a word here and there to guess at their general tone. 'BLACK BITCH ... NOT WANTED ... MONKEYS ... BACK TO THE JUNGLE ... KNOW WHAT'S GOOD FOR YOU ... WOGS...': the usual limited invective of prejudice. She closed her eyes briefly. Without sounding as if you were trying to make excuses, how did you explain

to someone who was not a native of your country that the
views expressed belonged to a tiny proportion of the
population, that the vast majority were happy to live and
let live? How did you sufficiently convey your own anger
and embarrassment? And why was it that the minority in
any community was always so disproportionately vocal?

'I just don't know what to say.' She stared at Vida Ray.
'I can't apologise: that would imply that I was in some way
answerable for the people – person – responsible for this
filth. I can only say I'm profoundly shocked, both on your
behalf and my own.'

'Vida came to see me this morning,' Natasha said,
'because she's had another one.'

'How long have these been coming, then?'

'Almost since we arrived,' Vida said.

Cassie leafed through the small pile of paper. 'No
envelopes?'

'I didn't keep them.'

'Did they arrive through the post?'

'They were hand-delivered,' said Vida. 'I kept hoping
they would eventually stop coming. But after the letter
which arrived this morning, I decided I ought to tell
someone. And Natasha has been kind...' Behind her
severe spectacles her eyes were full of sadness. 'There was
nothing like this in the States...'

'Five months ... that's dreadful. Have you contacted
the police?' asked Cassie.

'No.'

'What does your husband say?' It was so odd to hear
Vida speak that Cassie was still coming to terms with her
as an entity in her own right, rather than as Sammi's
adjunct.

Vida looked at Natasha. Natasha said: 'She hasn't
shown him any of them.'

'Why not?'

'Because it seems unfair to burden Sammi with this,' Vida explained. 'It's already hard enough for him to settle in to a different environment and establish a working relationship with his new colleagues.'

'But you haven't seen the latest one,' Natasha said. She pushed over a piece of paper half in and half out of an envelope.

Cassie took it out, read it, bit her lip. 'LEAVE FILTH,' the poisonous little missive read, 'OR TAKE THE CONSEQUENCES.' It was signed. FROM A PAID-UP MEMBER OF THE KEEP BRITAIN WHITE SOCIETY.

'Horrible, isn't it?' said Natasha.

Vida dropped her head into her hands and began to weep. 'I can't stand it,' she said. 'I am afraid now, all the time. For my husband, for myself.'

'Any idea who could be responsible?'

Vida shook her head. 'None at all. I suppose it must be one of our neighbours, someone local. I know that sometimes Sammi can be a bit...' Sniffing back tears, she did not finish the sentence.

'You'll have to go to the police,' Cassie said. 'It's the only sensible thing to do.' She looked from Natasha to Vida. The two of them resembled each other to a certain extent, though the delicacy of Natasha's Sri Lankan beauty was modified and enhanced by the other half of her heritage, which came from White Russian aristocracy who had fled St Petersburg before the Revolution.

'I can't.' Vida spoke firmly. 'If the hospital heard about this, they might wish Sammi to leave. I can't let that happen. They are involved with a gynaecological research programme which he has wanted to be part of ever since it was initiated. Otherwise...' she looked at Cassie and then at Natasha.

'Otherwise what?' Cassie asked.

'I was very happy in the States,' Vida whispered. 'I did not want to leave. My children are settled over there. But the chance came up and Sammi decided...'

'I was wondering whether your Paul might, you know...' Natasha said. She got up and brought over the coffee pot, filling a cup for Cassie, replenishing Vida's cup and her own. '...make a few discreet enquiries without bringing in the full power of the boys in blue and all that.'

'The ancient in blue, you mean,' Cassie said. The area made up of Larton Easewood and its environs was watched over by the benevolent eye of a bobby who was simply waiting to retire. This same dedicated policeman had just achieved national notoriety by being hauled up before his superiors for failing to meet some kind of quota, having made only four arrests in the past two years, three-quarters of them on the same night at the same time, when he chanced upon a trio of would-be joy-riders trying to break into a car.

'Whatever,' Natasha said. 'The thing is, this last letter seems to change things from mere abuse to a definite threat.'

'Yes,' said Cassie. 'I'll ring Paul.'

'Urgently,' Natasha said. 'Suppose someone attacks the Rays. Suppose something happened. They could be in danger.'

'What could happen?' Briefly Cassie touched Vida's arm. 'I don't want to play down any of this, but how could someone attack you or your husband? A gun? More arson attacks? Poisoned chocolates sent through the post or something? Whatever, it would be much too risky and the police would certainly launch a full-scale investigation. People who send anonymous letters usually get their kicks from doing just that: they don't move on to actual physical attack.' Though she spoke with assurance, she was not certain if what she said was true – there had recently been an extraordinary case in France which had started with letters and ended with not one murder but several.

'But you will speak to Paul, won't you?'

'If Vida's determined not to go to the police, yes, I will. But he's CID, you know, not involved with this sort of thing. And I know already that he'll advise the Rays to go to the police immediately.'

Cassie was conscious of impotence where Paul Walsh was concerned. She loved him, no question about that, if love meant having the hots for him, thinking about him whenever she had a spare moment and often when she did not, longing for him all the time. She believed he loved her. But whether she could persuade him to do something he did not want to do – or was not empowered to do – was quite another question.

'But you will at least ask him?'

'Of course.'

'Let us forget about my problems for the moment,' Vida said, 'and talk about other things.' She turned to Cassie. 'Natasha has told me of your business enterprise: how near is it to completion?'

'About three British Workmen and a lot of tea-drinking time away,' Cassie said gloomily.

'There's no reason why it shouldn't be finished by the middle of the summer,' said Natasha. 'I'll come over and kick some ass, if you like. I'm good at that.'

The three women laughed. 'When do you think you'll hear about your job,' said Cassie to Vida. 'You're looking for something in Oxford, I believe. At the John Radcliffe, is this?'

'The John Radcliffe?' Vida looked puzzled, wrinkling

her nose as her glasses slipped forward. 'This is a hospital, isn't it?'

'Yes.'

'Why should I be looking for a job in a hospital?'

'I thought your husband said...' began Natasha.

'Ah. I see where the confusion has been. I am Dr Ray, too, but mine is a doctorate in Theatre Studies,' said Vida. She shook the bracelets on her wrist so that they slid delicately down her arm. 'I have a degree from Pomona, in California, where my parents sent me for my BA, and then, when Sammi and I moved to the States, I took my Ph.D. there.'

'Is that where your black sheep gets his talent from?' asked Natasha.

Vida smiled. Dimples showed in her cheeks and she looked suddenly much younger. 'Talent. I don't know about that. Of course I am very proud of him, for many reasons. One of them being that he has taken his own course against all kinds of opposition from his father. Also, that he is beginning to make a name for himself, in spite of the fact that inevitably he is seen as an ethnic actor and the possible roles on offer will therefore be limited. The problem with Rashid is that although he has had many offers from Indian film companies, he wants to work in the West.' The dimples showed again. 'In Hollywood, of all places.'

'So if it's not at the hospital, what kind of job are you hoping to get?' asked Cassie.

'Nothing is certain at the moment. If things go well, I shall be attached to one of the younger colleges as a Visiting Fellow,' Vida said 'They are not so hidebound by tradition and English syllabuses and so on. But there is also a possibility in the other direction, at Bristol; the university has a very strong theatrical tradition and its drama courses are always heavily oversubscribed. I am still waiting to hear from both Oxford and Bristol. Or, since the posts on offer are part-time, maybe I shall be lucky and can take on both.'

'Your husband must be very proud of you,' Cassie said.

Vida looked quickly away. 'Yes, he is.' She did not sound convinced. 'He says, of course, that I do not need to work, but I like to have my own money then I do not have to consult with my husband on how to spend it.' In other words thought Cassie, she's subsidising the black sheep.

'There's an amateur dramatic company in Bellington,' Natasha said, scenting fresh blood.

'Is there?' Vida sounded cool.

'The Civic Theatre's actually quite historical, like two or three hundred years old.'

'Ah.' Vida raised delicate but unenthusiastic eyebrows.

'Maybe you could...' Belatedly, Natasha sensed that there was no point voicing whatever proposition she had in mind, and let it drop.

'I'm much more interested in experimental theatre, or community projects,' Vida said. 'Getting away from the tyranny of the proscenium arch, involving everyone, not just those who have set themselves up as somehow superior to the rest by adopting the label of Actor.'

'Isn't that what your black sheep – Rashid, I mean – is doing?' Cassie said.

'Indeed. We have had many arguments about this. But, of course, I speak from the directorial perspective rather than the performance-related one.'

The door of the kitchen burst open and Natasha's children rushed in. Some were crying, others were using inappropriate language of the Anglo-Saxon variety.

'Watch it, darlings,' Natasha said, slipping effort-
lessly from former-international-model-soon-to-be-busi-
nesswoman mode into her earth- mother role. 'We have
visitors. Daisy, why are you crying Borya, wipe your
nose, please. Mischa, leave those crisps alone or you
won't eat any supper, and Dima, fill the kettle and plug
it in, will you.'

Daisy howled louder and ran for her mother's arms.
'This big boy,' she sobbed.

'What about him?'

'He ... he ...' Five-year-old Daisy's lower lip trembled
and her big dark eyes over flowed.

'What did he do?' Natasha said.

'He ...'

'He *what*?' Over Daisy's head, Natasha frowned at the
other two women.

'He ... he showed me his willy.'

'Why should that make you cry? You've seen plenty of
willies before. Dima's and Borya's and Mischa's and
Daddy's ...'

'Yes, but theirs are just ordinary,' said Daisy, huge
tears plopping onto her school blouse.

'That's not what Sandra Middleton says,' Dimitri said,
attempting are evil sex-laden grin which was completely
spoiled by the fact that his fourteen-year-old voice had
not yet fully broken.

His mother ignored him. 'What was different about this
big boy's, then?'

'It was ...' Daisy clung to her mother's skirt, '... green.'

'*Green*?'

'It was only old Timmy Parsons,' Mikhail said. 'I *told*
her?'

'I can hardly bring myself to ask this,' said Cassie, 'but
why was old Timmy Parsons's willy green?'

73

'Five B has double art the last period of the afternoon,' said Dimitri, as if that explained it all. Which in a way, of course, it did.

Mikhail said: 'He's *such* a dreeb.'

'I'm only a little girl,' said Daisy, gulping. 'I'm not used to it.'

'I should hope not,' said her mother.

'He showed it to me, too,' said Boris. His chubby face was tear-streaked.

'And what did *you* do?'

'I got out my penknife and jabbed it,' explained Boris. 'So he hit me on the head with his school bag, and then Mischa hit him and so Timmy Parsons's girlfriend hit Dima and . . .'

'Sounds like a sub-teen version of *Reservoir Dogs*,' Cassie said. 'My head's reeling.' She rose. 'I'd better go.'

Driving away, she wondered if there was something wrong with her for never having felt the faintest urge to have a child.

Almost never.

She looked at her watch, and hesitated. She was already well to the west of the county. By the time she got to Bristol and found Haynes Crescent, it was more than likely that the former WPC Lockhart would be home.

She thought of telephoning ahead, but decided against it. She wanted to see the woman's face when she explained who she was and why she had come. If there *had* been something odd about Harry Swann's murder, she did not want to give the ex-policewoman a chance to prepare a story or an attitude. Better to show up unexpectedly. And if by any chance she was not there, Cassie had friends she could always go and visit.

Nonetheless, she slowed down the car at the edge of Larton Easewood. The lane stretched ahead of her

between banks of flat-flowered elder and fading haw-
thorn blossom. The red-brick Victorian building on the
other side of the road must be the Old School House,
where the Rays were living. She could see Charlie
Quartermain's handiwork in the long, narrow windows of
gothic design on the upper floor, and the stonework
which ran decoratively beneath the slate roof. At some
time, the house had been enlarged: she noticed the edge
of a conservatory, and an extension built of the same soft-
rose brick. A high flanking wall lined the drive and hid the
front door from the road: very convenient for people with
dog turds to dispose of and vicious correspondence to slip
through the letter-box. Across the road, a man emerged
from a gate set into the hedge and walked away from her
down the lane. That must be the paddock where the
cricket team played on Sundays.

She was using delaying tactics; she did not want to take
the plunge and drive to Bristol to confront someone who
had been a prime witness to the violent deed twenty years
back. Visiting the Boilermakers' Arms a few weeks ago
was one thing, even talking to Old Ruby and Bert, or
Kipper Naughton, inside the prison, had not involved her
directly with the events of that night.

But WPC Lockhart had been in the thick of it; if she
spoke to the woman, there would no longer be a skim of
third-party mediation between Cassie and what really had
occurred that night. Still she hesitated, the car engine
throbbing gently. This was primary source material and
she was reluctant to pick it up and turn its pages, for once
turned, she would never again be able to pretend that
none of it had ever happened.

In the end, forcing herself, she let in the clutch and
drove on towards the motorway and the road to Bristol.

76

6

Approaching the outskirts of the city along the M4, Cassie began to have doubts again about the wisdom of this impulsive trip. Partly because rain had begun to fall and the rubber bits of her windscreen wipers needed renewing. Partly because she had come without the piece of paper on which she had copied down the address and wasn't sure she had remembered it correctly. Twenty-seven Haynes Circle? Crescent? Something like that. And then again, Mrs Jill Davis might take strong exception to some total stranger showing up out of the blue, when she was about to sit down with a drink and chat to her husband about the day's events. Or cook supper. Or put the children to bed. She might not want to be reminded of what could well have been an exceedingly traumatic event, even if it was over twenty years ago.

She stopped at the next filling station and asked to look at their local telephone directory. She hoped that Mr and Mrs Ivan Davis did not have an unlisted phone number. DS Walsh had told her that all policemen did, as a matter of course – but these two had left the force years ago. On the other hand, old habits die hard. If they weren't in the book, she would have to go through the Yellow Pages and look at sporting goods stores, see if there was any clue there ... but they were listed. Twenty-seven Haines

Crescent, Warnford, Bristol. 'Warnford,' she said to the woman behind the cash desk. 'Where's that?'

'Take the turn for Shepton Mallet,' the woman said, in a soft Gloucestershire burr. 'It'll be signposted after that. Can't miss it.'

I can, Cassie thought, hurrying back to her car as cold rain swept across the garage forecourt. I could set out for Canterbury and end up in Cannes. Navigation was not her strongest talent, particularly if she was doing it for someone else. She remembered the rows she used to have with her former husband: setting out to stay with friends, ending up hopelessly lost, the car full of insults and recrimination and – on her part, certainly an increasing weariness. Irritatingly, however often she asked him to let her drive while he navigated, he refused, muttering about women drivers, declining to allow her to invade his male territory. 'Serve him right,' she said aloud. 'Macho twit.' She wondered if he were happy with his new wife and felt a momentary regret that the plans they had made for their future together had never worked out.

Haines Crescent was part of an exclusive modern estate of Executive-style Homes set amid flowering cherry trees and glades of silver birch. Efforts had been made to impart some defining individuality that would set each house apart from its neighbours but the goal was impossible to achieve when the bricks used were all so uniform and the windows and woodwork were identical on every one. Each one carried a square yellow sticker in the window, indicating that they were part of the Home Watch scheme. The executive-style gardens which accompanied these houses were immaculate, every shrub, every blade of grass and regimented flower looking as though it had been sprayed with wax polish and buffed to a high sheen. Looking at the spotless brick paths which led to the various front doors, Cassie hoped the soles of her shoes would pass muster.

Number twenty-seven differed from its neighbours in having a weeping willow on the unhedged lawn and two dormer windows set in its symmetrically tiled roof. The front door was painted forest-green and displayed an inordinate amount of shiny brass furniture. There was a car parked outside the double garage and lights on in the house; someone was obviously home.

She drove on past and pulled up alongside another sloping lawn which flowed to the meandering roadway with the smoothness of gloss paint. Now that she was so close, she wondered if she could go through with this. Artichoke-like, leaf after leaf of her secret self was being peeled away, right down to the tender heart; what frightened her was the possibility that when the last leaf was removed, there would be nothing there.

Leaning her head against the side window, she told herself that nobody was forcing her, she was here of her own volition. All she had to do was to drive away again, forget she had ever started to wonder about the past. For all these years she had coped, hadn't she? She had achieved, got a degree, a home, a career, friends. She functioned, didn't she, more than adequately? The answer was a definite yes. Yet, to her surprise, there were tears in her eyes for, try as she might to rationalise, she knew that whatever questions she put to Jill Davis, nee Lockhart, they were at least as much for her own sake as for her father's.

Talking several deep breaths, she turned the engine back on and drove further round Haines Crescent until she arrived again at number twenty-seven. She got out and almost ran up the path to ring the bell beside the front door. She knew that if Mrs Davis did not answer immediately, she would turn back, jump into her car and go home.

But the door was opened almost as soon as she rang the bell, as though she were expected. Cassie instantly recognised the woman who stood in front of her, sleek but defeated, as though getting to this place at this time had been almost too much for her. Once, a younger version of her had rocked Cassie in her arms, let Cassie cry against her chest. Once, she had sat with Cassie in the kitchen behind the public rooms of the Boiler-makers', and tried to explain that life would go on, that though it might be impossible to imagine it now, there would one day be something to look forward to again. And once, when Cassie had bolted through the back door and out away among the houses, this same woman had found her squeezed behind some shrub-hidden rocks along New River Walk, and coaxed her out, saying there was no need for her to go to live with Aunt Polly, promising that *of course* she could stay on at the pub with Gran, that there was no law which could force her to go to the Vicarage if she didn't want to.

Today, Jill Davis was trim and tidy, her blonde hair turning grey, her neat white blouse tucked into a neat red skirt. There was gold costume jewellery round her neck and attached to her ears: seeing her, Cassie immediately felt large and unkempt, hands the size of dictionaries, feet as big as frying-pans.

'Yes?' Mrs Davis looked beyond Cassie, clearly expect-ing someone else. 'Can I help you?'

'Mrs Davis?'

'Yes.'

'Mrs Davis...' Cassie's throat seized up again and she felt her eyes water. Darn it. She wanted to be cool. She wanted to be in control.

'Yes?' This time Mrs Davis's eyes met Cassie's and, momentarily, narrowed. A cautious look crossed her face.

'My name's Cassandra Swann,' Cassie blurted. 'I'd like to—'

'Swann?' There was a pause and then Mrs Davis sighed. 'You'd better come in.' She seemed to know exactly why Cassie was there.

She led the way into a comfortable living-room whose key decorative feature was pussyfooting prudence. The walls were painted an undaring magnolia, with a three-piece suite upholstered in cautious green; there was an unadventurous beige carpet on the floor. It was as though the Davises, uncertain of their own taste, were anxious to avoid offending anyone else's. There were uplighters on the walls, a small bookcase containing the Encyclopaedia Britannica and a few recent blockbusting paperbacks, a modern glass-fronted cabinet full of Lladro figures and a collection of Toby jugs. Beyond, through an archway, was an equally careful dining-room with flower prints on the walls and framed photographs standing on a modern teak sideboard. Squinting, Cassie could make out a wedding scene, the head and shoulders of a young man leaning sideways in a mortar board, a couple of portraits of children.

The house was warm and comfortable and smelled invitingly of macaroni cheese. A mock-coal fire flickered a welcome in the grate. Everything was expensively respectable, as bright and clean as if it had been bought yesterday, without any of the sense of accumulation over time, of keepsakes marking the milestones in a relationship, of mementoes handed down over loving generations. And there wasn't a single thing in either room that Cassie could have borne to live with.

'Sit down, Cassandra,' Mrs Davis said.

'Thank you.' Cassie sat down in one of the comfortable chairs. Without asking, Mrs Davis poured two whiskies into tumblers and handed one to Cassie. She looked down at her and gently shook her head. Without preamble, she said: 'Why have I always been sure that this would happen one day?'

'You know who I am?'

'I can make a pretty accurate guess.' Mrs Davis gathered her neat skirt under her aerobicked behind and sat down in one of the green armchairs. She stared at Cassie for a moment. 'You've come to ask about your father, haven't you?'

'I want to know who murdered him.'

Mrs Davis raised her eyebrows. 'What makes you think you'll find out, after all this time?'

Cassie twisted her hands about in her lap. 'I ... I think it's important that I at least try.'

'All right.' Mrs Davis seemed to understand.

'Nobody's ever been charged with my ... with Harry Swann's murder. Most murders are cleared up, in some way or another: why not this one?'

'We tried, my dear. Believe me. We always do, and your father was someone we liked and respected. But after the first enquiries, there wasn't anywhere much for us to look.'

'Why not?'

'The witnesses were all blind and deaf or suffering from acute memory loss. We simply couldn't pin anything on anyone. We brought everyone in that we could. We even charged a few of them with affray, assault, whatever we could, but we weren't able to make any more serious charges stick, partly because we didn't have the evidence and partly because I don't think any of them *did* see what went on. They all seemed genuinely shocked by what had happened.'

'So the Harry Swann case remains in the In tray, does it?'

'We never give up on a case,' Mrs Davis said. She looked through Cassie into the past, gently shaking her head. 'Handsome Harry Swann,' she said, her voice full of memory.

Cassie had to bite down on her lower lip to stop herself from crying out. *Dad...*

'We used to call him the King of Hearts, us cops,' Mrs Davis continued. 'I don't know what it's like up that way these days, but in my time, there was a fairly close relationship between the police and the local business community. Makes sense, when you think about it, especially for those in the catering trades. So I knew your father quite well, one way or another.'

'The King of Hearts?' Cassie said. *Dad, big, comfortable holding her, laughing, keeping her safe ...* The feel of his starched shirt collars against the side of her jaw came back to her, a memory perfectly preserved although she had not until now realised she possessed it still.

'Women loved him,' Mrs Davis said. 'And he loved women. Have you noticed how few men you could really say that about? They like screwing them, they like to have them around to cook for them and have their children, but they don't actually *like* them much. But your father...' Again she shook her head. 'He loved them, the look of them, the smell of them, the way they talked and laughed and thought.' She looked at Cassie and added quickly: 'I

don't mean he was promiscuous. He adored your mother
– everyone knew that – but when she died...'

'I hadn't realised.' But how could she have? For her, a
child, Harry Swann had filled the universe. Harry himself
would have had broader horizons.

'He was a good-looking man – well, you must have
known that – and he was available. Naturally women
threw themselves at him – all kinds of women. Harry liked
class, if you know what I mean,' Mrs Davis smiled
reminiscently. 'And class liked him.'

'Did you ever meet any of the women he went out
with?'

'I'd see him from time to time with someone, but I've
no idea who they were. When I said we established a close
relationship, I meant it was purely on a business level,
though we often dropped in to the Boilermakers' when
we were off-duty.'

'Does the name Brigid Fraser mean anything to you?'

Mrs Davis thought about it. 'Fraser?' She shook her
head. 'Can't say it does.'

'What about someone called Tony Spezzioli?'

'Where on earth did you hear about him?'

'I teach bridge in our local prison,' Cassie said. 'One of
the men in there – Kipper Naughton, he was called—'

'Heavens, yes,' said Mrs Davis. 'I remember Kipper
well. Wife ran off and left him to bring up his kids on his
own. Didn't something terrible happen to his daughter: a
hit-and-run accident, was it? Something likes that.' She
seemed younger, less contained, a flush of reminiscence
brightening; her face.

'—anyway, Kipper was there in the pub the night my
father died. He told me that this Spezzioli person had
pulled a knife—'

'That's how I got involved in the first place.' Mrs Ivan

Davis's eyes were bright. Cassie suspected that civilian life might have seemed pretty dull after her years on the force. 'I'd been keeping an eye on Spetzy because we'd had word that he was involved in drugs – that whole scene was just taking off in London in those days, and we still thought we had a chance of controlling it – so I was – not exactly following him, but making sure that I was around in the places he was around.'

'And that night?'

'He was lounging about outside the pub, the way they used to, him and some of his mates—' Again she shook her head. '—I still remember them, even after all this time: the Maloney twins Looney Barnes, a couple of others. I walked past them, just letting them know I was there, you see, giving them the old once-over, showing them that whatever they were up to, I was wise to them – pricing was much more of a community affair in those days. Then a couple of people, strangers, cane walking towards me, and before I really knew what was happening, they all started beating each other up. Fists and boots, you know the kind of thing.'

She broke off, smiling. She sipped at her whisky and glanced at her watch. 'My husband should be home soon. Would you like to stay for supper? We'd really love to have you; we don't of often get the chance to talk about the old days.'

Carrie started to shake her head but reflected that if she refused the invitation, she would be inconveniencing the no doubt hungry Davis if she had not finished what she had to ask before he returned. 'I'm not really very hungry,' she said – and wondered when she had last said that. 'And I don't want to interrupt your evening longer than I have to.'

'That's all right.' Jill Davis's smile was reminiscent.

'Thinking about it all, I'd forgotten just how much fun it all was.' In front of Cassie's eyes, she was metamorphosing from weary mother and wife into the eager young policewoman she must once have been. Is it marriage, or just life, that does that, Cassie wondered, that takes your enthusiasms, your hopes, and carefully smashes them one by one until you no longer bother to dream?

'What did you do when they started fighting?' she asked.

'Stepped up, told them to knock it off, told them I'd have them in the station soon as look at them, and then they all turned on me, knocked me to the pavement, started kicking me.'

'Were you surprised?'

'As a matter of fact, I was. It had certainly never happened to me before – there was still a bit of respect for the uniform in those days. *And* for women. Even though I was alone, it wasn't like the villains to start knocking a woman around – but I couldn't really see why they'd started fighting in the first place. The ones who'd just arrived: there was only two of them and neither of them seemed to be displaying any aggro, as far as I could see.'

'So you thought it was odd?'

'Definitely.' She nodded, biting her lip, thinking back. 'I never said so at the inquest – they weren't asking that kind of question – but now you've brought it all back, it was funny. And I'll tell you what else was strange...' She raised her hand and pressed a finger against the air between her and Cassie. 'They were kicking me, punching me, and I can't say it was a particularly pleasant experience, but those lads knew how to hurt. I mean, the Maloney twins had been in and out of nick for years, usually for some form of GBH. They certainly knew how land a paunch or put the boot in, but that night ... I was screaming my head off, of course, because it hurt, but, like I say, it could have been a lot worse.'

'You think they were holding back?'

'I didn't think so at the time, but looking back, yes, I think they might have been.'

'And then Tony Spetz pulled a knife, according to Kip Naughton.'

'*Some*body did. Might have been Spetzy, might have been one of the others. Either way, your dad heard the noise going on outside and came across to investigate and...' The vitality seemed to ebb from her as she sank back in her seat and looked down into her glass. 'That was the only violent death I was involved in during my years on the force.'

'But Tony Spezzioli was never charged?'

'That's partly because we never caught up with the little punk.'

'Why not?'

'Because after the first time we had him down to the station, he did a runner. The buzz on the street was that he went to Australia, changed his name, started again.'

'Where would he have got the money?'

'You tell me,' said Jill Davis 'He certainly didn't get it from that old lush who brought him up, Ruby Spezzioli, his aunt. She didn't have two pennies to rub together, and when she did, it all went on the booze.'

Things had changed, in that case. When Cassie had talked to Ruby Spezzioli, the old lady had not seemed to be suffering any financial hardship. And Kipper Naughton had mentioned the fact that she wasn't short of a bob or two.

'Doesn't that imply that someone helped him? Someone who wanted a convenient scapegoat and was prepared to pay?'

'Could be.' Again the former policewoman took over from the current wife and mother, turning the notion over in her mind. 'But one thing's for sure: if I was setting up a plan like that, I certainly wouldn't have involved Tony Spetz.'

'Why not?'

'He wasn't the most reliable villain I've ever had dealings with.' She laughed. 'If that doesn't sound ridiculous. For starters, he was too thick.'

'He seems to have managed to get himself to Australia.'

'Maybe. Maybe not. The CID chaps did go out to Oz but they never found a smell of him. They wondered if Spetzy and his chums had set them up, started the rumour to put them off the scent, but we didn't see that lot having the brains to dream that up. But even if they had...'

'What?'

'I'm afraid...' An apologetic expression crossed Mrs Davis's face. '...The only person who could have said for sure who killed Harry Swann was Harry Swann himself.'

Oh, Dad...

'Did he say anything before he died?' Cassie cleared her throat. 'Did you hear him speak?'

'Yes. Yes, I did. He came out onto the street and said something like: "What the fuck's going on out here?" And then his voice kind of changed. He said: "What're you doing here?" and then I think he shouted – I think he said "No, no!" and there was a kind of groan and he fell to the ground. And I think he said: "Why" I think I heard that, too. By the time I'd picked myself up off the pavement, the people who'd been standing around had all melted away, the way they do. I mean, because I'd seen them there, we were able to call in the twins and Looney Barnes and – oh, Jason Meacher, he was there too – and a couple of the others, but they all said...' Mrs Davis's voice dropped into a pseudo-cockney whine. '...they didn't know nothing, they hadn't seen nothing, wasn't their fault, if they was being charged they wanted to speak to their briefs, etc, etc.' She grimaced at remembered frustration. 'God. Sometimes you got sick and tired of them and their futile little lives.'

'My father said, "What are you doing here"?'

'Yes.'

'Like that? With that kind of emphasis? You said his voice changed.'

'It did. He said...' Mrs Davis closed her eyes and thrust her fingers through her careful hair as she tried to remember exactly, '...he said it as though – I haven't thought about it really that much, but as though he knew or recognised the person he was speaking to. "What're *you* doing here?" Like that. As though he were surprised to see the person there.'

'And then he said "Why?" Is that right?'

'Yes.'

'He could have been speaking to any of them, couldn't he?'

'Not if you think about it. The fact that he was surprised to see whoever it was he spoke to implies that it must have been one of the two people who came up – the ones I'd never seen before. Because he'd have known all the others, wouldn't he? After all, they were locals.'

'Of course they were.' Trying to slow down her swirling thoughts, Cassie said urgently: 'Can you remember anything at all about those two? The ones you didn't know?'

'It's all so long ago. And everything happened in split seconds. Don't forget that when Harry came out of the pub, I was lying on the ground being given the treatment

by at least three pairs of bovver boots. The only chance I
had to observe the couple who'd just arrived was in the
few moments before the lads jumped me.'

'Anything? Anything at all: an impression, a detail?'

Jill Davis pressed her hands to the sides of her head.
'One was a man, thirty or so, big bloke, six foot three at
least and burly with it. And the other—' She broke off. 'A
lad, wearing a cap, one of those tweed caps people wear in
the country. A young lad, twenty, twenty-one. Maybe a
bit more.' She leaned towards Cassie, her voice changing
dawn from brisk to maternal. 'Can I call you Cassandra?'

'Cassie.'

'I remember you, you know. Poor little thing. So
bewildered, so lost and frightened. And Harry's poor old
mum, your gran, absolutely devastated.'

'Don't,' Cassie said. 'Please don't.' But it was too late.
She started to cry, remembering with acid clarity the
frightened child she had been.

Mrs Davis also had tears in her eyes. 'I meant to keep in
touch, I really did, but when I came out of hospital after
the attack, Ivan and I decided to get married immediately
instead of waiting and then we moved away, and things
happened, the way they do. I hope, I really hope your life
has been all right.' She made an attempt at a smile. 'At
least you didn't end up in the Vicarage with that aunt of
yours.'

'I did,' Cassie said.

'But I thought—'

'My Gran died a couple of years later, when I was
thirteen. She had a massive heart attack one day. The
doctor said it must have happened at the end of the lunch-
hour, after closing time. She was – she died alone. She lay
there until I came home and ... and found her.' Oh God.
Gran, lying on her bed, dead eyes staring at the ceiling, a

fly buzzing in the corner of the window. Had she wanted a
hand to hold as she crossed the boundary between life and
death? Had she been glad to go? Distinctly Cassie
recalled the feel of Gran's cold face as she leaned over and
drew down the eyelids over those faded eyes, the house
quiet as a coffin around her. 'And in the end there was
nowhere else for me to go but to live with Uncle Sam and
Aunt Polly.'

'You poor thing – your aunt wasn't exactly what you'd
call warm-hearted, was she? She tried to come the lady of
the manor with me, and I didn't take kindly to it, I can tell
you.'

'If you thought she was awful, you should have met her
three daughters.' Cassie palmed away the tears and
managed a grin. 'The cousins from hell.'

'If they were anything like her...'

Cassie expelled a huge sigh. 'Look. Did you ever, at
any time, feel that my father's murder might have been a
set-up?'

'How do you mean?'

'You said that they weren't kicking you as hard as they
could have done. Is it possible that this wasn't simply a
brawl that got out of hand, but that the whole fight scene
was to distract attention from the real target?'

'Who might that have been?'

Cassie hesitated. Then she said: 'My dad.'

7

She did not sleep well that night. As she stared unseeing into the darkness, sharp-focused images punctured the layers of her mind, clear as capital letters. A man's silhouette against yellow light lying across the road, an arm raised against the bitter slash of a knife, thugs circled round a body on the ground, incredulous cries of horror as the drinkers in the Boilermakers' came rushing out. And always, somewhere in the background, their faces white against the dark, two people: a tall man and a lad, watching, doing nothing, while Harry Swann bled to death in the road. Shadows melting into shadows.

Yet, although the memories were clear, she could have seen none of this. While her father died, she had been asleep at the back of the pub, in the little room which overlooked backyards and creosoted fences, straggling roses and tool-sheds. She had a vague recollection of a police siren, her door being opened quietly and then closed again. It was not until the morning that they had told her what had happened.

In the end, she got up and went downstairs to make herself a mug of cocoa, then drank it in bed while finishing *Killing Me Softly*.

Around three-thirty, the telephone rang.

She froze for a moment, knowing who it would be and

the sort of thing the hated voice would say. The cold summons cut through the silent house, slicing across the dark corners of her bedroom. She shivered. One of these days he would come to the cottage and she would be alone and completely at his mercy. She knew this with a kind of helpless certainty. After a moment, she picked up the receiver, at the same time pressing the button to cut the connection, and laid it by the side of the set. Paul Walsh had given her an alarm which gave off a terrifying screech, but there was no one nearby to come to her aid. Even when Kathryn Kurtz was at home, Ivy Cottage was three hundred yards further down Back Lane: the chances that she would hear anything were minimal. Steve was aware of that: he had already made sure that she knew he had been to her home, had nosed around, had even logged some of her routines. Maybe she should get a real dog, since George, the ferocious German Shepherd she had invented in the hope of repelling him, had proved such a flop. Or maybe he would commit another assault on some young woman before he could get round to Cassie, and be sent back inside.

But it was both cowardly and immoral of her to hope that someone else would suffer in order that she might be saved from further fear.

She went downstairs to the kitchen again. After a moment's hesitation – if she let her fear of Steve dominate her life, she might as well move into sheltered accommodation right now – she pulled at the bolts on the back door and stepped out onto the dewy lawn. The morning air was sweet, scented with grass and lilac. A few birds were prematurely heralding the dawn; she could hear tentative frog croaks from the pond. Somewhere a rooster was limbering up for the morning alarm calls and the cough of a van wound along the line of a distant roadway. Cassie found comfort in these simplicities: murder and violence seemed to fade a little and after a few minutes she was able to go back to bed and eventually to fall asleep. It was nine-fifteen before she woke up and, remembering, reached out to replace the telephone. As soon as she had done so, it rang.

Was it Paul? She hadn't spoken to him for ages. 'Hello,' she said, snatching at what little thespian ability she possessed in an effort to sound like someone who had been up for hours.

'Cass: it's Natasha. Something terrible...' Natasha sounded almost incoherent.

'What?'

'People are so ... I just can't believe...'

'Is it the Rays again?'

'Someone's sent them – honestly, Cass, what kind of a mind could – a funeral wreath, can you imagine?'

'Was there some threat attached?' Cassie was fully awake now.

'A note. One of those florist's cards.'

'Did you see it? What did it say?'

'Something along the lines of In memory of Vida Ray, who did not heed the warning. Something like that.'

'It wasn't addressed to both of them?'

'No. Just to Vida.'

'Who delivered it?'

'A florist from Bellington.'

'Did you ring them?'

'As soon as Vida came round to tell me, I got on the phone to them immediately. The said it had been sent through Interflora, via some big flower shop in Knightsbridge.'

'And you rang Knightsbridge too?'

'Of course. They couldn't remember anything about

who'd ordered it, but their records show the sender came in yesterday. Cassie, I'm really upset about—'

'And this customer paid for it in cash, so there's no way of tracing anyone?'

'How did you know?'

'It's what I'd do, if I were into playing sick jokes on vulnerable people.'

'Is it a joke, Cass? Is that all it is?'

'Oh, Natasha.' Cassie sighed. 'Let's hope so – not that that would make it any better.'

'Have you had a chance to speak to Paul?'

'Not yet. He's away on a course at the moment but he ought to be back tomorrow. I'll tell him all about it as soon as he calls me. But the Rays really ought to go to the local police.'

'That's what I told her. But she – Vida, I mean – she keeps saying she doesn't want her husband's new job compromised in any way. And then, when I kept saying there was no way the hospital would see this kind of thing as *his* fault, she suddenly burst into tears and kept saying no police, no police.'

'Oh Lord,' Cassie said. 'You don't think it's him she's frightened of, do you?'

'If you really want to know, I think she's scared shitless of him. She had a mark on her neck today which...' Natasha's voice got lost in a choke of anger and dismay. Cassie knew that as a loved and loving wife, the mere idea of a husband offering violence to his partner was incomprehensible to her.

She said: 'Didn't the Knightsbridge shop think the message was a bit odd?'

'I asked them that but they couldn't have cared less. Some snotty manageress came on the line, said it wasn't their business to censor messages, merely to pass them on. You should see the thing, Cassie, the wreath: it's monstrous. I put it in my car and took it straight down to the Tidy Tip. Poor Vida: she's completely stunned.'

'I'm not surprised. Did you throw away the card too?'

'I wasn't thinking – just wanted to get rid of the thing. It was a crucifix, Cass, made of white roses. Hideous.' She paused. 'I suppose I shouldn't have chucked that card out, but it wasn't evidence, really, and if it came to a court case, the florist will have records.' There was a pause, then Natasha said: 'What disturbs one almost as much as the fact that the Rays are being persecuted like this—'

'Vida's being persecuted; Sammi doesn't know anything about it yet.'

'—Yes, well ... the most disturbing aspect is that it's one of us who's responsible. One of our very small community. I *hate* that. Every time I go out of the front gate and meet one of the neighbours, I think, are *you* the one shoving dogshit through people's letter-boxes? Are *you* the one who tried to burn someone's house down around their ears?'

'That's the worst of hellish behaviour like this: it seems to stain everything around it.'

'The awful thing is, I can't seem to think of anything to say to comfort that poor woman,' Natasha said helplessly.

'I know,' said Cassie. 'Look, do you know anyone in Larton Easewood who went up to London yesterday?'

'No.'

'Anyone with racially biased relatives in Knightsbridge?'

'I think the Rector's aunt has a flat near Harrods,' Natasha said. 'But she's about a hundred and three and spent most of her life as a Christian missionary out in India. Can't be her.'

'Is there a fledgling movement of the National Front Party, something like that?'

'No. Just a few frustrated Hockneys and Renoirs painting graffiti on the football pavilion on Saturday nights: swastikas and so on. But no slogans, no skin-heads, not really. Nobody's ever desecrated the church-yard – apart from leaving the odd used condom lying around. We've got Colonel Bartlett down the road, in Porch House, who's a fearful old bigot but since he's anti everything on principle, from women to broccoli, I don't think he counts.'

'Broccoli?'

'Nasty foreign rubbish. Not to mention Mussolini.'

'There's got to be a connection in there somewhere, if I just look hard enough.'

'Anyway, he's away at the moment, staying with one of his long-suffering daughters.'

'She doesn't live in Knightsbridge, I suppose.'

'Cold Christmas, actually.'

'"In memory of Vida Ray",' Cassie said ruminatively. '"Who did not heed the warning" – is that what it said?'

'As far as I remember.'

'What about the cricketing lot? Could it be any of them?'

'I thought about that. But most of them don't live here: they play here because we've got the pitch and the pavilion and score boards but they come from the surrounding villages. It's not even a regular side.'

'What about the ones who *are* from Larton Easewood?'

'Couldn't be more respectable. Canon Granger, for one. The bursar at St Christopher's. The manager of the supermarket at Bellington. Plus there's Simon Barnes, who's a medical student but who sometimes turns out if he's at home. His parents live in that big house on the other side of the green.'

'None of them sound like promising poison-pen material, do they?'

'Especially not the Rector.'

'Look, I can't promise a thing, but leave it with me.'

Not that there was much Cassie could do. She knew Paul Walsh would recommend going to the police: it was what any sensible person would do. On the other hand, she could understand Vida Ray's reluctance to do anything which might draw her husband's wrath – and his fists? – down on her if she could possibly avoid it. But in a community as small as Larton Easewood, it ought to be possible to find some clue as to the identity of the perpetrator. Perhaps a round-the-clock watch on the Old School House could be mounted; perhaps the Sinclair children could earn extra pocket money by keeping an eye open ... but that would mean telling them what was going on, and as the children of a mixed-race marriage themselves, they probably already knew more about racial persecution than they needed. In fact, prejudice was one of the very factors which had persuaded Natasha and Chris to leave London and move into the country in the first place.

Cassie stumbled downstairs for the third time that day, made some tea, gnawed an unsatisfactory stick of celery, ate half an unfilling grapefruit and went through the mail. One letter had her temporarily stumped. It came from the Education Officer at an open prison in the next county, and told her how much he had enjoyed *Killing Me Softly*, so much so that he wondered whether she would like to take up the post of Creative Writing Tutor at his establishment for a term. After staring at this for some time in bewilderment – how did he know she had been reading it?

And why, having read it, should that qualify her to teach creative writing? – she realised that somewhere an equally bewildered author must be puzzling over why he should have been invited to take a weekly bridge class at the same prison. Her first instinct was to chuck it in the bin, but if the author had the same instinct ... she put it to one side to follow up later. There was also a letter from somebody from an address in Mayfair, saying that he understood she occasionally acted as a professional bridge partner, and he would very much like to discuss this further, at her convenience. Yes, please, she thought. Playing as a professional partner was a lucrative way to add to her erratic – though beginning to steady – income.

Outside, the wind had dropped and the sun shone brightly on the garden. She could see the large posterior of the builders' foreman as he stood over the rotating concrete mixer like the compère at a bingo session. His thinner workmates were inside the outbuildings, knocking down walls, creating a huge amount of dust which billowed into the garden and had already covered the nearest plants. Even with the windows shut, she could hear the grinding and bashing plus the heavy throb of their ghetto-blasters turned up to full volume.

Yesterday, she had left Warnford before Ivan Davis came home, but his wife had promised that if she remembered anything at all, however trivial it might seem, she would get in touch at once. Meanwhile, it was a question of deciding between choking to death on dust while over-dosing on heavy metal, or going to London. An easy choice.

'What'll it be?' The landlord of the Boilermakers' obviously didn't recognise her although it was only a few weeks since her earlier visit.

'An orange juice, please,' Cassie said. Last time, he had been both unfriendly and patronising; she did not feel inclined to lay on the charm. She looked along the bar to where she had expected to see Old Ruby raising a dainty glass of gin and tonic to her ancient lips. 'And a packet of ready-salted cri—' But the words died before she could finish uttering them. A vision of Primula and Hyacinth, emaciated and skeletal in their dinky wedding outfits, plastered itself like blown newspaper against the inside of her forehead. And there was Uncle Sam's birthday luncheon the next Sunday ... Gritting her teeth, she said: 'On second thoughts, just the juice.'

'Dieting, are we?' the landlord smirked.

What if we were? It was none of his damn business. Cassie raised offputting eyebrows and did not bother to answer. After a ladylike sip, she nodded at the vacant stool against the wall of the bar and said: 'Where's Old Ruby, then?'

'Poor old girl – haven't you heard?'

Would I be asking if I had, dork? 'No.'

'Terrible, just terrible. Dunno where you are these days, do you?'

'That depends on—'

'Kids! I dunno.' The landlord raised his overabundant eyebrows and shook his head. 'It's not like my young days, I can tell you that. Had some respect then, even if we weren't exactly little angels, but nowadays – it's bloody disgraceful. If you ask me, they have things a damn sight too easy for their own—' He was well launched on one of those interminable Great Bores of Today monologues, and Cassie thought it might be some time before anyone would interrupt him with requests for refills, since there was no more than a handful of people in the room: a couple of pensioners, a couple of late lunchers, a fleshy man of about forty-five who was sitting by the window over a pint of Guinness.

She swallowed her orange juice and banged the glass down on the counter. 'I'll have another of those,' she said authoritatively, stopping him in mid-flow. While he was reaching beneath the counter for bottle and opener, she said: 'What happened to Old Ruby?'

'I dunno,' he said, straightening up. 'Kids these days, they think they've—'

'Did someone mug her or what?'

'Mug her. No, they just bleeding murdered the poor old cow, didn't they?'

'Murdered?' Cassie felt suddenly cold.

'Yeah. Far as the police can make out, someone broke in while she was round here – one of our regulars was Old Ruby, you could set your clock by her – and lay in wait for her and then when she got home, stabbed her to death with her own bread knife, made off with her pension. It's bloody disgraceful, helpless old thing like that.'

'Stabbed?' Cassie could not keep the horror from her voice.

'Thirty-six separate wounds, according to the coppers. You'd hardly credit it, would you. 'Ere, wasn't you round this way a few weeks back?'

'As a matter of—' Cassie fidgeted with her glass, feeling very far from happy. Kipper Naughton had suggested that Old Ruby was being 'taken care of'; now, it seemed, she had been taken care of in the most definitive way possible. Could it have anything to do with Cassie's own recent enquiries?

'Yeah, I remember now,' the landlord went on. He leaned across the thick mahogany counter and rested on his elbow. 'Came in asking for Old Ruby, didn't you? It was just after that that the old girl snuffed it.'

'I'm really sorry to—'

'Yer. I remember you now. Thought it was a bit odd, you coming in just now and knowing her name. Some story about your dad owning the place twenty years ago, wasn't it?'

'It wasn't a story, it was the truth,' Cassie said. 'Look; there's a picture of him over there on the wall.' She slipped off her stool and walked between the small round tables to where a framed colour photograph hung above what had once been the fireplace but had now been boarded up. She had noticed it last time she was here: a crowd of men and women in the ludicrous fab gear of the Seventies, with Harry Swann the middle of the flares and flowered shirts and hideous sideburns.

'I was on that trip,' someone said behind her.

Cassie turned. The man who had been drinking Guinness had joined her and was looking up at the photograph.

'Were you?'

'That's me, there, see? Standing at the back.' He peered more closely then pointed to a lad in an embroidered afghan waistcoat with hair standing out round his head as if he'd just stuck his finger into an electric-light socket. 'Gordon Bennett, what did we think we looked like?'

'Dedicated followers of fashion,' Cassie said.

'Dedicated bunch of wankers, if you ask me.' He looked at Cassie. 'Meacher's the name. Jason Meacher.'

Involuntarily, Cassie stepped back. Jason Meacher was one of the men who had been hanging round outside the pub on the night of Harry Swann's death. It seemed this was still his local, even after so many years. Could she – dare she? – question him? Looking behind her, she saw the landlord staring intently at them both.

She turned back to the photograph. 'Where were you all going? Was it a trip to the seaside or something?' she said, and was surprised that her voice sounded perfectly normal.

'No, we was off to Haydock Park. Harry Swann always liked a nice day at the races.'

Cassie came to a decision. 'Look, Mr Meacher, would you let me buy you a refill?'

He seemed surprised. 'OK. Don't mind if I do.'

'I'll bring it over to your table.' While she ordered another Guinness, Cassie wondered whether she should admit to being Harry Swann's daughter. There seemed no point in concealing the fact: even if he had not overheard what she said to the landlord about it, the man would undoubtedly tell him when she'd gone. On the other hand, wouldn't she be exposing herself unnecessarily? Suppose – by some stretch of the imagination – he were the one responsible for Old Ruby's murder – though she had absolutely no reason for thinking that he was.

As she walked over to Meacher's tables she decided she would have to come clean if she was to get anything out of him.

'Harry Swann was my father,' she said, as he took a long pull at his drink.

'Is that a fact?' He didn't seem particularly interested.

'Don't you think it's strange that nobody's ever been charged with his murder?'

He shrugged, eyeing her over the top of his glass. 'It was an accident.'

'You were here yourself, that night, weren't you?'

He gave her a cautious look but did not try to deny it. 'What if I was?'

'Did you see what happened?'

'No.'

'Come on, Mr Meacher. According to my information,

you were right in the middle of it all. You must have seen something.'

'I didn't. We was hanging round outside – I told the Old Bill at the time – and these two blokes nobody ever seen before come up, and suddenly there was a fight, bird on the floor being kicked about, knives out, and your dad—' Meacher looked down at the table. 'Honest, it was all over in a few seconds.'

'What about those two who appeared? You say you'd never seen them before: can you remember anything about them?'

'One was a big bloke. The other was a just a kid – didn't look as if he'd even started shaving.'

'Anything else?'

'The kid had a cap on, hair kind of bundled up inside it. Other than that . . .' Meacher lifted his glass again and took a long swig.

'Would you recognise either of them again?'

'What, after all this time? Leave it out, lady. Only saw them for a couple of seconds before we was all pitching in – I still don't really know how the whole thing ever got started. And soon as we realised what'd happened, your dad and all, we was off out of there. I mean, no one ever meant to do Harry in, he just got in the way.'

'You think someone else was supposed to be knifed?'

'I'm not saying that.' Meacher wiped Guinness foam off his upper lip. 'The knife was probably just for show, like. No one was supposed to get stuck.'

'Whose knife was it?'

'No idea.'

'Not Tony Spezzioli's, then?'

His expression this time was as much angry as suspicious. 'Look, why're you in here asking all these questions if you already know so bleeding much?'

'As I explained, Harry Swann was my father,' Cassie said. 'I'd like to sort a few things out.' She stared at him, hoping the tears would not rise again. 'I *need* to.'

He nodded. 'Take your point. But far's I know, Tony Spetz didn't carry no knives. Not then, not ever.'

'Why did he disappear, then?'

'Di'n't want to get fitted up by the Bill, did he? Wiv a record like he'd got, he'd've bin inside with a murder charge wrapped round his neck and tied with a bow before you could say "knife", know what I mean?'

'If it wasn't his knife, whose was it?'

'Dunno.' He shrugged, looking away from her towards the dirty window and the traffic thundering past outside in the road.

'Do you know where Tony Spezzioli went?'

'No idea.' His gaze slid away from hers. She wondered if he was lying.

'Someone said something about him going to Australia.'

'Dunno nothing about it.' Unease glistened on his face like sweat.

Cassie changed tack, nodding over at the group photo on the wall. 'Did my father often organise trips to the races?'

'Two or three times a year. Loved the track, did Harry. But mostly, he went on his own.'

'Did Tony Spezzioli ever go on one of these trips?'

'Course he did. Wasn't much else for us to do . . . gave us a bit of a break, like.'

'Is he in that photograph?' Cassie nodded over at the fireplace.

'Can't remember,' Meacher said. 'Probably was. Usually came: liked a bit of an outing, did Spetzy.'

'Show me.'

Meacher got up and walked over the photograph again, followed by Cassie. His gaze wandered over the fading picture. 'Yer. There he is, at the back. Got his hands on Old Ruby's shoulders, see?'

Cassie peered closer. 'That boy with the curls?'

'That's him.'

Tony Spezzioli, despite his Latin name, had a square Anglo-Saxon face under an untidy crop of dark curly hair. And in front of him was a tiny chirpy figure, Old Ruby, not so old then, the aunt who had brought him up. Not, it appeared, with much success.

'When you went to the races, did you ever see Harry Swann there with someone?' asked Cassie

Meacher frowned. 'How d'you mean?'

'A woman, perhaps.'

'Oh, a woman. He had lots of those, did Harry.' Belatedly, remembering that the woman at his side was Harry's daughter, he added: 'So they said, but I could be—'

'It's all right. I know about that. I just wondered if you could identify any of these women, whether you knew any he spent more time with than others.'

'There *was* some bird he used to meet up with at the race-tracks,' Meacher said. 'Not my sort, I must say. Bit too cut-glass for my taste.'

'How old was she?'

He grinned, showing discoloured teeth. 'You're not supposed to ask a woman's age.'

'Young,' Cassie said patiently. 'Old? Somewhere in between?'

'Pretty young. Dolly-bird type – you know, long hair and skirts so short, you could see what she'd had for breakfast.' Meacher smiled reminiscently. 'Them were the days, all right.'

'Do you remember her name?'

'Can't say as I ever knew it,' Meacher said, after thinking about the question. He drained his pint, leaving a pattern like ecru lace over the inside of the glass. 'No. Definitely not.'

From her bag, Cassie pulled out the photograph of Harry Swann with the woman Quartermain had identified as Brigid Fraser. 'Was this her?'

'Blimey,' exclaimed Meacher. 'He never dressed up like that when he went racing with us lot, I can tell you. Looks a right toff, dunny?'

'What about the woman?'

Meacher scratched at his unshaven jaw. 'Couldn't really say.' He tapped the photograph. 'Can't see her face, for one thing. Might be the one I saw him with but I wouldn't swear ... Like I say, you can't see her face, can you? I only saw him with her a couple of times, from a distance, like. And it was a long time ago.'

There was a different librarian on duty in the reference section, a stern woman with startling eyebrows. When Cassie asked to see copies of the newspapers over the past few weeks, she appeared to take it as a personal affront – frowning, staring at Cassie with an expression of defiant dislike – though eventually she got up from her desk and opened a cupboard set into one of the walls.

'How far back?' she grated, Ivan-the-Terrible style.

Cassie calculated. 'Six weeks, please.'

Glaring, the librarian picked out an armful of papers, dumped them onto a table and returned to her desk without further speech.

'Thank you,' Cassie called after her. 'Very much.'

The accounts of Ruby Spezzioli's death did not differ substantially from what the landlord at the Boilermakers' had already told her. Someone had broken into Ruby's house, waited for her on the first floor and then pushed her downstairs. She had died, not from the fall, but from the subsequent horrific assault with a bread knife taken from her own kitchen, after which the murderer had ransacked the house before making off with what remained of Ruby's pension – just picked up that day from the post office – and various pieces of jewellery, electronic equipment, of which Ruby possessed a surprising amount, and a couple of fur coats. A niece had appeared to testify to the loss of these articles: it was suggested that Ruby might have had considerable quantities of cash hidden about the house, of which the thief could have had prior knowledge.

The knife attack seemed gratuitous, violence simply for the sake of it. Cassie could not bear to think of the frightened old lady lying damaged in the hallway, watching her attacker come down the stairs with her knife in his hand. She must have known he was going to kill her, though Cassie devoutly hoped that she had drunk enough gin at the pub beforehand to deaden at least some of the fear and the pain.

A witness had described seeing someone slipping through the backyard gate into the alley which ran behind the houses but could offer no more than a vague description of someone who was neither tall nor short, young nor old, male or female. The landlord of the pub had been convinced that children were responsible; reading the local weekly free-sheet, Cassie could see why. In the past few months, children had terrorised old age pensioners, smashed up empty properties, vandalised homes where the owners were away. But even in these violent times, surely children did not stab old ladies to death.

However, something else was bothering Cassie. For

years, Old Ruby had been dropping in to the Boilermakers' every lunch-time and every evening, drinking
her gin and tonics, staggering home to fall asleep until
the next day when she started again. And then one
day Cassandra Swann, professional bridge teacher and
orphan, shows up asking questions about her father's
murder, and within days, Old Ruby, aunt of the suspect
Tony Spezzioli, is killed

You'd have to be pretty thick not to wonder if there was
some connection between the two facts.

And if there was, that put Cassie Swann not only in the
position of being – albeit unwittingly – an accomplice to
murder, but also in the direct line of fire herself.

Didn't it?

8

As Cassie walked along the grassy path between the side of the cottage and her tumbledown shed-cum-garage, the white cat appeared from the direction of the pond and padded through the grass to wind round her ankles with the soft insistence of spilled emulsion. She bent to stroke it, at the same time checking it out for tell-tale flakes of goldfish. Twice already she had restocked the pond but with the combined forces of the herons and the cat against them, the goldfish were having a hard time hanging in there.

Peace had settled over the place. The workmen had gone for the day, leaving everything albinoed beneath a coating of powdered plaster. White grass, white gravel, white hedges. White beer cans. Low-wattage evening sunshine added a theatrical kind of illumination so that the garden looked as though it had been dreamed up by an avant-garde set designer. Beyond the hedge at the end, fields spread across the sloping landscape: blue-green with springing barley, sunshiny yellow where the farmer had planted oilseed rape.

Pushing aside the ivy strands hanging over the back porch, she was about to insert her key in the lock, when the door swung open. Jesus. Someone was already inside the house. Her lungs froze. Was it Steve? Had he broken in while she was gone? Was he waiting to pounce on her, to rip her face apart? She stepped back onto the grass, away from the porch, ready to turn and run. Behind her, the cat yowled, wrenching its tail from beneath her foot and streaking towards the safety of the hedge. Then from the kitchen, someone called her name.

'Paul!' Cassie burst in through the door 'Oh, God. I thought ... I thought ...'

Detective Sergeant Walsh was sitting at the kitchen table, confronting a bottle of red wine and two glasses: He stood up as she launched herself towards him and opened his arms. 'You thought I was waiting in here with a Stanley knife in my hand, ready to draw patterns on that pretty face?'

'Yes.'

'Christ, I'll cut his balls off if I ever catch up with him,' Walsh said violently. 'Scaring you like this.' He smiled at her. 'You're so beautiful, Cass. Have I told you that?'

'Not recently.'

He poured wine into the second glass. 'Got any plans for this evening?'

'I have now.'

'Are they the same plans as mine?'

'Probably.'

'Good.' He put his arms around her again.

The two of them gazed into each other's eyes. His were hazel, with dark flecks in them. Cassie loved him. His beautiful mouth brushed her eyelids and she sighed. 'How long can you stay?' she asked.

'At least until the morning – unless some emergency crops up.'

An emergency meant violence, a vanished child, a life forcefully snatched from its owner. 'Something nearly always does,' Cassie said sadly. They had never spent more than a few hours together, time grabbed from busy schedules, their shared moments all too often broken by calls from Walsh's superiors.

'I'm afraid it goes with the territory.'

'These fragments have I shored against my ruin,' said Cassie. 'Oh Paul: wouldn't it be wonderful to have longer together? A whole day? Forty-eight hours?' And even as she said it, wished she had not. Perhaps their relationship needed exactly this longing for more, perhaps it thrived on the urgency of never having enough time in each other's company. Perhaps if they were together for a longer stretch they would bore each other, find they possessed irreconcilable views, discover that neither was truly what each perceived the other to be.

'I've got some leave coming up soon. We could go away together. Abroad, even. Paris, Madrid, Vienna: whatever turns you on.'

'*You* turn me on,' said Cassie. She began to undo the buttons of his shirt as he pulled her blouse up out of her jeans and reached beneath it to hold her breasts in his hands.

'Beautiful,' he said. 'Fantastic.'

'What are we going for today,' said Cassie. 'The hurly-burly of the *chaise longue*?'

'We did the hurly-burly bit last time.'

'Then we'll just have to settle for the deep peace of the double bed.'

'I'll drink to that,' Walsh said, draining his glass before pulling her towards the boxed-in stairs which led up to her bedroom.

'Paul.'

'Mmm?'

'What's the best way to deal with poison-pen letters when the person getting them doesn't want to get involved with the police?'

'Ignore them.'

'Suppose there's more than letters involved.'

'Dog crap, do you mean? Petrol bombs? Rotting garbage on the doorstep?'

'That kind of thing.'

He turned to her and pulled her closer towards him, flattening her breasts against his chest. 'I take it you're not asking this simply out of curiosity.'

'No.'

'Is this racially motivated?'

'It seems to be. At least, members of a minority group living in a local all-white community are involved.'

'Publicity,' said Walsh. 'That'll kill it stone dead. Let the local all-white community know what's going on. Most people don't like unfair play. Most of us root for the underdog. One bad apple in the barrel doesn't mean everyone holds racist views. Publicise it, and the community itself will sort it out.'

'Trouble is...' Cassie burrowed closer to Walsh, '...the husband doesn't know, and the wife wants to keep it that way.' She explained the situation.

'If she won't tell him, more fool her.'

'Can't you do anything?'

'Darling, until they call us in, no one can do anything. And even if they did, it wouldn't be me who'd handle it.'

'I mean, in a private kind of way.'

He drew back and looked down at her lying in his arms. 'Are you serious, Cass? Are you really suggesting that I spend my spare time keeping an eye out for suspicious characters carrying shovelfuls of dog-shit?' Walsh's unsympathetic tone had nothing to do with lack of compassion and everything to do with the pragmatism of a police force already stretched way beyond the limits.

Put like that, of course she didn't. 'Given the circumstances, what would you do?'

'I already told you.' He bent his head and kissed the tip of her nose. 'Can we change the subject? We have so little time together and I really don't want to waste it talking about how to help people determined not to help themselves.'

She knew he was right. She pulled his hips towards hers. '*You* can help yourself as much as you like,' she said softly.

So he did.

At three-twenty in the morning, the telephone rang. Cassie was instantly awake. As she reached for the receiver, ready to cut the connection, Walsh pulled her arm back and lifted it himself. 'What the fuck do you want, you scumbag?' he growled, holding the handset away from his ear so that Cassie could listen in.

At the other end, she clearly heard Steve's voice. 'Stick it up your ass, you pig bastard.'

'I know who you are,' Walsh said.

'So what, fucking pig, fucking motherfucker?'

'Try this trick again,' said Walsh, his voice murderous, 'and you'll be sitting in a cell stuffing your balls back up your nose.'

'Hang on, fucker, while I try to stop trembling.'

'You'd better believe me, you piece of shit,' Walsh said and slammed the receiver back on its rest. He lay against the pillows, his body taut, his mouth set in a tight, angry line, breathing hard through his nose.

'Was that what they call a frank exchange of views?'

Cassie said lightly, hoping to reduce the charged atmosphere

'That about covers it,' said Walsh shortly. He put his hands behind his head, not looking at her, quivering with rage and tension. She saw that he had left her, had moved into policeman mode, no longer Lover but Law Enforcer. When he was like this, she found him pretty intimidating.

'Thanks for handling it,' she began but he was not listening.

'Christ, I hate them,' he said, his chest rising and falling under her hand. 'I *hate* those fucking bastards who think they're better than everyone else and don't give a shit who they trample on in their efforts to prove it. Fuck them, fuck the lot of them.'

She said nothing.

'God,' Walsh said. A tremor started up somewhere deep in his body. 'I'd like to shoot the bastards. Especially *that* one.' He jerked his head savagely towards the phone. 'Half an hour with me would wipe some of the cockiness out of him, believe me.'

Which was exactly how innocent men found themselves spending years of their lives behind bars, paying for crimes they had not committed. 'Shoot them?' said Cassie. 'That's a bit sweeping. A lot of criminals deserve sympathy, not blame. Some of their backgrounds, the way they were brought up ... They can't all help what they are. I often meet men in the prison who—'

'Spare me,' Walsh said harshly. 'I don't want to hear your wishy-washy bleeding-heart views, thanks. In my book, either you're a good guy or you're not.'

'Paul, how you can take such a simplistic view of things? Nothing is that cut and dried, nothing's all black or all white. Even *white* isn't all white.'

'It has to be for me, Cassie. I'm a copper. It's like being a doctor, if you let yourself get too involved with your patients, you'd throw up the job the first time you saw a deformed baby, a child with meningitis, someone dying. So you learn to stand somewhere on the outside, to suppress your emotions. I can't afford to think that there are grey areas where the fucking villains aren't as bad as I think they are, where they deserve my sympathy. I can't afford to see them as anything but wicked or I'd never be able to get on with my job.'

'But that's tantamount to—'

'Ssh,' he said, his mouth against her cheek.

'Seriously, Paul. You can't take that attitude. People aren't animals. Any more than you are. A lot of what you call villains have never been given a chance, they were hideously abused as chi—'

He rolled onto his side and put his hand across her mouth. 'Cassie. We're in bed together and this isn't exactly my idea of pillow talk. Couldn't we discuss something else?'

She twisted away from him. 'You wouldn't be so damn patronising if I were a man.'

'I wouldn't be lying naked in bed with you if you were a man.'

'Paul, you're being—'

He moved his hand down across her belly and into the soft place between her thighs. 'I love you,' he said.

Cassie let it drop. He was right: this was neither the time nor the place for such discussion. Nonetheless, villain and cop, what were they but two sides of the same coin? The disloyal thought crept into her head that if Walsh's attitudes were typical of the police as a whole, then the government's plans to arm them could be the first step on the road towards legalising death squads. But who was she to take a high moral stance when she felt exactly as Walsh did about Steve?

Later, drowsing in Walsh's arms, she remembered Steve's words. He had seemed to know exactly who Walsh was. He had called Walsh 'pig'. That must mean that he knew Walsh was with the police. That must mean that he was still watching her, that he might even be outside the cottage that very minute. Beyond the light cast by the lamp on the bedside table, the shadows in the bedroom seemed to solidify, slabs of darkness edged with fear.

Even later, lying wakeful with her arms around Walsh's sleeping body, Cassie wondered if it had helped that he had tackled Steve on the telephone. Did she feel any safer? Quite the contrary. Somewhere out there, Steve still roamed like a tiger, no longer merely dangerous, but angry now, and vengeful.

Natasha came through the back door into the kitchen, her face grim. Cassie looked up from a dutiful breakfast of grapefruit juice, milkless tea and one slice of toast spread with Marmite. When those damned weddings were over, she was really going to pig out ... 'What's up?' she said, stifling thoughts of the way butter melts into just-made toast, the marbled curl of a Cumberland sausage, creamy mounds of scrambled eggs fried tomatoes.

For an answer, Natasha flung a piece of paper down on the table 'Vida found this on the doormat yesterday,' she said.

Cassie looked down at it. A sheet taken from a pad which could have been bought in any stationer's shop, anywhere. Words written with a fine-point felt-tip pen. HE'S FIRST. THEN YOU. She read the short message several times. 'She's *got* to go to the police,' she said.

'She absolutely refuses,' said Natasha.

'Unless she does, nobody can do much to help her.'

'She's terrified for her husband's position.'

'I spoke to Paul,' said Cassie. 'His reaction was exactly what I predicted. They can do nothing unless she calls them in.'

'But isn't this an outright threat?'

'It could be. But if she wants help, she'll have to...' Cassie didn't finish the sentence.

'Damn it!' Natasha put a kettle on to boil then opened a cupboard and found coffee beans, a grinder, the push-down glass jug.

'Why does she bring them to you, anyway?' Cassie said.

'Isn't it obvious? I'm the only person who's tried to be friendly, as far as I can make out. Besides, she's desperate.'

'Not desperate enough to get proper help.'

'She's suicidal, Cassandra.'

'Why do you say that?'

'She said so.'

'I wondered if you were talking about the scars on her wrists.'

'You've noticed them too?'

'I could hardly not, the way she shakes her bracelets around.'

'But that reinforces my point. If she's already tried it once, this is exactly the sort of thing that's likely to push her over the edge. Which is why she needs to know that there's someone on her side.'

'Us, do you mean.'

'Of course us. I mean, hear she is, alone in an alien country, and this sort of thing starts happening. It's terrible.'

'I know.' Cassie looked at the message again. HE'S
FIRST. THEN YOU. 'Has Sammi seen this one?'

'No.'

'Don't you think he should? If it's some kind of death
threat against him, then he ought to have the option of
calling in the police, getting protection.'

'That's what I said to Vida. She's beginning to realise
that she can't keep it to herself any longer, that she's
going to have to tell him – and the police, too.' Natasha
slammed coffee beans into the electric grinder and
switched it on at the wall. 'Of course, we could do it
ourselves, Cass.'

'Do what?' Cassie had to shout to be heard over the
furious noise.

Natasha switched off the leaned against the counter,
folding her arms across her chest. In jeans and a washed-
out denim shirt, she looked about eighteen. 'Uh...' She
gave a visible gulp. '*We* could tell Sammi.'

'Oh, no.' Cassie said. 'No we can't. No way.'

'*I* can't.'

'What makes you think I can?'

'For one thing, you're bigger than I am.'

'Et tu, Brute?'

I don't mean around the hips, you idiot – though you
are, of course, because that's the way you're built. I
mean, you're more of an authority figure than I am.'
Natasha emptied the ground coffee into the glass jug and
poured boiling water over it.

'How did you work that one out?'

'For a start, you're a very imposing woman, as you must
know.'

'If you dare call me Junoesque...'

'And you're his bridge teacher.'

'*What*? You mean, taking the guy for a weekly bridge

class gives me the right to interfere with his private life? Tash, I can't go against Vida's wishes: she must have a good reason for not telling him – which may or may not be the fact that she's scared of him.'

'Do it, Cass.' Natasha pressed the plunger down, pushing the coffee grounds to the bottom of the jug. 'For my sake.'

From the moment Cassie had seen the first note, she had realised that whether she wanted to or not, she would somehow end up involved. None the less, she tried. 'Excuse me,' she said. 'But I think you've got me confused with someone who gives a damn.'

'No, I haven't. You *do* give a damn – not just about the Rays but about your fellows in general. And even more, about me. And my children.'

Cassie pushed her cup around on the table. She should have known better than to hope that Natasha would not pick up on one very obvious aspect of the anonymous letters. If they were racially motivated, then Natasha herself was a natural target. Might even be the next to be attacked. 'Besides, you've always known you'd be the one who would have to talk to Sammi.'

If 'twere done ... Cassie pushed away from the table and stood up. 'OK. I'll do it right now.'

'On the phone?'

'What else do you want me to do?'

'Make an appointment to see him.'

'On what grounds?'

'Say you're having trouble with your periods.'

'Oh please,' groaned Cassie.

'Say you're pregnant. Say you're trying to *get* pregnant and can't.'

'He's a consultant, for God's sake.' Cassie found the number of the hospital in the directory and began dialling. 'I wouldn't get to see him in the first instance if I were the Virgin Mary carrying sextuplets.'

The hospital exchange answered, asking whom she wanted. She adopted an official kind of voice and said she wanted to speak to Dr Sammi Ray, only to be told that he was not currently available. When Cassie asked if he could be contacted somewhere else, she was informed that he sent up to London twice a week to see patients at a private hospital near Sloane Square.

'Sloane Square?'

'Yes.'

'And he goes up every week?'

'Yes. He specialises in—'

'Thank you.' Cassie said

'Who is this, please?'

Cassie replaced the receiver. 'Tash,' she said slowly.

'What?'

'I've just had a rather horrible idea.'

'Tell me.'

'We know that the wreath was ordered from a Knightsbridge florist, don't we?'

'We do.'

'What we didn't know – until now – is that Dr Sammi Ray goes up to London twice a week. To Knightsbridge.'

The two friends stared at each other. Then Natasha put down her coffee cup and bit down on her lower lip. 'Oh Gods' she said. 'So what are we thinking here?'

'We're trying hard not to jump to hasty and ill-founded conclusions said Cassie. 'But I think we're wondering whether Dr Sammi has a motive for getting rid of his wife. I think we're wondering whether he might not be responsible for the whole campaign against her, with a view eventually to doing something or other rather terminal to her, or even driving her to suicide again, and at the same time casting suspicion away from himself and onto someone else, some murderous bigot living in or near Larton who never existed in the first place.'

'I wish we weren't thinking that,' Natasha said 'I hate all this. I hate people who make other people suffer. I hate bullies.' Her eyes filled with tears; she looked exactly like Daisy.

'If we're right, he may be not just a bully but a potentially murderous bully.'

'If you could have seen the bewildered look on that poor woman's face. She just can't believe that anyone could hate her and her husband for being different from them. If we have to tell her it's been Sammi all along who's been doing this...' She broke off. 'If she's already talking about killing herself – you don't seriously think that Sammi's trying to drive her to it, do you? Because if so, it's about the cruellest thing I ever heard.'

'It's just a theory,' Cassie said hastily. 'Not even based on fact. Let's hope it stays that way.'

A frightful noise broke out in the garden as the two thin workmen appeared round the side of the cottage. One had a giant state-of-the-art radio balanced on his shoulder, tuned at top volume to Radio 1, the other was carrying a plastic bag full of cans of beer. Under his arm was a copy of the *Daily Mirror*.

'My,' said Cassie. 'There's a couple all set for a hard day at the coal-face, if ever I've seen one.'

'Hi ho, hi ho, it's off to work we go.' Natasha raised her coffee cup to her lips.

Cassie opened the window and made turn-it-down-for-Chrissake gestures which the two men pretended not to see. 'I had it written into the contract that they weren't supposed to play that bloody thing above a certain level,' she said.

'Perhaps they can't read.'

'If I go out and make a fuss, they turn it down but the minute I've gone, they just turn it up again.'

Natasha stood up. 'Your problem is you're too sweet.'

'Moi?'

'You think you're tough but you're much *much* too sweet.' Natasha bent and planted a kiss on her friend's forehead. 'Leave it to me,' she said briskly.

While she was gone, Cassie looked again at the note on the table. In the context of the preceding threats, it was menacing. On the other hand, outside it, the words could have been no more than a simple statement of fact. Sammi Ray's involvement in the terrorising of his wife had seemed so possible a few moments ago: briefly she had seen the whole scheme plain. Now, doubt crept in. Quite apart from the fact that she had absolutely no reason beyond a random coincidence of location to go on, it was a complicated way to get rid of a wife.

Maybe it would not be a bad idea to drop in at the Knightsbridge florist and make some enquiries. Perhaps a personal approach would yield more information than Natasha's phone call had about the person who had placed the order for that wreath. And if by any chance it implicated Sammi, then they would at least have a solid basis from which to proceed.

9

'Cass? It's me.' The voice at the other end of the phone was breathy, like a child's. The sort of voice which belonged to a pygmy in size eight jeans and a skimpy top. Or to one half of a pair of diminutive twins.

'Hello, Primula.' Cassie made a real effort to expunge any sourness from her voice. Though still a struggle, this was slightly less difficult than it had once been. Since her cousin had become pregnant, after years of trying, some of the acid seemed to have evaporated from the relationship between the two of them. Cassie liked to think that Primula had changed more than she herself had. 'How's things?' She decided that she could handle anything as long as Primula didn't start banging on about her boobs.

'Are you coming home on Sunday?' demanded Primula.

'Home?'

'To the Vicarage,' Primula said, enunciating clearly as though she were speaking to a foreigner. 'For Father's birthday party.'

'Uh...' In all the years, Cassie had never once considered the Vicarage home.

'Don't say you'd forgotten.' Primula blew a chiding breath into the receiver. 'Honestly, Cass.'

'Of course I haven't.'

'Derek and I will be staying with Hyacinth and Eric for the weekend and were just wondering whether you'd like to drive down with us on Sunday morning.'

'Us meaning you and Derek?'

'Of course. And Hyacinth and Eric, of course. Plus these days, I suppose, baby makes three.' The smugness of Primula's maternal little laugh made Cassie want to crush beer cans against her forehead, but she tried to keep calm. It was bad enough to feel morally inferior for being several sizes larger than the twins; to feel that she had somehow failed to make the grade because she had no children herself was a bit too much. Sometimes she thought that Primula only rang up when she was running low on paragon injections and needed a booster shot; she reminded herself that no one could make her feel inferior without her consent. The trouble was, Primula had never bothered to ask for it.

Briefly, she pictured the drive down to the Vicarage if she accepted her cousin's invitation. Primula would talk endlessly about episiotomies, stretch marks, ante-natal clinics and swollen ankles, while Derek the Headmaster snuffled into his moustache and discussed sperm counts – oh *God* – or the number of miles to the gallon his new second-hand Cavalier could do. Hyacinth would be snide. And Eric the Estate Agent would either boast about the latest housing bargains he'd managed to offload onto unsuspecting buyers, or try to grope her. Or both.

'Actually, I've got something on that morning,' she said.

'But I told you last time I rang that Mother's planning a celebration lunch this time, not a dinner party.'

'I mean, in the earlier half of the morning,' said Cassie hastily.

'We can wait for you.'

'I'm ... I'm not sure exactly where I'll be.'

'You *have* kept the day free, haven't you?'

'I already said so. Look, much better you go without me and I'll arrive under my own steam.'

'*You* won't be late, will you?' Primula said sharply. 'Mother won't be too pleased.'

'Story of my life,' Cassie said. Aunt Polly had made a lifetime's career out of not being too pleased, especially if her niece was involved.

'What?'

'Don't worry: I'll be there at the right time, with my hair brushed, my shoes shined and Uncle Sam's present in my hand.'

'We bought him a sweater,' Primula said.

'Why?'

'Why?' Primula seemed nonplussed by the question.

'He's got quite a few of those already.'

'It's a really nice one – we saw it in one of those mail order catalogues.'

'I bet that was Derek's idea.'

'How did you guess?'

Because only someone as monumentally boring as Derek could have come up with such a monumentally boring gift. Not to mention superfluous. 'Call it woman's instinct,' said Cassie.

'What did *you* get him?'

'A one-way ticket to Tahiti.'

'To where?'

'I bought him a wheelbarrow.'

'A wheelbarrow,' Primula said in a dead voice.

'Yes.' Cassie smiled secretly. For once she was OK, for once she'd done the right thing. 'Do you remember, last time we were at the Vicarage he was going on about the rickety state of his wheelbarrow?'

'Yes,' said Primula. 'I wish we'd thought of it.'

'Never mind. At least somebody did.'

'Yes, but...' Even Primula could not bring herself to voice the thought that it would have been more fitting for Uncle Sam's daughter, rather than his niece, to have been the somebody in question.

Cassie pulled a deep breath into her lungs, knowing she would have to take the plunge some time. 'So, Prim, how are you? How's the pregnancy going?' Not the boobs, *please*.

'Oh, just fine, thanks,' Primula said. 'Everything's marvellous, actually. At least ... I'm getting quite a lot of backache, though I've stopped throwing up in the morning, the way I did at first. And I keep having these weird kind of tremors, funny little cramps, like labour pains, sort of. I've got a bit of toxaemia, too: last time I went to the clinic, the doctor said I should be resting more, but you know how it is, with a home and a husband to care for you can't really—' she broke off. 'I really envy you, Cass, not being married any more.'

Piss off, Cassie thought. 'Yes, it does have its advantages.' One of them being that you didn't have to spend your spare time with Derek the Headmaster.

'But the worst thing is my breasts,' said Primula, while Cassie stifled a moan. 'You should see them, Cass...'

'No thanks.'

'... Great ballooning things, with these giant blue veins all over them, and nipples the size of traffic bollards. You wouldn't believe how absolutely huge I am: there's four months to go and I'm already wearing a size 38D...' She prattled on, pretending to be unaware of the fact that Cassie had been wearing size 38D since she was fourteen.

'...doctor says this, Derek says that ... baby ... breathing exercises ... elderly primagravida ... Beatrix Potter frieze ... baby ... blah blah blah ... aren't you?'

Cassie had temporarily lost the thread. 'Aren't I what?'

'Do you ever listen when I'm talking to you, Cassandra?'

'Quite often, Primula.'

'I was just saying, aren't you just longing to be pregnant too?'

'Christ, no!' It came out more explosively than Cassie had intended. Despite the occasional weaknesses, at the moment the idea had all the charm of an invitation to share a cell with Hannibal Lecter; the thought that she might be reduced to the level of swapping anecdotes about tremors and nipples with anyone at all, let alone with Primula, brought her out in a cold sweat.

'Don't worry, Cass. One day you will be. I know,' Primula said teasingly, 'how jealous you are, really, even if you try to pretend you aren't.'

'I am *not* pretending.' Cassie had never satisfactorily worked out whether Primula spent time practising being nasty or it just came naturally.

'I'll have to go,' Primula said. 'Derek's just come in.' She put her hand over the receiver for a moment, then uncovered it and said: 'He sends his love, by the way.'

'Gosh.'

'So, we'll see you at lunch-time on Sunday.'

'I wouldn't miss it for anything.'

The phone replaced, Cassie reflected that having to go to the Vicarage on Sunday might be marginally less ghastly than she expected. If she could get Uncle Sam on one side, she could perhaps pump him about her father. He had never talked about Harry Swann before, but with a glass or two of celebratory plonk inside him, he might be persuaded to part with information which could be helpful in her search for more detail about Harry's death.

From the escritoire, she took the photograph of her father and the woman tentatively identified as Brigid Fraser, breeder and trainer of horses. Although his face was familiar, it was the photograph she recognised, rather than the man. He was separated from her, not only by time, but also by the lapses of memory. If she closed her eyes, she could almost smell the Brylcreem on his hair, almost see the way the strong hairs clustered on his wrist around his watch-strap, almost feel the security of his pillowing thighs when she sat on his knee with his arms around her. But his face had gone, erased from her recollection by time. Sometimes, waking suddenly in the night, she would think she heard his voice – '*What are* you *doing here*?' – but she could no longer be sure that her recall was true. For years she had sought to distance herself from him: sometimes a conscious blocking out of the past had been the only way to survive the inclement rigours of the Vicarage. Now that she was finally allowing herself to remember, it was no wonder that the mind's eye faltered.

Some things she would never forget, however. Aunt Polly visiting with the girls, after her mother's death, for instance. Gran had been excited: she had loved Sarah, her daughter-in-law, and was delighted at the chance to entertain Sarah's sister-in-law. 'We'll give them a really slap-up tea,' she had said. 'What do you think, Cassie?'

'Trifle,' suggested Cassie. 'And jelly.'

'Some of them nice chipolatas from the butcher.'

'Crisps.'

'I'll make some ham sandwiches, too. Here, Cass, what about a bit of corned beef, too?'

'Lovely, Gran.'

'And tea. She doesn't sound like much of a drinker, your aunt. I'll get in some of that la-di-da stuff, Earl Grey or something, just in case she doesn't like our sort of tea.'

In the event, faced with a heaped table, Aunt Polly had accepted a cup of tea and a ham sandwich, half of which she left at the side of her plate. Rose and the twins were allowed a small bowl of Gran's best trifle, with many an admonition about not spoiling their appetites for dinner, once they got home. The twins evidently found something comic about Cass's pink nylon party dress, which she had been allowed to wear specially for the occasion; they had sat opposite her in little tartan kilts and white frilly-collared blouses, nudging each other, while a flush of shame had turned Cassie scarlet. Watching Gran's face, Gran's recognition that she had somehow let Sarah down without knowing quite how, Cassie had felt loathing branch like coral in her heart. If this hateful woman, these cousins, were the family of a man who was in the God business, then she herself would espouse paganism in whatever form she could. If these were la-di-dah manners, then she would remain determinedly coarse. She had had no idea, then, that she would end up living under the same roof as Aunt Polly and her daughters, but even if she had, would not have changed her views. It was unfortunate that proximity had bred a bewildered dichotomy in her.

There was a knock at the door. When she opened it, she found a man standing outside. Middling tall, hair dark and boyishly unruly, black poloneck under a herringbone tweed jacket, brown eyes. Cute. Adorable things like this did not turn up on the doorstep every day of the week.

'Hello,' she said, trying to keep the suggestive overtones out of her voice and at the same time reminding herself how much she loved Paul Walsh.

'Miss Cassandra Swann?'

'Yes.'

'My name's Tim Gardiner.' He paused, and then said defeatedly: 'You won't have heard of me,' in the tone of one who none the less hopes he is wrong.

'Should I have done?'

'*Killing Me Softly*?' he said, raising tentative eyebrows.

'Uh...' The name was vaguely familiar. 'Look, why don't you come in? I was just having coffee.' She would not normally have invited complete strangers in with such insouciance, but there was something comfortable about Mr Gardiner.

'Coffee,' he said. 'That would be wonderful. He followed her into the sitting-room and looked around. 'What a lovely room.'

Cassie always felt awkward when someone praised her home. To express gratitude for the compliment was to gather to oneself approval which was properly intended for the place rather than the person who inhabited it. To ignore it was ill-mannered.

'The cottage is very old,' she said. 'About four hundred years old, as a matter of fact. The walls are two feet thick in some places.' Just like me, she nearly added.

'It isn't so much the room,' said Gardiner, 'as—'

'What?' she breathed. Was he going to say: 'as the woman in it. The *gorgeous* woman in it?

No such luck. '—as the way you've arranged it. Very welcoming. Very ... personal.' He reached out a finger and brushed it lightly across the edge of a picture. 'I love that.'

Cassie did, too. It was a water-colour of a cornfield which had been painted by her maternal grandmother. He stopped in front of her bookcases, as though looking for something and then, evidently not finding it, stooped beneath the lintel and followed her into the kitchen 'And real coffee,' he said, as he saw the coffee pot on the table.

'Is there any other kind?'

'Not only is there, but people drink it and actually think they're having the coffee experience. In fact, people even write books about advertisements for the stuff these days.' He looked wistful. 'Mind you, if I'd been asked, I'd have written one too. Tremendous commercial idea.'

'Do I take it you're a writer?'

'Actually, I am.'

Cassie's brain finally clicked into gear. 'Do I also take it you've recently been asked to conduct an evening class in bridge at Lansdowne Prison?'

'I was almost as surprised at the suggestion as you must have been to be asked to become Creative Writing Tutor for a term.' He laughed. 'Anyway, I spoke to the Education Officer, and sorted it out. He gave me your name and address, just in case, and since I was passing nearby, I decided to drop in. I do hope you don't mind. It was one of those spur-of-the-minute things which, in my experience, so often lead to disaster and grief. I hope this time will prove an exception.'

'You don't look like a man much acquainted with grief.' All the lines of his face turned upward, as though he had been happy most of his life.

'Don't I? Believe me, appearances are often deceptive. The life of an author is one of almost constant personal rejection.' His puppy-dog eyes were sad. He winced suddenly, his coffee jerking from cup to saucer, as a gigantic chord of music: split the air, followed by a heat so loud and insistent that the kitchen vibrated.

Cassie leaped to her feet and slammed the window shut. 'Those bloody men,' she said. 'Just a minute.'

She raced outside to the outbuildings inside which the

two thin workmen were sitting against the stripped-down wall, reading the paper with the ghetto-blaster between them, while the fat one, unfazed by the noise, spoke to his bookie on his portable phone. 'Yer, Jim, I'll have a tenner each way on California Dreaming and a fiver to win on—'

'Switch that bloody row off!' Cassie yelled.

'You what?' One of the workmen looked up from the paper with an air of hurt surprise.

'Turn that noise down or I'll have you for breach of contract,' Cassie said more calmly. She unclenched her fists, conscious of the attractive Tim Gardiner watching her through the window and aware that as a picture of serene womanhood, she was falling down badly.

'What noise?'

'That damn radio of yours. I told your boss that I work at home and I have to have quiet.'

Grudgingly, one of the men turned the volume control knob a fraction. 'Lower than that,' ordered Cassie. 'And that ... and that ... as the sound crept down.

'Can't hardly hear it now,' grumbled the other one when she finally nodded approval.

'Yes, well, you're not here to listen to the radio, you're here to get on with turning this hellhole into a civilised commercial enterprise,' Cassie said sharply. 'And if that fucking radio gets any louder when I go back to the house, I'm going to throw it into the pond.'

'That's what the lady said yesterday,' said the fat man, his negotiations completed.

'The difference between her and me is that I mean it,' Cassie said firmly.

'That's what *she* said.'

'Want to risk it?'

Muttering, they folded up the newspaper and began to cast about them for their equipment. The fat one set the concrete mixer going. The white cat watched from the porch. Order of a kind was restored.

Back in the house, she found Gardiner in the sitting-room, studying the books which covered one of the uneven walls. 'You've got a lot of Robin Plunkett,' he said. 'We obviously share an admiration for his work.'

'He's my godfather,' Cassie said.

'My goodness...' Gardiner's eyes glowed when he smiled. He looked as if he were about ten years older than she was. 'Look...' He glanced at his watch. 'This really was an impulse visit, but why don't we have dinner together some time?'

'Why not?' said Cassie, cool as ham, though her impulse was to shout Yo, baby!

'I'll give you a ring in the next couple of days, all right?'

'Lovely.'

'You can tell me about your godfather.'

'And you can tell me about your disasters.'

'It's a deal.' Gardiner touched her hand briefly before he went out into the sunshine and walked between the flower beds to the gate set in the hedge. Cassie smiled as she watched him go. Mmmm, she thought. Very tasty.

And what a contrast to Charlie Quartermain, who arrived fifteen minutes later, carrying a dozen yellow roses, a plastic bag and a bottle of Montrachet. ''Ello, darlin',' he bellowed, stooping beneath the ceiling beams as she let him into the sitting-room.

'Good morning, Charles.'

'Thought you might like some lunch,' he said, banging the wine down on the inlaid top of Robin's William IV games table.

'That's very kind of you, but—' She picked up the bottle and moved into the kitchen.

'Smoked trout, sparrowgrass, fresh baked rolls...'

Charlie peered into the bag) '... quails' eggs – gotta mate with a quails' egg shop – and a dozen ripe peaches.' He wrenched open the back door and went into the garden. 'Let's have a butcher's at what's going on here, then.'

Before she could stop him, he was walking rapidly towards the building works, where the workmen were exchanging meaningful grins, obviously believing him to be her lover.

What a thought. 'Charlie,' she said, following him. 'There's really no need...'

But it was too late. 'What you call that?' he said, Pointing at a piece of timber which had been plastered into one of the walls. 'That supposed to be seasoned wood?'

'It *is* seasoned, mate,' the fat foreman said, chucking away his cigarette and leaving it to smoulder in the middle of a lavender bush. 'All guaranteed. Says so in the contract.'

'If that's seasoned,' Charlie said, 'I'm Rudolf Nureyev.' He shook his big head. 'Sorry, lads, but that is coming out. And what's going on above those two windows? Thought Miss Swann had asked for the stonework to be left exposed, not plastered over.'

'The lads did that while I was off sick,' said the big workmen defensively. 'We was going to uncover them later.'

'And beans don't make you fart,' Charlie said rudely.

Cassie had already pointed out the places where the original wall had been plastered over, and been given the same excuse. She would never have known that the timber was unseasoned. What amazed her most was that Charlie, who had asked to look at the architect's plans some weeks ago, should have remembered so many details of them.

His face had dropped into an expression of saddened disbelief. He shook his head slowly. 'I hope you lot weren't trying to take advantage of Miss Swann, just because she's a woman,' he said. 'That wouldn't be very clever. That would definitely be out of order.'

There was a mafia-sharp edge to his voice which brought the foreman out in a sweat. 'Course not, mate. Like I said, we was going to –'

'Gordon Bennett, looks like amateur night at the Builders' Ball round here,' Charlie interrupted. 'Look at that bloody piping. It's off.'

'Already made a note of it.' The foreman began to bluster. 'It's in hand, mate. Keep your hair on.'

'Won't take you long to put things right, lads, will it?' Charlie said 'Otherwise, you're doing a good job. I like that bit of fancy brickwork at the back.'

Cassie was impressed. He'd told them off but also praised them. Returning to the kitchen, she found the corkscrew. Let the men think what they liked about the relationship between her and Charlie: much as she hated to admit it, they'd probably do a better job if they thought she had a man to look after her interests.

'They're OK,' Charlie said, coming back to the house. 'Just need a bit of an eye kept on 'em. They're bound to try it on, especially with a lovely little thing like you.'

For once, she let it pass, except for the fleeting thought that perhaps to a man as big as Quartermain, she really did seem small. 'Trouble is, when I go and inspect what they've done, I'm not always sure exactly what I'm supposed to be keeping my eye on,' she concluded.

'I'll pop round again next week, see what they're up to, if you like.' Charlie tore open the bag of rolls and began to stuff one into his capacious mouth. Crumbs rained. Two or three of them lodged in his chest hair, areas of which were visible through his bulging shirt buttons. 'I love smoked trout, don't you? More subtle than smoked salmon.'

'Yes.' Difficult to imagine Tim Gardiner eating like that. Difficult to imagine anything but a wild beast eating like that. 'How was Cologne, Charlie?'

'Dresden was fine, thanks. Didn't stay long, though. Had to come back early.'

'Oh?'

'My dad. Had one of his turns.'

'I'm sorry.' Gran used to have turns, when her legs went funny and her face grey, when she would clutch at her chest and grow breathless.

'Lives on his own,' Charlie said. 'Gotta nice flat in the Smoke, nice neighbours and that, but you can't help worrying about them, can you?'

'No,' agreed Cassie – if you've got someone to worry about, that is. For some reason, she had always assumed that Charlie had no family; the thought that somewhere there was a Quartermain parent was vaguely alarming. 'How old is your father?'

'Coming up to seventy,' Charlie said with evident pride. 'Actually, it's nearer eighty, but he lies about his age. Tell you what, girl. He's always on at me to bring him over to meet you; why don't I—'

'But he doesn't know me.'

'Heard all about you, though.'

Every single time she found herself feeling a faint strand of empathy with Quartermain, he managed to blow it. 'Has he really?' she said. What story had he fed his father about the relationship between himself and the bridge teacher?

'Yuss,' said Charlie, seemingly oblivious to the ice in

her voice. 'Ever so pleased, he is. He's always saying he wants to see me settled before he goes.' Quartermain's phlegm-coloured eyes bulged piously at the ceiling.

Reluctantly, Cassie put down the quail egg into which she had just daintily bitten. 'What exactly is it that he's pleased about?'

'You, girl. And me. Us.'

'Charles' Cassie said through clenched jaws. 'There *is* no us.'

'I'm not going to tell him that, am I?'

'Why not? It's the truth.'

'Anyway, thought it might be nice, now the summer's come, to bring him over one Sunday. Bit of a change from the big city, give him a chance to breathe some country air. What do you say?'

Good old Charlie. Always twanging at the heartstrings. If she refused, she would be churlishly denying an old man a pleasant day out. If she agreed, she would have to endure God knew what kind of nudging expectation on the part of Charlie's father.

'I say it's bloody blackmail,' Cassie said.

'Blackmail's an ugly word, Cassandra.'

'You're not giving me any choice, are you?'

'No,' Charlie said cheerfully. 'That's settled then. What about next Sunday?'

'I can't. It's my uncle's birthday.'

'Sunday after?'

She wanted to refuse, using intemperate language and violent gestures. But she knew, from past experience, that once the suggestion had been made, it would alchemise into some sort of agreement by her that Charlie's father could come. So the sooner she got it over, the sooner the thought of it would cease to haunt her.

Exasperatedly, she clicked her tongue against the roof

of her mouth. 'Oh, all right,' she said, and made no pretence of looking forward to it.

He seemed not to notice. 'By the way, you were wanting Biddy Fraser's address, weren't you?'

'Yes.'

'Here.' He wrote it down for her.

'Thank you.'

He smiled. 'Ever so good of you, Cass, to have us for lunch –'

'Who said anything about—'

'—When I tell him, the old boy'll be pissing himself.'

Not literally, Cassie hoped.

When he had gone, she thought about her own father. Harry Swann. She was supposed to be trying to find out who might have been responsible for his death. Somehow she was going to have to trace the two strangers: the big man and the smaller one with the cap. How? Where to start looking? Her difficulty was compounded by the fact of her own deep reluctance. Each step she took back into the past was like setting out on a narrow unrailed bridge across a gorge. She did not want to dig up the events of twenty years ago, yet, at the same time, she knew that unless she did so, she herself would always remain – much as she resisted such psychobabble – emotionally stunted.

For the moment, and disregarding Tony Spezzioli and his aunt, she still had two sources of information to check out. One was her uncle, who must surely know something more than the mere facts. The other was Brigid Fraser. Was Charlie right in confirming that she was the woman in the photograph with Harry Swann? It was almost impossible to reconcile that half-visible face with the pared-down contours of the woman she had seen on the television screen after the Grand National. And even if they were one and the same woman, what connection could she possibly have had with Harry Swann's death?

Tenuous, Cassie told herself. Insubstantial to a degree. She could just imagine Ms Fraser's expression if she showed up at her house asking whether she had had anything to do with the murder of a man twenty years before. Even if she had, she wasn't going to admit it, especially if she had got away with it for all this to me. And, besides, what possible reason could there be?

Harry Swann, the King of Hearts, Jill Davis had called him. Could it be one of those affairs of the heart, a jealous husband getting rid of his wife's lover in the hope of recapturing her affections? Charlie Quartermain had said something about Ms Fraser's husband going off, leaving her: did that add strength to the supposition, or did it weaken it? Cassie looked again at the photograph: did they look like lovers? He had an arm around her shoulders while she clutched a big leather handbag to herself, like a shield. The camera had not captured any sign of a special bond between the pair: the two of them gazed at the photographer without a hint of a shared secret or a mutual passion.

Cassie stared out of the window at the workmen, who moved about uneasily, not realising that she did not really see them.

She knew there was only ever going to be one way to find out if Brigid Fraser was implicated in the death of her father, and that was to go and visit the woman.

142

10

But the visit to Brigid Fraser was going to have to be postponed. The next morning, as Cassie stood waiting for the kettle to boil and watching the workmen flick their filter-tips into the goldfish pond, DS Walsh passed the window and, knocking lightly, came in through the back door.

'What a surprise,' Cassie said.

'Not a pleasant one, I'm afraid.' There was a heaviness about his voice which prepared her for bad news. He picked an apple from the bowl on the dresser and noisily bit into it.

'What's wrong?'

'Those people you told me about, who'd been getting the anonymous letters: what was their name?' he asked.

'Ray,' she said. 'Sammi and Vida Ray. Why? What's happened?'

'There's been a suspicious death,' Walsh said.

'Who's died?'

'The husband. Dr Sammi Ray.'

'Oh, my God,' Cassie said softly. HE'S FIRST. The words flickered in her mind. THEN YOU. 'Where was this?'

'He was found in his car outside some flats near Gloucester Road tube station. By another consultant, as it happens, haematologist at Guy's. He glanced in as he walked by and recognised the briefcase on the back seat as a doctor's bag. Took a closer look, since most medics these days are very careful about leaving their gear in full view, because of the possibility of drug-related break-ins, and saw the body.'

The body. Cassie was stunned. The fact of Sammi Ray's death seemed too enormous for her to grasp. She tried to hold onto it but it kept slipping away from her. Sammi Ray was dead. Was it because he did not heed the warning? Was murder the ultimate step in the poison-pen writer's campaign to terrorise the Rays out of the village? Not that motivation mattered particularly, compared with the unremitting fact that a man lay dead who only a short time ago had been alive. The thought swelled and bloomed in Cassie's brain like a malignant flower. She sat down at the table and rested her face in her hands. She had not liked Ray, nor approved of him, indeed, she had hardly known him. Nonetheless, she found herself disproportionately upset by the news of his death.

'...Otherwise he might quite easily not have been found for a while. The body was lying across the front seats, under a rug, not noticeable at all at first glance,' Paul was saying.

'When did this happen?' Cassie's voice fluttered in her throat, weak as a fledgling.

'They haven't got the pathologist's full report yet but the assumption is that he was killed some time last night, or early this morning.'

'Any suspects?'

'The London boys are working on the theory that he might have tried to tackle a thief, someone after drugs, and got clobbered for his pains. When they discovered that the victim lived in Larton Easewood and got onto us, as the local branch of the CID, I remembered you asking about anonymous letters and seeing that he's an asiatic gentleman, I put two and two together and thought it might be worth checking it out with you. Is it the same bloke?'

Cassie nodded.

'Thought so.'

'Has his wife been told?'

'There's a WPC with her now. And a neighbour...' He looked down at a notebook and ruffled a couple of pages, '...a Mrs Natasha Sinclair.'

'We were invited to dinner at the Sinclairs' the other day, but you weren't able to make it...' Cassie said vaguely, her mind still spinning. She thought of something else. 'Why didn't his wife raise the alarm when he didn't come home?'

'Apparently he rang up from London and said he would have to stay up there overnight.'

'Did he really?'

'A conscientious husband, apparently, our Sammi,' Walsh said. 'Always let his missus know if he was going to be late, that kind of thing.'

'Ah.' Maybe later Cassie could voice her feelings about just how conscientious a husband Sammi had been; for now she would keep them to herself.

'Apparently it was quite usual: she didn't think anything of it. In fact, she told our WPC that she was rather relieved, since her son had come down for the evening and things were a bit sticky between the two men, the lad being an actor and refusing to get what his father called a proper job. From what I can make out, spent more of his time resting than acting.'

'She told me.'

'Seems that having spent the evening chatting about this and that, his prospects and so on, he decided to stay the night, since his dad wasn't going to be coming home, and the two of them went up to bed around ten-thirty. He left early the next morning, before his mother was awake.'

'Poor woman.' What would Vida be feeling now, realising that while she slept, her husband lay dead at the hand of a stranger? Would she wish she had, after all, told him about the poison-pen letters.

As though following the same train of thought, Walsh said: 'Tell me a bit more about those poison-pen letters.'

'Natasha Sinclair's the one you should ask. She was the person on the spot. And she actually saw the wreath.'

'Wreath? Nobody's mentioned a wreath.'

'One of those funeral wreaths, in the shape of a cross. But I only know what Natasha told me. I didn't see it for myself.'

'We'll hear what Mrs Sinclair's got to say a bit later. As the liaising officer, I'll be taking statements from everyone down here who might be connected with Dr Ray.' Walsh coughed awkwardly. 'I'm really sorry this should have happened. Friends of yours, and everything.' He stood behind her, a man unused to displaying emotion, gripping her shoulders in an attempt at comfort.

Cassie knew how difficult he found it to move between the role of policeman and that of simple citizen. She reached up and covered his hands with her own. 'Not friends, exactly. They were both in my bridge class. I knew Dr Ray's wife better than I knew him.' Again Cassie paused, keeping back her suspicions about the way Sammi might have physically mistreated his wife. Although she had no intention of permanently with-holding the information, it was another item she would rather tell Walsh later, at a more suitable time. 'Are you linking the death with the letters?'

'At this stage we're simply in the business of information gathering. But obviously they'll have to be taken into account,' Walsh said. His grip tightened. 'Cass...'

'Yes?'

'You know that I really do love you, don't you?'

The question had an ominous ring 'I like to think so,' she said. 'Why are you asking?'

'I can't discuss it now.'

'So there's something to discuss, is there?'

Abruptly, he let go of her and walked towards the door. 'I'd better go. I'll keep in touch.' He smiled at her and stepped outside. The kitchen darkened momentarily as he passed the windows, his solid frame blocking out the light. He had left without saying goodbye, a habit Cassie was only just coming to terms with.

The telephone rang. 'Cassie. Natasha here. You simply won't believe what's happened. Sammi Ray's been—'

'I know'

'I went over to the Rays' house as soon as I heard. I'm phoning from there now.'

'Do you want me to join you? I've got private lessons most of the day, but I'll get there as soon as I can – early evening probably.'

'That would be good. There's not much we can do for Vida, but at least she won't be alone until her children get here, later today. They're flying in from the States. The son's in London somewhere—'

'The black sheep son, is this?'

'There's only one. His name's Rashid, if I remember rightly – but she hasn't been able to get hold of him yet to tell him what's happened. There's a policewoman here, but it's not the same as having friends around at a time like this.'

'Friends: is that what we are, Natasha?'

'Whether we are or not, we're fellow humans, and men fear death as children fear to go in the dark.'

Cassie said: 'I'll be there as soon as I can.'

Her last call of the afternoon was at the church hall in Steepleton, where a group of senior citizens were psyching themselves up for an arduous few weeks of sunbathing and bridge-playing in Portugal, later in the year. They were a jolly crowd, well pleased with their lot, content to have a weekly visit to the hairdresser, a big TV set in the lounge, food on the table. Occasionally one of them would reminisce about the years before or during the war, the appalling working conditions they had endured in their younger days, growing up without the benefit of the Welfare State, the difference between their lives and those of their parents: there was a palpable atmosphere of contentment with their collective lot, of never having had it so good, which Cassie always enjoyed.

Then it was on to Larton Easewood. *HE'S FIRST. THEN YOU*. All the way there, the words throbbed and bounced in her brain. *HE'S FIRST* . . . and now Sammi was dead. Was Vida also in danger?

The centre of Bellington was shut tight, gutters sleazy with litter in the yellow light of a summer evening. Neon signs flickered red and blue above deserted pavements. Outside an amusement arcade, a crowd of youths stood ratpacked, faces empty and unfocused. There was a pool of vomit outside the Midland Bank. Once this had been a thriving town centre but Town Centre Virus had struck and now many of the shops were boarded up, their former customers sucked into the convenience of the supermarkets which ringed the town. Those which were left were mostly insurance agencies, building societies or charity shops on short lease. No one sold goods any more.

Even the chainstores were beginning to defect to the edge
of town, their sites encroaching further and further into
the countryside with each year that passed, nibbling away
at green belts and open fields. Soon, the whole country
would be one vast shopping mall. Someone had thrown a
stone through the window of the shut-down pizza parlour
in the High Street, the cracks radiating out from a central
point like the rays of a stylised silver sun; disregarded, a
burglar alarm screamed on the wall of the Citizens'
Advice Bureau offices.

Along the river bank, where the town began to slip
away towards the countryside again, expensive cars were
parked one behind the other, their radios turned up to full
volume. Ice-T and the Beastie Boys throbbed, while the
teenaged drivers leaned against their vehicles in their
drug-pushers' uniform of baggy trousers and high-top
trainers, waiting for deals to go down. New citizens who
needed no advice, who would not have listened if it were
offered. Their girls lay across the bonnets of their cars like
photo-ops at the Motor Show, and laughed vacuously
every now and then. And women died beneath the
hooves of horses, thought Cassie, to give these girls the
vote.

There was movement on the river, canoeists, rowing
club shells preparing for Henley, raucous youths splashing about in hired craft, guffawing loudly at not very
much, burps and swear words rolling over the surface of
the water. As she passed, Cassie realised she had
forgotten to ask how Sammi had died: she tried not to
think about it. Nonetheless, her mind raced from possibility to possibility like a trapped bird. A shot from
behind, perhaps, plastering Sammi's handsome face over
the windscreen, unless the killer had held a pillow over his
face or something. Strangulation would have been easy, a

tie, for instance, whipped round his neck, a pair of tights, a belt. What about a knife? A blow with some heavy object? A plastic bag yanked suddenly over Sammi's unsuspecting head and – don't think about it. She shuddered. So many ways to kill, but in the end, only one way to die.

Though she concentrated on the road, the pictures kept returning. Walsh had mentioned the possibility of a car thief, but surely a car thief would not have wasted time stuffing Sammi's body into the car and covering it with a rug before going off on foot, would he? It would have been far more logical for him to take Sammi's keys and drive the car off, leaving the body behind. She tried to imagine someone hidden inside the back of the car, waiting for Sammi to climb into the front seat.

Was it the writer of the letters? And if so, what did he look like, this man who had threatened and terrorised his neighbours, who crept through the shadows to drop his ugly messages on their doormat? Had he watched to see how his victims reacted to the sly poison of his words? Had he rejoiced to see Vida grow ever more frightened? Had he wondered why Sammi, kept in ignorance, showed no signs of fear? It could have been a woman, of course. Anonymous letter writing was supposed to be a woman's weapon.

She recalled the man who had emerged into the lane from the cricket field behind the Old School House. The groundsman, probably; it would be easy to check out. He had lacked the rural accessory of a dog so what else could he have been doing? She strained to remember if that was just before the Rays had received another letter – but even if it had been, the man had made no attempt to conceal himself. Yet it was certainly true that Vida at that time had been sitting in Natasha's kitchen, leaving the coast clear for hand-delivered mail. Another thing to check out.

When Cassie nosed her car into the brick-paved area behind the wing wall which shielded one side of the Old School House from the road, Natasha was waiting for her in the porch. She stood with her arms wrapped round her chest, looking haggard, her eyes red

'How's Vida?' Cassie asked.

'She's been sedated. Oh God, Cassie: it's been so painful to watch. She didn't cry, she just sat there, trembling all over, in shock, her face gone completely grey. In the end, they had to give her something to make her go to sleep.'

'Poor thing.'

'It's not that she's distraught exactly. More as if something has broken inside her. Whatever we thought about Sammi, she obviously loved him.'

'Maybe he was really lovable.' The two friends walked through the heavy arched doorway into the hall. 'Maybe he didn't beat her up at all. We have only our own nasty imaginations to thank for thinking that he did.'

Tears rolled down Natasha's face. 'I just can't believe it. And the worst thing of all...'

'What, Tash?' Cassie took her friend's arm, knowing what she was going to say.

'I keep thinking about *me* – about us. If this maniac's killed Sammi, who's next in the firing line? And what else might he do?'

'Don't be silly,' Cassie soothed.

'Is it silly? I'm not exactly a WASP, am I?'

'If he was going to write letters to you, he'd have done it before the Rays arrived.'

'They might just have been the catalyst. The final straw

or something. And now Sammi's ... It wasn't that I particularly liked him, but to think that he's dead...'

'Not just dead, but murdered.'

'And in such a dreadful way.'

Cassie cleared her throat. 'Uh ... how, exactly?'

'Oh, Cassie, so awful. He was garrotted. What a thing to have to tell his children. They're still trying to get hold of the son, by the way. He's not at the number his mother gave me, so we've had to leave messages all over the place.'

'He probably stopped off to see a girlfriend or something on his way back to London. He was here last night, apparently.'

'The rest of the family will be arriving from London tonight. There's an uncle – Sammi's older brother – coming down later. I've laid in some supplies for them and made up some beds. There's plenty of room.'

The square hall where children's coats and shoebags had once hung smelled of floorwax and spices. In the large living-room beyond, ornately carved furniture of reddish wood sat against the walls. Framed miniatures of eastern design were hung in orderly arrangements: turbaned princes riding out to war, long-haired ladies languorous under berried trees, musicians sitting cross-legged on flowered grass while tigers strolled behind them. Two porcelain elephants stood on either side of the fireplace.

A young woman constable appeared at the other end of the room where once the village children learned their lessons. 'She's asleep,' she said. 'I'm going to make some tea: would you like some?'

'Thanks,' Cassie said. All she wanted was for none of this to have happened, but the WPO looked as if she needed to do something.

The telephone rang and the policewoman snatched it up. 'Yes? Yes? Fine. Yes, someone will be here.' She put down the receiver and said: 'The daughters. Calling from Heathrow. They've hired a car and should be here in about an hour and a half.' She turned towards the back of the house where the kitchen was, then stopped. 'If the telephone rings again, answer it, will you? We're hoping the son will call. He still doesn't know what's happened to his father.'

'You'll tell him, will you?'

'I shall have to.' A gloomy expression crossed her face. 'The worst part of my job is having to give people bad news.'

When she had disappeared, Cassie said: 'Presumably she's not the only person on the case, is she?'

'There were other police here when I arrived. A couple from London and a local man – not your Paul, though.'

'He's involved in some capacity,' said Cassie. 'Liaising with the police in London, I think. I presume Vida showed the letters to them.'

'She didn't, actually.'

'Why not?'

'Well...'

'Well what?'

'Actually ... she's got rid of them.'

'But they're evidence.' Cassie was scandalised. 'Surely she can't have been so stupid as to destroy them.'

'You wouldn't have thought so, but she said that when her son was here last night, she showed them to him, and because it was the first time she'd been able to discuss them with someone in the family, she just flipped. All the worry and fear that she's been hiding all these weeks just overcame her and she started sobbing and having hysterics, so he advised her to burn them right then so that she wouldn't go on brooding about them. He said it was all nonsense, and made her put a match to the lot of them in the kitchen sink.'

'How stupid can you get?'

'They didn't realise at the time that the poison-pen writer was up in London, knocking Sammi on the head,' said Natasha.

'We don't know for certain that he did. The Metropolitan Police think it was a druggie break-in which went wrong. It was Paul Walsh who linked Sammi Ray to the letters, because I'd asked him earlier what was the best way to handle them.'

'It's all so unbelievable,' said Natasha. 'I've been racking my brains for days, trying to think who could be responsible.'

'What about the cricket team? There's twelve suspects there, for a start.'

'Plus assorted hangers-on and supporters and believe me, some of them are fanatical about the game.'

'So they wouldn't react kindly to Sammi threatening to take them to court if any more sixes crashed into his garden.'

'Except, as I said before, most of them live outside the village.'

'In fact, didn't you say before that only three of them live here?'

'That's right. And the person responsible for those letters more or less has to live fairly close by, since anyone coming in on a regular basis to drop them through the door would certainly have been noticed. You can't sneeze in Larton Easewood without someone saying "Bless you".'

'So, apart from the cricket team lot, who are your other suspects?'

'I came up with two people – but they're just possibles, you understand: I'm certainly not accusing anyone, nor even suggesting that they were responsible. I mean, I only—'

'Just give it to me,' Cassie interrupted. 'These people aren't going to end up sewing mailbags for the rest of their lives, just because you thought they might be capable of writing nasty letters to people.'

'OK. One's a retired dentist, came from South Africa years ago, and I only mention him because although *I've* never heard him make overtly racist statements, I understand that he does have some pretty twisted views about white supremacy and what he calls "undesirables".'

'Hey, tell him to come over and see me sometime. I've got some pretty twisted views about dentists which I'd love to share with him.'

'He and I were on the Harvest Festival committee last year and he had a hard time being civil to me, let alone listening to anything I might want to contribute.'

'He might just hate women.'

'He's married.'

'That means he likes them?'

'Perhaps it's just black women he can't stand. Not that I'm particularly black, but that's how he perceives me.'

'Moron.' How anyone could display even the most covert kind of prejudice against a creature as rare and beautiful as Natasha was entirely beyond Cassie.

'My other suspect,' continued Natasha, avoiding Cassie's eyes, 'is Lolly Hayden White.'

'What?' Cassie laughed disbelievingly. 'The Honourable, do you mean?'

'Yes.'

'But that's ridiculous. She's a pillar of the county and a close friend of Mercy Laughton, Giles's mother. I've

155

played bridge with her several times. In fact I was playing with her just the other afternoon.'

'Not everyone shares your belief that if you play bridge you must be saintlier than Mother Teresa,' Natasha said, voice tart as gooseberries.

'I know, but—'

'Lolly may play a decent game of bridge but she also has a real motive for trying to drive out the Rays: she's wanted to buy the Old School House for ages because, in case you didn't know, her youngest daughter lives in Bellington and she wants to be near at hand because of the grandchildren.'

'There are other houses, aren't there?'

'Yes, but she's set her heart on the Old School House. Her mother taught there, centuries ago, when it really was the village school. It's come up for sale four times in the past eight years, and every time she thinks she's got it, something happens to prevent it. When it was last on the market, six months or so ago, she offered the asking price before it even got into the agents' hands.'

'So what happened?'

'We never really heard all the ins and outs, but I think Sammi Ray must have snuck in and offered the owner – he lives in London and used the place as a weekend cottage – considerably more than he was asking. Lolly couldn't believe it'd slipped out of her grasp yet again. She was absolutely furious.'

'How do you know?'

'Because not only did she tell everyone, she actually went round there, the day after they moved in and made a terrible fuss. Completely lost control. Shouted and screamed, called them all sorts of names, things I'd never have believed she would say. Said they were cheats and had no right to be living there, the house was morally hers and if they had a shred of British decency – well, you can imagine the sort of thing.'

'She was brought up in some far-flung post of Empires, wasn't she?'

'Kenya, I think.'

'Ah.'

'Not that that means a thing,' Natasha said hastily, as though she feared the Thought Police were on patrol and was determined to demonstrate her political correctness.

'Of course not. But you can't seriously be suggesting that Lolly might have murdered Sammi just to get her hands on the Old School House.'

'I'm only pointing out that she did have a kind of motive for writing the letters, in the hope of driving them out.'

'Pretty tenuous.' But Cassie was frowning, remembering Lolly's poor performance last time they had played bridge together. Was it due to something more than an off day? Was the Macbeth Factor to blame: an uneasy conscience affecting her game? Or had she been preoccupied by something even more sinister: the planning of further attacks on the Rays, perhaps, or even of Sammi's murder? But that was impossible: no way could frail little Lolly have murdered the handsome doctor. On the other hand, a garrotte didn't require all that much strength to be effective, did it?

Outside, a car door slammed. Voices could be heard. Someone rapped at the front door then lifted the heavy round latch and walked into the hall. Three women. Cassie was slightly nonplussed. For some reason she had imagined that the Ray children who were doing so well at American universities would be male. At first sight, the three of them were as like as a string of matched pearls. Behind them, a man in a peaked cap brought luggage in from the car and stowed it in the hall. Awkwardly Cassie and Natasha stood up as the three came towards them, one behind the other. They wore saris and spectacles, with a great many pieces of clanking jewellery. All three had clearly been crying in the past few minutes.

'I'm Dina Ray,' the first one said. 'And these are my sisters. Shula and Rita.'

'We are so very sorry about your father's death.' Natasha said. 'It has been a most terrible shock.'

'Would you like a cup of tea?' Cassie felt diffident at offering the women refreshment in their own home. 'There's a policewoman . . .' She gestured vaguely towards the kitchen.

'Is Rashid not here?' either Shula or Rita asked.

'Not yet. But your uncle is coming soon.'

The three women fluttered among themselves. 'And Mammi? Where is our mother?'

'She's asleep,' Natasha explained. 'They gave her something to calm her; naturally she was terribly shocked.'

'We'll go and peek at her,' Dina decided.

Before they could do so, through the open front door they all heard another car pull up.

'Perhaps that's Uncle Dev,' one of the daughters said. All three spoke with markedly transatlantic accents. They stood in a forlorn multicoloured group in the middle of the big room, gazing hopefully at the door.

Two men came hurrying into the house. The first was in his fifties, barrel-shaped in an expensive suit and black silk tie, his handsome moustachioed face proclaiming his kinship to the dead Sammi Ray. The second man who had followed him lingered by the door, red-eyed, his mouth drawn down as though he were a child trying not to cry. Sammi and Vida's black sheep was young, good-looking, dressed like a male model. He gave a brief unhappy smile as the three Indian women moved forward with little cries of 'Uncle Dev!', 'Rash!' and they all began to embrace each other, sobbing.

'Come on,' Cassie said quietly to Natasha. 'I think we should just slip out and leave them together.'

'Yea. You'll come back to the house, won't you?'

'I'd rather get home, if you don't mind.'

And all the way back to Honeysuckle Cottage, Cassie tried to work out whether there was any significance at all in the fact that Rashid Ray was the young man who had been in Blackwell's, the last time she was in Oxford.

11

Cassie got up early the next day. Standing on the scales in the bathroom, she squinted down at the register. *What*? Surely some mistake. Bending closer, she watched the needle waver on either side of the impossible total. She stepped off, removed her pearl earrings and clipped her toenails then stepped back on again. Not a blind bit of difference. Despair gripped her. This really wasn't fair. All those weeks of celery, all those hours of abstinence, and for what? The hell with it all. She went downstairs and cooked eggs and bacon, found an English muffin at the back of the freezer and toasted it, spread butter and jam generously over the two halves, and felt a kinder, gentler woman for it. Replete, she sat for ten minutes on the seat outside the back door, taking in the smell of dewy leaves and the sound of birds. The heatwave continued: she enjoyed the early sunlight, knowing that by midday it would be too fierce to be out in. The white cat joined her, followed by its sidekick, a tortoiseshell kitten. Fetching them a saucer each of milk, she listened to their contented purrs; pity it took more than that to make people purr.

Later she drove through the clean morning air to Welback, just over the border into Hampshire. Nearly at her destination, she stopped to admire a classic view of horses strung along the skyline as they took their morning exercise along the ridge of the downs. Come to Dick Francis country...

Ten minutes later she was turning into the drive which led to Brigid Fraser's stables. A sanded road, bounded on either side by white picket fencing, led towards a long, low, two-storey house. Red brick laid in herringbone patterns between dark-stained beams. Stone lintels surrounding leaded windows. Clay roof tiles. Built in the Twenties, Cassie estimated, some self-made man's Tudor dream come true.

The working part of the yard clearly lay somewhere behind the house. Waiting for someone to answer the front-door bell, she could hear equestrian snorts, an occasional whinny, rough male shouts, machinery whirring, the persistent splash of water. Footsteps eventually approached on the other side of the thick wooden door. Keys were turned. Someone tugged ineffectually at the handle. A voice called, though she could not understand what it said, or even if it was directed at her. She pressed an ear to the sun-scoured surface and as she did so, the door opened suddenly.

'We usually use the back entrance,' the woman facing her said brusquely. Brigid Fraser was easily recognisable from her brief TV appearance on Grand National Day. Up close, her complexion was deeply weathered and there were nicotined edges to her front teeth. Today she wore baggy jeans and a green padded jerkin over a short-sleeved blue-and-white-check blouse. Despite the teeth and the jerkin, she was still a handsome woman, though smaller than she had seemed on the screen. In a way Cassie could not define, there was something familiar about her.

'You don't know me—' Cassie began.

'I know.' Brigid Fraser's voice was brisk. 'What're you

selling: insurance, encyclopaedias or God? Because we don't want any of them, thanks very much.' The door began to close.

'No,' said Cassie. 'I'm not selling anything. My name's Swann. Cassandra Swann.'

The door's motion stopped and it slowly opened again. 'Who?'

Cassie knew the other woman had heard perfectly well the first time. 'Cassandra Swann,' she said, less tentatively now.

'That's what I thought you said.'

'Harry Swann's daughter.'

'I know whose daughter you are.' Brigid Fraser's look was unhappy. 'This is something of a surprise.'

'I'm sure it is.'

'I must say I rather thought that period of my life was over for good.' The door was swung wider. 'I suppose you'd better come in,' she said reluctantly.

Her reaction to Cassie was curiously similar to Jill Davis's. She led the way into a comfortably shabby sitting-room, full of old sofas covered in faded split-seamed chintz and even older retrievers, two of which were lying in front of the empty grate where a massive arrangement of dried flowers bloomed. Turning to Cassie, she said, 'Do you mind farting?'

'Excuse me?' Was this a politely worded order to break wind, or a veiled warning that Brigid herself might?

'It's just that Cleo and Daphne do rather tend to foul the atmosphere, and if you don't like dogs...'

'I think I'll probably survive.' Cassie sat down as far away from the dogs as she could. Dusty sunlight slanted in through the windows; there were roses here and there, generously crammed into bowls, spilling petals onto unpolished surfaces.

'Now,' said Ms Fraser. She perched herself on the arm of one of the sofas as though indicating that the interview would have to be a short one. She gave Cassie an appraising look. 'Yes. You've turned out just as pretty as your father always said you would.'

'Um...'

'So how can I help you?'

Cassie had pondered exactly this question during the drive down. How *could* Brigid Fraser help her? Perhaps not at all, perhaps only a little, perhaps a lot. Whichever, she had come to the conclusion that the bold approach was the best one, so wasted no time.

'Were you and my father lovers?' she said.

Brigid did not seem to mind the question. 'Yes,' she said simply. 'We were—' Breaking off, she said: 'Should I ask for some identification?'

'I've got my—'

But before Cassie could finish, Ms Fraser added: 'On the other hand, you don't look as if you've come to steal the spoons.'

'I've already got some of those.'

'When your father and I first met,' Brigid said, evidently feeling some need to explain, 'he was a widower. It was in the tea tent at Market Rasen. I'd gone with some friends – my husband and I didn't have any horses running that day – and someone jerked my elbow so that I spilt a cup of tea down Harry's jacket.' She stopped.

'And?'

'I sat down on the ground and began to cry. It was terrible. My friends were absolutely nonplussed, and your poor father ... Nobody knew, you see. Nobody'd ever realised.'

'Realised what?'

One of the dogs produced a slow eructation; it was difficult to gauge whether from fore or aft.

'I'd been married for nearly six years,' Ms Fraser said, 'to a man who – well, these days I suppose you'd call him psychotic. Or psychopathic – I'm not too well up on the correct jargon. Certainly he was mentally unbalanced. A wife-beater, a woman hater. Sadistic, cruel, an absolute domestic tyrant. Anyway, having spilt the tea over your father, I was waiting for him to lam into me, I was waiting for the blows. Because if that had been Jerry . . .'

'Why hadn't you left him?'

'Good question. Because, I suppose, by the time I realised just what I'd married, I'd already been terrorised into not being able even to think without his permission. Besides, there wasn't anywhere for me to go. I had no money of my own – it was all tied up in this place. My parents wouldn't have me: they'd warned me not to marry him in the first place. My brother was – is – a religious fanatic who would have turned me away without a second thought if I'd shown up saying I was going to leave Jeremy. Looking back, it seems ridiculous that I had so little confidence in myself, but at the time, I felt . . . I felt absolutely alone, so I stayed where I was. Better the devil you know . . .' She lapsed into silence.

'And then you met my father.'

Brigid's face brightened at the memory. 'He was wonderful. So big, so safe and comforting.'

'I remember.'

'And you'll probably also reminder that he had the most beautiful voice.'

'Yes.'

'The kind of voice that makes you realise everything was all right, that nothing was ever going to hurt you while he was around.'

'Yes,' Cassie said again. She was not going to break down or get emotional and weepy, but inside her chest her heart leaped with longing to be once more in the circle of her father's arms. Perhaps all adult daughters felt like that, especially if their lives had turned sour. There are stains on the heart which can never be obliterated. What surprised her was the fact that she was experiencing considerably more than a twinge of pique at this stranger's evident familiarity with Harry Swann. 'So what happened after you'd covered my dad with tea?'

'He picked me up, pulled me to my feet, put his arm round me and led me outside. I'd never seen him before but he knew who I was, because he'd seen me around at other race meetings. He took me somewhere behind the stands and put his arms around me. Just let me weep a bit, then asked me what was wrong. So I told him. It just came pouring out.' She smiled wryly, looking off to the side. 'Actually, it was the first time in my life that anyone had ever listened to me.'

Last time Cassie had heard those words it was inside Her Majesty's prison at Bellington. She opened her mouth to reply but Brigid, the conversational bit between her teeth, had started up again.

'I know I don't sound like someone who never had any confidence, but it's the truth. That's why I liked horses so much better than people – and still do. That's why this place is so important to me. Horses love you without any question – a bit like dogs.' She glanced over at Cleo or Daphne, as one of them eased itself, and waved her hand under her nose. 'Phew! Aren't they awful?' she asked fondly.

'They are rather.'

'Can't help it, poor old girls. Anyway, the point is, I

came from a wealthy middle-class family, right schools, right references, right connections. But the whole system's geared – have you ever noticed? – to men, not to rather awkward women like me.'

'I wouldn't know. I never had the right connections.'

'In my world, if you don't fit in, heaven help you.'

'Not just in your world...'

'So I can't tell you what a relief it was to just sort of let go. I'd been hiding things for years but with Harry I never had to hide anything.' Brigid Fraser smiled. 'Anyway, you didn't come here to listen to my reminiscences about your father, I'm sure.'

'I came,' Cassie said carefully, 'because I want to know what happened to him. And why.'

'I don't know, my dear. If you're talking about his death, I really know absolutely nothing.'

'I'm sure, you see, that it wasn't a random killing.'

To her surprise, the blood drained from Brigid Fraser's weather-beaten features, leaving them a curious biscuity colour. 'Why do you say that?'

'I've talked to the policewoman who was involved, and to some of the other people who were hanging around at the time. It's as if the whole incident – the attack on the policewoman, the fight – was engineered deliberately to get at my father.'

'Oh, no!'

'We've got no proof at all, but that's how it's beginning to look. Obviously I'd like to know why. And, of course, who was responsible. The police seem to have drawn a blank right from the start, and it's so long ago now that it's probably impossible to find out.'

'No,' Ms Fraser said again. The words came out as a kind of Baskerville howl. 'No. No. Please.' The sound was incongruous, more suited to some deserted graveyard at dead of night or a blasted heath surrounded by swirling mists than to this room full of dust and sunshine and roses.

'Mrs Fraser, can I . . .'

'You think he was killed on purpose?' The question was no more than a whisper.

'I'm coming to that conclusion, yes.'

'Oh God. I loved him,' Brigid said suddenly. 'We were going to get married. He was my . . . he was everything to me.' She stared distantly at Cassie, as though seeing her across a gulch crammed with broken dreams. 'It can't have been—' She broke off.

'What can't?' Cassie said.

'Not Jeremy. Please, not Jerry.'

'Your former husband?'

'It *can't* have been him.' She sat with her face in her hands for a while, then said in a low voice: 'I did wonder briefly at the time whether he might have had anything to do with it. But he couldn't have: he'd gone by then. He'd left me, left the country.'

'Where did he go?'

'He had some distant cousins farming in Australia,' said Brigid. 'He went out to join them, as far as I know. But we didn't keep in touch. He might equally have gone to Scotland, or the States. All I know is, he said he was going to Australia.'

Australia: where Tony Spezzioli was supposed to have gone after the murder. Was this more or less than a coincidence?

'I've never seen him since,' Brigid said. 'Thank God.'

'Do you think he might have come back to murder my father?'

'It's the sort of thing he would do. The kind of senseless violent cruel thing.'

'What motive would he have?'

'Just getting back at me would be enough.' Brigid
shook her head. 'But it couldn't have been him.'

'Why not?'

'Because he didn't know about Harry, I swear he
didn't.'

'Could someone have told him?'

Sighing, Brigid said: 'I suppose so. But who? We were
extremely discreet at first – though to be quite honest,
there wasn't much to be discreet about, since I wasn't
exactly keen on sex, after years of what amounted to
marital rape.'

'I see.'

'The whole point about my relationship with your
father was that it didn't start out as a love affair, it was
much more of a rescue operation. I know he'd have said
the same. After all, we came from rather different walks
of life.'

'How precisely do you mean?' Cassie asked carefully.

'Well, I mean ... he ran a pub, for goodness sake. It's
not exactly...' Brigid abandoned the sentence, while
resentment simmered in Cassie's brain. 'Anyway, I can't
tell you what it meant to me to have someone to confide
in, someone to feel safe with. It was only gradually that
things ... ripened between us.'

'Mmm.' Cassie did not want to interrupt Ms Fraser,
whose words were emerging as though they had been
buried, djinn-like, deep inside her, until Cassie chanced
by with the magic phrase of release. On the other hand,
the pique she had originally felt at hearing her speak in
such familiar terms about Harry Swann was fast ripening
into something fairly close to full-blown jealousy.

'And once Jerry had buggered off, it didn't seem to
matter about keeping the relationship secret. Harry came
here quite often – not as often as I'd have liked, of course,

but he had a little girl to – he had you to look after – and we certainly didn't try to hide it. Why should we? Especially after the divorce came through.'

'Who divorced whom?'

'I petitioned against Jeremy, on the grounds of desertion, though I could have cited cruelty or something. It was Harry who gave me the courage to go ahead with it.'

'How long after you got the decree was my father killed?'

'About three months.'

'Just supposing that your husband was involved, why would he have waited until the divorce went through?'

'It was he who walked out,' Brigid Fraser said. 'Perhaps it wasn't until then that he even realised there was another man in my life.'

'If he was in Australia by then, who might have told him?'

'Anyone, really.'

'It would have to be someone who knew you both, wouldn't it?'

Brigid thought about this then nodded. 'I suppose so.'

'Was there someone here, working for you perhaps, or living nearby, who was particularly close to him? A woman, maybe?'

'He was close with just about any woman who crossed his path. For some reason, they all seemed to fall over themselves for him. I can't blame them, really: I'd been the same when I first met him, before I knew just what he was capable of. When he wanted, he could be extraordinarily charming. And he was handsome, too, in that boiled red way that the English gentry go in for. You know: blond curls and rosy cheeks and glinting Saxon eyes. Talk about the bloody knave of hearts.'

'Sorry?'

The smile on Brigid's face was bitter. 'You remember the nursery rhyme: the knave of hearts, he took those tarts, all on a summer's day? In Jeremy's case it was on a winter's day, too, not to mention spring and autumn. And they always *were* tarts, too. Cheap tarts. You can't imagine how it hurt, the first time I found him in bed with a woman – in *our* bed. We'd only been married a month. It was after that that he started to beat me up, as if he no longer needed to keep up the pretence that he was an ordinary decent man.'

'But you can't think of anyone in particular who might have acted as a spy for him?'

'Not really.'

'Not among the staff?'

'There was a stable lad who left here more or less when he did, but other than that...'

'Were they loyal to him or to you?'

'To me, mostly, I'd have said. After all, I'd done most of the hiring. We'd bought this place together, you see. We both had money left to us – me considerably more than him, I may say – and then I got his share as part of the divorce settlement.'

'Did he mind that?'

'I've really no idea. Probably. But there was no way *I* was going to give up everything I'd worked for.'

'So that might have been a reason for him wanting to get back at you in some way.'

'It could. I didn't think of that – but back then, I was simply concentrating on getting through the days on my own. Not just coping with the business, but also realising that I was never going to see Harry again.'

'What about Jeremy's relatives? A doting mother, for instance?'

'There was a mother – she's dead now – but she always

seemed to hate him even more than I do . Dreadful old bag – obviously she must have been part of why he turned out as he did. I doubt if she'd have been communicating with him. She even refused to come to the wedding.'

'Any siblings?'

'A sister; she lives in Norfolk. I only met her a couple of times but she didn't seem to like Jeremy much, either.'

'Did the police interview you when my father was murdered?'

'No. Why should they?'

'If you and he were having an affair ...'

'I don't think they knew. Our lives were lived separately. He was in London, I was down here. He always came to see me, not vice versa – because of you, actually. Sometimes we went away together for the odd night or weekend. My family owns a tiny little cottage near the Welsh border, outside Ross-on-Wye.' She looked wistful. 'It's beautiful there, so isolated. The perfect place for lovers.' She fingered the heart-shaped locket which hung on a chain round her neck. 'That's where he gave me this, actually. It's all I have of him: I never take it off.'

'Mmm,' Cassie said again. As a matter of fact, she did not really want to hear this. Nor did she wish to know that her father had been going to marry Brigid Fraser. Especially when she was not sure she believed it. Or was she simply being childish?

'Nobody uses it now. My brother wanted to sell it when my parents died – he lives in the Dordogne these days – but I refused. In the end, I had to buy him out. I go up there sometimes, not very often, just to remember Harry and the happy times we had there.' She shook her shoulders about and shivered like someone who had just emerged from a cold, swift-flowing stream. 'So, no: the police didn't speak to me, nor did I see any point in contacting them. I mean, as far as I knew, the whole thing was just another unfortunate incident, a pub brawl. And besides, I was so completely devastated...'

'You've not married again.'

'No. I've never seen the point. Apart from this place, Harry was all I ever wanted and ... well, that didn't work out, did it?' Brigid shrugged casually, but Cassie could see how much it mattered still.

'Look: I'm sorry to belabour the point, but when I mentioned the fact that it might have been a put-up job, that the fight outside the Boilermakers' could have been staged as a diversion while my father was stabbed, you immediately thought of your husband.'

'Because if you're right, then it was exactly the sort of thing I an imagine him doing.'

'Murder?' Cassie said. 'That's strong stuff.'

'He was a spoiler, he liked to ruin things. He even had a go at this place...' Brigid tightened her lips, as if in pain. 'If he set his mind to it, I'm certain he wouldn't have any difficulty persuading himself to kill someone else. But as I said, he'd emigrated to Australia by then. Surely even Jerry wouldn't have come all the way back here even for a chance to ruin my life yet more than he already had. I can't think of any other reason.'

'Have you kept up with him?'

'How do you mean?'

'Do you know whether he's married again, got children, making a success of things?'

Brigid Fraser's face indicated indecision. Then she said: 'As it happens, I do. Most amazing coincidence but I was leafing through some newspaper magazine the other day and there was an article about Englishwomen married to men farming in the outback and how they coped with the hard life out there. To my astonishment, one of them was married to Jeremy. There was even a picture of him looking grizzled and sunbleached, in khaki shorts and a safari shirt – you know the kind of thing.'

'I saw that too.' Cassie remembered the piece quite well. A filler piece about women married to Ozzies, wives from the Home Counties who spent their days coated in moisturiser, desperately trying to recreate the lives they had left behind among the sunbaked Australian hills and the hundreds of miles of merciless red soil. It had all seemed about as close to hell as anyone would want to get. 'That's the only news you've had?'

'The only news I want, thank you.' Ms Fraser smiled oddly. 'I stared like an idiot at the wife in the photographs, looking for the tell-tale signs that Jerry was up to his old tricks: the long sleeves, the sunglasses, the slightly crooked smile. They were all there, but in that climate you probably need the sleeves and the glasses for protection against the sun. And anyone's smile would be crooked, with nothing but Jeremy and sheep for company.'

'Did you ever speak to his mother about him?'

'Not if I could help it. As a matter of fact, I ran into Sheila – the mother – at Ascot one year, yonks ago now, but we steered jolly clear of Jeremy as a conversational subject, I can tell you. And as I said, she's dead now.'

'What about the sister?'

'She's dropped in here a few times, on her way down to Cornwall. I think she feels sorry about what happened – but we don't discuss the past, and I've never even been sure that she knows what a bastard her brother was. And probably still is.'

'Was there any . . .' Cassie hesitated. 'Did you ever get the impression that my father was mixed up in something a bit dodgy?'

'What sort of thing?' Brigid was already shaking her head.

'I don't know. The newspaper reports just mentioned something about drugs or prostitution or something – without being at all specific. I wondered if that could have been the motive behind his killing.'

'Your father was a good man. He hated dishonesty, cruelty of any kind. I'm not going to say he went round trying not to step on ants, but basically he was ... well, *good*.' She smiled oddly. 'Perhaps too much so.'

Cassie had to force herself to concentrate on her questions. How unfair it all was, how poignant, that just as she reached the age when she was able to appreciate the sort of human being her father had been, he should have been killed. 'Does the name Tony Spezzioli mean anything to you?' she asked.

Brigid hesitated, frowning slightly. 'I'm sure I've heard that name somewhere, but I can't think where it was.'

It was the very first connection Cassie had had between the different sides of her father's life. 'Please,' she said, 'Try to remember where. It could be important.'

'I will. It's an unusual name, I couldn't mistake it for anything else, could I?'

'Not really.'

'And I want to tell you, Cassandra, that if there is the slightest possibility that Jeremy was in any way responsible for your father's murder, I will do everything I can to see that he pays for it.' She clenched her fists. 'If he was, he obviously must have changed your life for the worse and he certainly ruined mine.' Brigid stood up. 'Would you like to see round the stables? And then have some coffee?'

'Thank you.'

* * *

The tiled passage between the back door and the kitchen was lined with photographs. There were three or four of people gathered in groups outside in the stable yard where Cassie had just spent half an hour, but horses predominated, handsome, well-bred, bright-eyed. Most of them were proudly alone, blanketed or blinkered, or simply freestanding; occasionally they were being held back by diminutive lads. There was a photograph of a younger Brigid Fraser astride a fine-looking black: it was easy to see why Harry Swann might have fallen in love with her.

'That's my horse,' Brigid said. 'I named him after your father.'

'Handsome Harry,' said Cassie.

'The Second. Harry himself will always be the first.'

Cassie was about to pull out the photograph of her father and the woman who must have been Brigid, all those years ago. But selfishness restrained her. Suppose Brigid asked if she could have it? Would it be possible to refuse? Deciding that it probably would not, Cassie did not mention it.

'Is Fraser your married name?' she asked, just before she left.

'Yes. I should probably have changed it but somehow...'

'Will you give me the name and address of your former sister-in-law?'

'Of course.'

'And the cousins in Australia, too.'

'I've absolutely no idea who they were or what their name was. But here's the sister's number. As I said, she's the only one I keep in any sort of touch with.' Brigid Fraser tore a sheet from a pad on the wall and wrote the number down. 'If I think of where I heard that name you mentioned – Spitzalino, was it?'

'Spezzioli.' Cassie wrote it down.

'Right: I'll definitely get in touch. By the way, how did you get onto me in the first place? It was hardly common knowledge that your father and I were connected.'

'It was something of a coincidence . . .' Cassie explained about Grand National Day, a horse named Handsome Harry the Third. And Charlie Quartermain, of course.

'Quartermain? That name seems familiar.'

'Years ago he came here to do some work on your window surrounds.'

'Good heavens, yes. I remember him well. A big chap.' Brigid wrinkled her weather-beaten nose. 'Very NOSD.'

'Sorry?'

'Not Our Sort, Dear,' explained Brigid blithely. Cassie's egalitarian hackles lifted briefly then sank back into place as she reminded herself that this crude piece of snobbery more or less reflected her own feelings about Charlie. 'But I had to admire him,' Brigid continued. 'He'd had the courage to do what I couldn't.'

'What was that?'

'Throw up everything and start again.'

'Wrestling, do you mean?'

'Wrestling? No, he was studying law, he told me.'

'What?'

'He said he'd only recently realised that what he really wanted to do was work with his hands, do something with his life that had some meaning, so he abandoned his law studies and apprenticed himself to a stone mason.'

'Yes. Well.' Cassie raced in before she could decide that she'd made a mistake in bringing it up. 'Actually, Mr Quartermain told me that there'd been some problems here.'

'What kind of problems?'

'Rumours about, I don't know, horse doping or something.'

'Yes.' Brigid twisted her sunburned hands together. 'Yes. It was just about the last straw, really. Finding out that my husband had jeopardised our whole business by trying to fix a race, ruining any reputation we might have achieved ... I think that's part of why he left, realising that he was only a couple of steps ahead of the police. But I can't tell you the relief when he went. It was years before I dared to believe that he wasn't going to come back. Even now, I wake up sometimes and panic at the thought that he might reappear.'

The two women walked together to Cassie's car. Cassie handed over one of her business cards. 'There's my telephone number and address.'

'Bridge,' said Ms Fraser, examining it. 'Nancy, my former sister-in-law, plays a lot of bridge.' Standing by the driver's window as Cassie hooked on her seat-belt, she said: 'And if I sound as though I loathe my former husband, it's because I do. And always will. By the same token, I loved your father. And always will.'

Cassie put her hand over the roughened one which clutched at the wound-down window. 'Me too,' she said.

'Please come and see me again, Cassandra. You're so like he was, so strong and calm. So ... restful, somehow.'

Strong? Calm? Restful: Cassie thought about that one. Was she those things? She certainly did not feel them. Was restful a good thing to be? Didn't it almost equate with boring? And what was wrong with her that she couldn't simply accept the remark as a tribute, rather than searching in and around it for any negative undertones which might be lurking within?

And as for Charlie Quartermain: she tried to imagine

him in a barrister's wig, or handling the details of a complicated lawsuit. Absolutely out of the question. She laughed delightedly: 'Come off it, Charlie,' she said aloud.

12

Aunt Polly and her eldest daughter, Rose, were both
excellent cooks, and she food at Uncle Sam's birthday
party just about compensated for everything else, even
though every mouthful Cassie took was watched with such
disapproving intensity that she half expected it to putrefy
on her fork before it had a chance to reach her lips. Primula
wore an unnecessarily ballooning maternity outfit in
scarlet cotton with a teeny lace collar, which made her look
like an eager tomato, and kept putting a hand on her almost
non-existent bump. Rose and Hyacinth were aggressively
small. Eric the Estate Agent and Derek the Headmaster
proved once again what a pair of dreebs they were. Cassie
could never decide which was the more tedious, though
both of them seemed to have undergone the same charisma
by-pass operation. Eric, however, although he had fewer
topics of discussion than Derek, did still show an occasional spark of what Cassie assumed was deliberate
humour. Over coffee, both of them insisted on giving long-
winded speeches in praise of their father-in-law, but at
least Eric's included quite an amusing joke, even though
the punchline was smutty enough to cause Aunt's Polly's
lips to draw back from her teeth like a mad mare's.

Cassie was still laughing at it when she realised how far
the temperature in the dining-room had fallen and that her
aunt and her cousins were gazing at her with frosty

reproach. Even after all these years, she was still not acclimatised to the way things were at the Vicarage: to this sense of imprisonment, of wings clipped and spontaneities stifled. Of enjoyment denied.

Her cousins began a tiresome dispute about clearing the table and doing the washing-up, each one trying to outdo the others in laying up for themselves treasure in heaven.

'Let me do the—'

'No, let *me*–'

'But you did all the–'

'I *like* scouring saucepans.'

Cassie didn't. Nor did she have any intention of getting involved, especially since she knew there was a large and efficient dishwasher in the kitchen.

'How about a turn round the garden, Uncle Sam?' she said, while the twins threw bilious glances at her, grudging Marthas to her unlikely Mary.

'What a pleasant idea,' twinkled her uncle. 'We could even go and look at my new wheelbarrow again.'

More sour looks from the Ugly Sisters. Not that Rose and the girls *were* ugly: that had always been part of the trouble. Not that they were even that unpleasant: it was more a question of personality clash. 'Yet Cassie would never be able to forget the years in which she had yearned for a Fairy Godmother, for a pumpkin coach to take her away from all this, for a prince carrying a pair of custom-made gloss slippers on a cushion.

Beyond the french windows, the Vicarage garden ran alongside the wall of the churchyard and then sloped down to a sluggish bit of river over which a rickety plank led to another meadow where cows ambled and buttercups shone. Sedate lawn and disciplined borders below the house gave way to first a semi-derelict tennis court end then to a small orchard, a tangle of uncut grass where sunlight dripped through rambling roses and unkempt falls of syringa and clematis. The green air sparkled the smell of honeysuckle was almost overpowering. Somewhere in among the leaves and blossom was Uncle Sam's Snug, a wooden summerhouse to which he often repaired in order to smoke a pipe or two and write his Sunday sermon. A couple of elderly deck-chairs sat outside; on the thick slice of treetrunk which acted as a garden table between them was a tray containing a glass and the remains of a pitcher of Aunt Polly's homemade lemonade in which floated two dead wasps. Uncle Sam's panama hat lay among the juicy grasses.

'It all looks as if it's come straight out of some country living magazine,' said Cassie. The Vicarage ought to have been an idyllic place in which to grow up, but every Eden has its serpents, and this one had been no exception, containing four examples of the species, all of them slimline.

'How blessed we are,' Uncle Sam said, a trifle tendentiously.

'All this, and heaven too.'

He squinted at her through pipe smoke, wondering if she was taking the piss. 'Quite right, my dear.' He settled into one of the deck-chairs and waved at the other. 'You want to ask my advice, don't you, Cassandra?'

'Not so much your advice as—'

'Dare I wonder whether it involves a young man?' Uncle Sam asked with gut-wrenching roguishness.

'He who dares doesn't always win, Uncle Sam.'

'Sorry?'

'You can wonder, but I'm afraid no men are involved. At least, not in the sense you mean.'

'What a disappointment.' Uncle Sam leaned towards his niece and touched her knee. 'One thing you must never forget, my child, is that you are just as good as anybody else.'

This seemed unusually perspicacious of him. And something she would have appreciated hearing from him years ago, when sometimes it seemed as though the whole ethos of the Vicarage was directed at proving that she was not.

'Just because you have not yet found the Right Man does not mean that he does not exist,' opined Uncle Sam, puffing clouds of Old Peculiar Something-or-other into the air. Did he realise it smelled exactly like cannabis?

'Uncle Sam, please. I like the way my life is, thank you very much. I'm not looking for a husbands –' which wasn't to say that if one showed up, she might not at least consider him '– and you're quite right, I do want to ask you something. But not for advice. I want you to tell me everything you know about my father's death.'

Uncle Sam jerked upright, choking momentarily on his own pipe smoke. He coughed vigorously for some seconds in what Cassie perceived as a useful time-gaining ploy. Finally, he said: 'My dear Cassandra, I know regretfully little about it. In fact, virtually nothing, beyond what appeared in the papers at the time, and the small amount of information the police were able to provide us with.'

'That's ridiculous. You were family.'

'I know but ...' He sketched helplessness in the air, the nearest he ever came to criticising the women of his family for their lack of charity to others.

'What about him as a man?'

'Again, I didn't know him nearly as well as I ought to have done. For various reasons ... we didn't meet very often, unfortunately. What I saw of him, I liked. A good, honest, worthy man.'

Cassie longed to tell her uncle what a patronising asshole he could sometimes be, but decided that if she was to

extract anything else from him, it might be wiser to keep
the opinion to herself. As he uttered his condescending
platitudes, she easily understood why the relationship
between God and herself was not one based on mutual
affection. Nor even on mutual respect – at least, not on
Cassie's part. Because it didn't say a lot for God, quite
honestly, if he allowed himself to be waited upon by such
milquetoast fence-sitting servants as Uncle Sam, did it?

It was becoming obvious that if she wanted solid information – if, indeed, there was any – she would have to go to
Aunt Polly. Much as she hated the idea, her aunt would be
the one who had at her fingertips any gossip there might be.
In addition, Aunt Polly was not restrained by her
husband's need to adhere to the basic principles of
Christianity, nor did she possess his reluctance to speak ill
of the dead, especially if the dead had once been his
brother-in-law.

'I can't pretend we weren't a little dismayed when your
mother expressed a wish to marry him,' Uncle Sam went
on. 'As I said, a splendid fellow, your father, but not quite
what *my* father had in mind for his daughter – for Sarah.'

My Father, the Judge. My Grandfather, the Anal
Retentive, if the photographs were anything to go by.

'What exactly *did* he want for her?'

'He wanted her to be ... well, I suppose, *happy.*'

'Is that why he never spoke to her again when she
married her choice instead of his?'

'You sound very bitter, Cassandra.'

'Too right.'

'I think my father feared that Sarah would not be living
up to her potential. As you know, she took a Double First
at Cambridge, and was expected to do tremendously well
in her chosen career at the bar.'

'Daddy's little girl.'

'And then, to throw it all up for a common – for a publican, however decent and honorable a profession it might be . . .'

'Where do you stand on scribes and pharisees?' Cassie said. Between them, as heavy as undigested Christmas pudding, sat a wealth of biblical bad-mouthing about publicans. Synonymous with sinners, weren't they? Scum, for the most part. Useful mainly as an indicator of New Testament reptilian lowlife?

'Cassandra . . .'

'He made my mother very happy.'

'I'm sure he did.' The expression on her uncle's face was one of stony disapproval.

'She never regretted marrying my father, not for a single moment. Never,' insisted Cassie.

'Of course she didn't,' soothed Uncle Sam, skilled in the diplomatic feather-stroking of ruffled women.

'But anyway, I'm not asking you about their marriage, I'm more interested in hearing what you picked up about him after my mother's death.'

'As I say, we didn't see a lot of him.'

'When you did, what did you talk about?'

'You, a lot of the time. Your cousins. Gardens. Your father was a very keen gardener, as you know.'

'I didn't know that.'

'He was.'

'But there wasn't much of a garden at the pub. No more than a bit of backyard with a couple of scraggly rosebushes over the back fence.'

'A garden is a lovesome thing, God wot.'

Jesus. Cassie sometimes wondered whether Uncle Sally was suffering from premature senility. Would Sarah, had she not died, have grown as tedious as her brother? They were brought up together, after all, came from the same gene pool. But the notion was inconceivable: Sarah had been a free spirit, she had followed where her star led, thrown up her brilliant career for the sake of True Love. That was how Gran put it, at any rate, and Cassie had never seen any reason to doubt it.

'So, apart from my father being fond of gardening,' Cassie said, striving to keep her voice acid-free, 'there's nothing more you can tell me about him?'

'Not really.' Uncle Sam was being decidedly evasive.

'In spite of the fact that your only sister was married to him for nearly ten years?'

'Circumstances were not always ideal.'

What he probably meant was that Aunt Polly refused to have a common publican and sinner in the house. It would have damaged her fragile ego had, say, one of her friends dropped in and found some large, loose man with the wrong accent lounging about all over the furniture spitting on the carpet, telling coarse jokes and scratching his balls. Never mind that Harry Swann had not been remotely like that. Never mind that he was a kind, loving, generous-hearted man. Never mind that he would have ... There were angry tears in Cassie's eyes as she heaved her self out of the lowslung deck-chair. 'I'll see if Aunt Polly knows anything more than you do,' she said and stalked off through the apple trees to the house. After her came the wistful sound of Uncle Sam's voice:

'I'm sorry, Cassandra.'

He probably was, too. But also incapable of cutting through the divisions of upbringing and education to see the real Harry Swann beneath. But who was she to cast the first stone? Wasn't she just as obstinate and prejudiced about Charlie Quartermain?

Aunt Polly sat thinly in the drawing-room, doing something dainty with an embroidery frame. 'Cassandra,' she said. Her smile would have had toads racing off in search of harrows.

'Harry Swann,' Cassie said abruptly.

'What about him?'

'I've never asked either you or my uncle for information about his death.'

'Why do you want to drag all this up again?'

'Because it's suddenly become rather important to me to find out how and why he died.'

'Surely you know he was killed in some kind of street brawl.'

'If I can prove to myself that that's all it was, I'll have to accept it. But—'

'What makes you think it was anything more?'

'I've been making enquiries. For instance, I've spoken to the policewoman who was there at the time, and one or two other people, and there seems to be a suspicion that it was something more than a mere accident, something more than a man getting in the way of a knife which was never intended for him.'

'What on earth are you saying?' Aunt Polly set aside her embroidery and put both hands neatly in her lap, at the same time fixing Cassie with a hard stare. The stare was an attempt to conceal the fact that she had drunk a little more than her customary two glasses of white wine. Perhaps she didn't realise that the tip of her nose, which was deeply flushed, was a dead giveaway.

'I'm saying that I think he was specifically, rather than randomly, murdered,' Cassie said. 'What I can't work out is why. I've discovered that he had a – a woman friend at that time, and that she had a violent husband. I've spoken to her too and it's possible that he could have been responsible. So I'm wondering if you know anything, anything at all, which might help me prove it.'

Aunt Polly pressed the back of her hand against her forehead. 'Street brawls. Violent husbands. This sort of thing is completely alien to me, Cassandra.'

'To me too, Aunt Polly.'

The hard stare softened fractionally. There was the slightest of bends in the angle of Aunt Polly's backbone. 'We haven't always got on in the past,' she said, unexpectedly.

'You can say that again.'

'I know you blame me for this.'

Cassandra held her aunt's gaze, saying nothing.

'However, I should point out that you were a difficult child, a turbulent child, particularly compared with your cousins.'

'What did you expect?'

'Your presence in our family was, to put it bluntly, disruptive. I may not always have handled that in the right way, but the blame was not all on my side,' Aunt Polly said coldly.

'I was a child, for God's sake,' cried Cassie, ignoring her aunt's wince at her blasphemy. 'I'd lost my parents, my grandmother, my home. I came from a different background: quite apart from grieving, how did you expect me to fit in?'

To her astonishment, instead of some acid rejoinder, her aunt stared down at her hands. Blood rushed into her pale face. She picked up her embroidery. 'Perhaps I expected too much,' she said quietly. 'Perhaps I didn't always deal with you in the most tactful or even kindly way.'

Cassie frowned. This was definitely not the Aunt Polly she knew and, for the most part, loathed. She wanted to ask if everything was all right, except that it might have sounded sarcastic.

'It's my father I'm really interested in,' she said, and when her aunt sighed a little, was conscious of having been somewhat less than gracious. It was the first time in their joint lives that her aunt had spoken in a personal way to her and perhaps she should have seized the moment, run with it, used it to try and remove from the abscess of their relationship some of the poison while the opportunity was there.

'I don't know if I can help you.'

'This woman he was seeing...'

'A horse breeder,' said Aunt Polly. 'Trainer. Whatever they call them. She had a horse running in this year's Grand National. Handsome Harry the Third.'

'How did you know that?'

'I made it my business to know. She was called Brigid Fraser, ran a stables down in Wiltshire or Hampshire or somewhere.'

'If you know that much, perhaps you know something about her husband.'

'Jeremy Fraser. His mother used to live in Norfolk and was a distant cousin of friends of mine.'

It was like accessing a database. Press the right button and all the relevant information flashed up. 'What about him? Would you agree with his former wife, who thinks he might well have been capable of killing someone?'

'I can't possibly answer that question. If he was, it's not exactly the sort of thing you'd expect his mother to have confided, even to her cousins, is it? According to them, she blamed the breakup of his first marriage on the girl. Said she was extravagant, wilful, unfaithful. Said she could hardly blame her son if he went with other women.'

'But she would say that, wouldn't she?' said Cassie. Brigid Fraser had not seemed to fit this profile. Bossy she almost certainly was, but wilful? And there was no large evidence of extravagance about the place: everything was of good quality, but nothing was new – except the computer in the office, and these days, that was a necessity rather than a luxury. As for unfaithful, there had been a painful ring of truth about Brigid Fraser's description of herself as a thoroughly battered wife.

'She wasn't the only person in your father's life, of course,' Aunt Polly said suddenly.

'Oh?'

'There were always women around. Harry had an undeniable charm – one always saw why Sarah should have...' Aunt Polly's mouth tightened and she smoothed her skirt across her knees.

'Did he charm you, Aunt Polly?' The question was intended ironically, but to Cassie's amazement, her aunt reddened.

'Don't be ridiculous, child,' she snapped, not looking at Cassie. 'About these other women, most of them weren't serious.'

'How do you know?'

'Because he told me.'

'He what?' Try as she might, Cassie simply could not imagine the circumstances in which Aunt Polly and Harry Swann could have got close enough to discuss what was, in essence, sex. This was definitely something to put into cold storage until she had the chance to take it out and give it some quality time.

Aunt Polly did not seem to realise that she had disconcerted her niece. 'Perhaps if you'd had a stepmother, things might have been different...' She sighed again. 'I'm afraid he never really got over your mother's death. I will say for Harry that he was very careful not to get you mixed up with any of them. He told me once that he didn't want you to forget Sarah, and until he was absolutely certain he had found someone who could take her place, he preferred to keep you right away from the more earthy side of his life.'

'Was Brigid Fraser just earthy? Or serious, as well?'

'I'm not sure.'

'She told me they were going to get married.'

'If they were, Harry didn't tell me.'

'He wasn't involved in anything criminal, was he?'

'No. Definitely not.'

'How can you be so certain?'

Once again Aunt Polly put down her embroidery frame. 'Because I contacted the police when he was killed. And – please don't flare up at this, Cassandra – because I had already engaged a private detective to look into him.'

'You'd *what*?'

'It was at the time your uncle was being talked about as a possible candidate for a bishopric.' There was a wealth of disappointment in Aunt Polly's tone. 'Given your father's occupation, and the part of London in which he chose to pursue it, it seemed a wise precaution. Think of the headlines if he had been involved in anything shady. Bishop's Brother-in-law in Massage Parlour Scandal, that sort of thing.'

'It could just as easily have been Publican's Brother-in-law in Rent Boy Scandal,' said Cassie, angrily.

'You're being facetious, Cassandra. Can you imagine your uncle mixed up in something so sordid?'

'About as easily as I could imagine my father. Why should a man who keeps a pub be any more likely to rent a boy or go to a massage parlour than a bishop?'

'That's a question which hardly deserves an answer,' said Aunt Polly, after vainly trying to think of one.

Stay lucky, Cassie thought: at least God hadn't been brought into it. 'And if either of them did so far forget themselves, what, when you get right down to it, is so wrong with either?' She waited, but Aunt Polly merely closed her eyes and breathed in through her nose, indicating long-suffering and pained forbearance. 'Anyway,' continued Cassie, 'having checked him out as suitable brother-in-law material, you discovered that he wasn't running around with a load of habitual criminals.'

'I did.'

'That must have been a relief.'

'However, in the course of investigations, the man I hired did learn that that woman – the trainer – had been operating a bit close to the line at one point. Or her husband had.'

'It was her husband – I asked her about that. She implied that the best thing about it was that the police were asking questions so her husband emigrated to Australia before they could pin anything on him.'

'All so unsavoury,' murmured Aunt Polly.

Cassie got up. 'Do you still keep old newspapers?'

'Yes. They're in the laundry outhouse, as always.'

'Can I look through them? I'm trying to find an article I read not long ago and it would be much easier if you happen to have it here.'

'Help yourself, my dear.'

My dear? Driving away later, Cassie wondered what had got into Aunt Polly, apart from a surfeit of Rheinhessen. In twenty years, she had never heard a term of endearment from her aunt. Nor, in all that time, had she learned as much about her as she had in a single afternoon.

Whose fault was that? Perhaps she herself was as much to blame for the distance which lay between them as her aunt was. It was obvious that at the very least, Aunt Polly had felt some kind of *tendress* for Harry Swann – how far had *that* gone? – and that the feeling must, to a certain extent have been reciprocated. Had they – *could* they have kept together? It was almost inconceivable – but not completely. It cast a new light on Uncle Sam's wife to imagine her in bed with her brother-in-law, if she ever had been. Perhaps that was why she disapproved so much of Cassie and her background: it was a kind of defence mechanism for having been seduced by it herself.

And then there was the detective: how in the world had a woman like Aunt Polly known how to find a private eye? Was that something you looked up in the Yellow Pages? Had she done the whole Raymond Chandler bit, gone to his sleazy downtown office over a takeaway curry shop wearing a hat with a veil, told him she wanted the goods on Handsome Harry, talked tough? It seemed unlikely.

Meanwhile, there was Brigid Fraser's husband to look into. The Vicarage laundry had long been a collection point for the parish's thrown-out newspapers, cans, bottles, old clothes, any kind of discarded rubbish which could be used either for recycling or selling for charity. In the boot of the car was a bundle of colour supplements Cassie had removed, one of which, she was fairly sure, contained the article to which Brigid Fraser had referred, about life as a farmer's wife in Oz. Cassie could hardly wait to get home and read it again. Because although the evidence was, admittedly, little more than circumstantial, increasingly it looked as though Jeremy Fraser was at least implicated in – if he was not the actual perpetrator of – Harry Swann's murder.

13

'Paul? It's Cassie.'

'Yes?'

Just like that. Bald. Impersonal. No endearments. No warmth in the voice. But Cassie had learned the hard way that when DS Walsh was working, his short-term memory seemed to pack up. So even if, say, only two hours earlier he had been bonking her on the kitchen table, he was still perfectly capable of addressing her as though she were not only a total stranger but in addition, one who had just uttered some distasteful obscenity which he had decided for the moment to ignore.

'I was wondering how the Sammi Ray case was going,' she said, tentatively.

'We're still pursuing our enquiries.'

'I didn't think you'd decided to bin the paperwork and join a formation dancing team instead.'

Walsh did not react. His voice was worse than cold, it was indifferent. 'Did you want to ask me anything in particular?'

Only why you haven't rung me for ages, she wanted to reply. Only why you said the other day that you really do love me, because – stop me if I'm wrong – isn't that the kiss of death? *I love you* is fine. *I really do love you* comes across as about as genuine as an MFI chiffonier. 'Only to see if you'd discovered anything further in the case.'

'We haven't.'

'Oh. Right.'

So much for that, then. Silly me for bothering to call. Humiliated Cassie had barely replaced the receiver before the phone rang again.

'It's Tim Gardiner here. You may not remember me...'

'Uh...' She was still thinking about Paul Walsh, her gut twisting with anticipation of further rejection.

'I don't seem to make much impression on people,' he said dejectedly.

Was this false modesty or the result of a lack of confidence which came near to matching Cassie's own? And if the latter, was it endemic to all writers, or just to this particular one? She pulled herself away from Walsh in the future and concentrated on Gardiner in the present.

'*Killing Me Softly*, right?' she said.

'Also *Dead Bawd, Death by Chocolate, The Last Waltz, Love Me to Death*, etc., etc.'

'That sounds like a lot of books.'

'It is. I'm on my tenth one now.'

'Have the all been published?'

'Yes, thank God.'

'How long have you been a writer?'

'About six years.'

'You *have* been chur—'

'*Please*! If we are to enjoy an evening together, the setting up of which was the reason for this call, then I must warn you that there are two or three phrases which can instantly turn even the most placid of writers into a raging homicide. And one of them is the "churning." ' Gardiner paused. 'You *were* going to say "churning", weren't you?'

'Yes. Sorry , how thoughtless of me.'

'If Robin Plunkett is your godfather, he must have told you that the life of a writer is all blood, sweat and tears.'

'Many times. Particularly when he's sitting over an extended lunch in France, waiting for the second bottle to arrive.'

'Did I also mention angst?'

'Angst goes with the territory. According to my godfather.'

'Which is why "churning" has me running for my sawn-off shotgun.'

'What other phrases should I avoid?'

'Do you write under your own name?' said Gardiner. 'That's a good one to steer well clear of. In fact, that's an absolute killer.'

'Why?'

'Because the sub-text is: I've never heard of you'

'I'll try and remember that. Anything else?'

'I didn't like your last book can lead to a certain amount of teeth-grinding.'

'I've only read one of yours and I enjoyed it.'

'Good. Now, are you going to allow me to take you out for dinner in the extremely near future?'

Ought I to feel disloyal? Cassie asked herself. I mean, what about Paul, the man I am supposed to love, the man I was in bed with only a couple of days ago? 'I certainly am,' she said.

'Tomorrow?'

'Great.'

'I'll pick you up at seven-thirty.'

Cassie dropped in to see Natasha on her way home from an afternoon's bridge on the other side of Bellington.

'Any more news of the Rays?' she said, sitting at the kitchen table and nibbling at a slice of freshly baked lemon sponge.

'Not so far. Vida's still under sedation; the son's more or less collapsed and the daughters have got up just about everybody's nose from Canon Granger to the chap that goes round selling vegetables out of a pram.'

'How'd they do that?'

Wearily, Natasha said: 'They must take after their late father. They're going to make some poor girl the most godawful mothers-in-law. Bossy, interfering ... can you imagine having the nerve to tell the Rector he was too high church for an English village and he ought to introduce a more demotic note?'

'She's got a point. Last time I went into the church at Larton Easewood, I almost choked to death on the incense fumes.'

'Rite A, she told him. It's like a red rag to a bull to mention Rite A to the Canon. Apparently he nearly had a stroke. Told her she was an impudent hussy.'

'Let he who is without sin,' Cassie said. 'Considering the reason why he's no longer attached to Winchester Cathedral, I would think a little low-church breast-beating might be more in order.'

'Be that as it may, one of the other girls showed up at the rectory at eight o'clock yesterday morning to complain about the bellringers practising the night before. Poor Canon Granger had barely opened his *Times* before she was haranguing him at the breakfast table, saying it would be more suitable if the practice were held in the middle of the day when most people were at work.'

'I hope he turned the other cheek.'

'The other side of his tongue, more like. The rough side. The Canon doesn't suffer fools gladly. Especially female ones. He pointed out, in unchristian terms, that most of the bellringers were also at work in the middle of the day, which is precisely why practices are held in the evening. I gather – via the housekeeper – that he suggested that if she didn't like it, she could go back to the banana tree from which she must recently have descended, and she's now consulting the Race Relations Board.'

'You *are* joking, aren't you?'

'That last bit,' Natasha conceded, pouring boiling water onto Orange Pekoe, 'may have become a little exaggerated in the telling.'

'How did they manage to antagonise the man with the vegetables?'

'By pointing out that he'd do better if he kept them refrigerated.'

'A refrigerated pram? Sounds like one for the Patent Office.'

'And last night they all came racing out of the house *en masse* to shriek at Edwina Standing's dog. Nearly gave the poor old thing a heart attack. Said they'd call in the lawyers if the dog trespassed on their parents' land again. I tell you, the whole village is up in arms.'

'Where's the son – Rashid?'

'Still confined to his bed, I think. We haven't seen him, but the doctor told me he's been calling in every day and the boy's gone into a deep depression.'

'Is that what the rest of us call mourning?'

'Probably.'

'He was down here the night his father was killed, wasn't he?'

'Yes.'

'Would he have come if Sammi had been around?'

'I've no idea.'

'I mean, it seems odd that he planned a visit to see his parents if he didn't get on with his father.'

'*You* don't get on with your aunt and uncle and cousins Yet you showed up for your uncle's birthday, didn't you?'

'I suppose so.'

'Not all families are as dysfunctional as yours, Cass. Even if the father disapproved, Rashid could still have been behaving like a dutiful son. Or maybe he wanted to discuss a loan to tide him over, or getting a proper job ... any number of things, really ...'

'It must have been a bit of a relief when Sammi rang to say he couldn't get home that night.'

'So I gathered. It meant that mother and son could enjoy the evening together, instead of having to listen to Sammi laying down the law.'

'And they went to bed about ten-thirty?'

'According to Vida.' Natasha frowned. 'What is this, Cassie? I'm not the Ray Family Expert. Why are you asking all these questions?'

'Just wondering, really. I mean, wasn't it a bit odd of him to persuade his mother to destroy all those poison-pen letters?'

'A bit stupid, perhaps. But not necessarily odd, not if he cares about her, didn't want her constantly worrying about it ... and especially if he understood why she didn't want to involve his father.' Passing Cassie a mug of tea, Natasha said: 'You aren't trying to fix Rashid up as the villain, are you?'

'I like to look at all the possibilities.'

'The other day you thought Sammi himself might be responsible.'

'Only in the same way you thought your bigoted dentist

or Lolly Haden White might be. Talking of which, surely somebody must have seen someone delivering those letters or sticking burning rags through the door.'

'Not if you think about it. That wing wall completely hides the front door from public view – and you could easily approach from the field behind. They seem to have been delivered late in the evening, too, when most of the village is either in bed or watching telly. Besides, nobody knows about it – except the person responsible and Vida. And us, of course.'

'I suppose that's why Paul said that publicity was the way to handle it,' said Cassie. 'The more people know about what's been going on, the more likely it is that someone will remember seeing someone skulking about. Talking of which...' She explained about the man she had seen emerging from the sports ground. 'I wondered if it was your retired dentist.'

'What did he look like?'

'A man, mostly. Nothing exceptional: no hunchbacks or gammy legs or—'

'In that case, it wasn't the dentist. He doesn't exactly limp but he's definitely got a lopsided walk.'

'Is there a groundsman?'

'No. The cricket team have a rota for mowing and rolling and marking out the pitch before matches. There's only a wooden summerhouse, not a proper pavilion, and the team captain hangs onto the key for it. It was probably him you saw, checking the place to see that it hadn't been overrun by would-be arsonists or gluesniffers or something.'

'The captain's one of the three team members who live locally, is he?'

'Yes Major Timson.'

'Ah, a military man?'

'Once, yes. He served with one of those fancy regiments: the Royal Blues or the Ghurkas or something. Now, he's the Bursar for St Christopher's, over at Swainton.'

Cassie tried to remember if the man she had seen had possessed a military bearing. Or a bursarial one, for that matter. 'If he's the team captain, presumably he'd have been particularly fed up with Sammi's moans about cricket balls, wouldn't he? As the one in charge of things.'

'He was pretty annoyed,' said Natasha. 'Sammi was threatening to obtain an injunction until they'd sorted things out. That would have put paid to the rest of the games set up for this season.'

'And now Sammi's dead, there's no threat to the fixtures list?'

'Presumably not.' Natasha made disbelieving faces. 'You don't seriously imagine that Major Timson killed Sammi, do you?'

'The selfish hope of a season's fame,' Cassie said. 'It can get to you.'

'Something certainly got to Sammi, but I very much doubt if it was Major Tim.'

'Why don't you do a little nosing around? Check out where he was the night Sammi was killed. Ditto Lolly. And while you're at it, the dentist.'

'Why me? I'm a mother, for God's sake, not a private eye. Besides,' said Natasha defiantly, 'if you really want to know, I'm too frightened.'

'I understand that. But since I don't live here, *I* can't do it: I'd end up being ridden out of the village on a rail. But it would be perfectly natural for *you* to ask, when you're buying groceries in the village shop, for instance, or meeting the kids off the school bus.'

'People would smell a rat immediately if I started doing

either,' said Natasha. 'The village shop is far too pricey for me, and I've never met the children off the bus, nor do I intend to start doing so. Anyway, none of it's really our problem, is it?'

'Wasn't it you who told me that no man is an island?'

'I quoted Bacon at you, not Donne.'

'Either way, I think you should ask around – for Vida's sake, if for nothing else.'

Natasha clucked irritatedly. 'Why can't we leave it to the police? We've told them everything know.'

'Mmm.'

'Haven't we?'

'Sort of.'

'Cassandra Swann: what have you been keeping back?'

Cassie was saved from replying by a man at the door who was selling compost. By the time Natasha had decided whether she wanted two, bags or four, or, indeed, any bags at all, Cassie was on her feet making sounds of departure. In the car, she tried to analyse why she had withheld from Walsh the information she had so genuinely wanted to give him. Like, for instance, the fact that Sammi Ray might well be thoughtful enough to ring his wife to say he would not be coming home, but at the same time, his attitude to her was dictatorial to say the very least. That she seemed to have an inordinate number of bruises. By not passing on the information was she hampering the course of Walsh's enquiries? It seemed unlikely. The police probably had good reason to be of the opinion that this was one of those random murders. She had nothing to feel guilty about.

She managed not to feel guilty until she was in the sitting-room of Honeysuckle Cottage with a drink in her hand, watching the television screen, where a complacent Tory MP pontificated about family values. Sometimes she thought these people were even more out of touch than the Royals – and there weren't too many family values going begging among that lot, for a start. 'One-parent families ... lack of discipline ... traditional values ... adultery ... divorce ... breakdown of our society! ... he ranted, talcumed jowls bulging with self-satisfaction, while Cassie rootled around for the channel changer and switched off.

Should she not call DS Walsh and tell him everything she knew or suspected? The answer was obviously yes. As an honest citizen, a dutiful one, she had no other choice. So why did she feel such relutance to do so? In the end, it boiled down to the fact that she could not bear the way his voice would not change when he heard hers.

This demanded further introspection. Was she really prepared to withhold what might be significant information for a reason so contemptibly trivial? Was she that petty? Well, yes: she rather thought she was. Surely, however involved a man was in his work he ought to respond with some show of affection to the sound of his beloved on the phone. If he did not, what did it make her: nothing but a person with whom he – contemptible phrase – had sex? And further, had she responded to Tim Gardiner with such libidinous alacrity as some unacknowledged way of getting back at Paul?

Tossing back the contents of her glass and slopping more whisky into it, she told herself that the onus was not on her.

Meanwhile, she had other things to do. Heaving herself out of her chair and averting her eyes from the way her wrists bulged as she did so – it had to be fat: not even Arnie Schwarzennegger had muscles on his wrists – she went out to the shed-cum-garage in front of which she had earlier parked her car. In the boot was the bundle of

newspaper colour supplements which she had brought
home from the Vicarage the previous Sunday; she hefted
it out and lugged it into the kitchen. It didn't take her long
to find the issue which had carried a feature about English
wives in the Australian outback. She pulled it from the
pile and took it back to the sitting-room.

Half a dozen women were featured, all with names like
Melinda or Kate. Some were shown astride a tractor or a
horse; others swung Scarlett O'Hara fashion on verandas.
Four of them featured a husband in the background, each
of whom had a complexion like a handmade shoe and
wore a shirt with epaulettes. One of the husbands was
called Jeremy. Nobody in the article was surnamed
Fraser.

Had she missed something? Brigid Fraser had distinctly
said that her former husband was one of those in the
article yet Cassie, reading through it again, could find
nothing which indicated that any of the four men pictured
had ever been married to a Wiltshire horse trainer.
Perhaps he had adopted a new name to go with his new
country, odd though that might be. In which case, it was
idle to speculate which of the men it was. Or had Fraser
been Brigid's maiden name? Lots of women reverted to
the name they were born with when they got divorced.
But Aunt Polly had referred to the husband as Jeremy
Fraser. And Cassie herself, she now remembered, had
asked the question already.

Cassie switched on the television again and tried to
concentrate on a programme about giant turtles, but the
discrepancy continued to niggle at her. It was always
possible that there had been a similar article in another
colour supplement, but it seemed unlikely. She considered the possibilities while, on the screen, pigeon-toed
shells from which ancient faces protruded headed down

dunes of white sand towards the sea. In the end, she dialled Brigid Fraser's number, only to be informed by a woman with a broad Gloucestershire accent that Mrs Fraser would not be back until late that evening.

Exhaustion overwhelmed her. Depression, too. She suspected that whatever answer Ms Fraser gave to her questions, it would not advance the search for Harry Swann's killer. The trail was cold – what else could it be after so many years? And even supposing that by some miracle she discovered who was really responsible for his death, and why, what then? What did it matter any longer? What difference could it make now?

She started awake, dry-mouthed and stiff; there were tears in her eyes and a crick in her neck from falling asleep in the armchair. The grandfather clock showed that it was nearly two o'clock in the morning. She had been dreaming, vividly, of a man with hair which glinted in the glow from the street lamps, her father's voice saying: 'What're *you* doing here?', the shine of a knifeblade, blood on a London pavement. Light had spilled from a suddenly opened door, reflecting off the round end of a beer can rolling in the gutter, a bicyclist had passed, there had been ugly faces, ugly words.

She shivered, aware of long-forgotten menace. Something had woken her and as she shook off the blur of sleep she realised what it had been. Instantly she was up and switching off the sitting-room lamps, adrenalin pumping through her body. Someone had turned the heavy latch of the front door: there was no mistaking that particular noise. A metallic click as the handle was lifted, a low squeak as it was turned. She stood in the suddenly darkened room, her breath rushing in and out of her lungs, the sooty taste of fear clogging the back of her throat. Steve? Was it Steve? Had he been standing outside, peering in at the lighted room, watching her as she slept? She crept around the ground floor of the cottage, staring out into the night. She tried to identify alien movement, inimical shadows, but despite the pale light of a half-grown moon, could see nothing.

She found the telephone and holding it up to the window in order to see the numbers, dialled Paul Walsh's home.

'It's me,' she said, when he answered.

'Hello.' He sounded as if he could barely remember who she was. 'What's up?'

'I'm sorry to call so late, but someone's outside the house, a prowler or something.'

'How do you know?'

'Because they tried the front door.' She began to gabble. 'Oh God, Paul, suppose it's Steve, suppose he breaks in and starts to—'

'Calm down,' he said. 'Calm down. I'll get a call sent out, see that a patrol car comes round as soon as possible, OK?' And before she could break down and demean herself by begging him to come, added: 'It'll be a lot quicker than me trying to get over to you.'

He was right. Of course it was. So why did she feel so resentful? Why could she not avoid the thought that if she had similarly called upon Charlie Quartermain, he would have been at the cottage, protecting her, almost before she had replaced the receiver?

Much later, after the police had been and flashed torches all round the garden, talked in loud and comforting voices, drunk tea in the kitchen and finally gone away with noisy reassurances of driving by again very soon, she went to bed. But not to sleep.

She lay propped up against the pillows until the new day had pushed darkness to the edge of the sky, her ears alert to the faintest sound. She lay with her eyes closed, visualising the street off the Holloway Road where she had grown up. It had scarcely changed in the years which had passed since her removal to the Vicarage. A certain amount of gentrification had taken place: front doors painted in trendy colours, hanging baskets, modern shop windows, that sort of thing, but basically the street had remained as seedy as it always had been.

And while she strained to hear something which wasn't there, she reflected that if she had wanted an answer to the question of what difference it would make if she were to stumble over evidence pointing to her father's killer, she had it now. The only way she was going to exorcise those increasingly disturbing dreams was to find out who was responsible for them.

She would have to go to London again. Like DS Walsh, she was going to pursue her enquiries.

14

Before she left the house, Cassie telephoned Brigid Fraser again. The same Gloucestershire accent as before answered; this time Brigid was home, not hiding her annoyance at having to leave whatever she had been doing.

'Yes?' she said impatiently.

'It's Cassie Swann here. I was looking through that magazine article, the one about Englishwomen in Australia—'

'I remember.'

'And I couldn't quite see which one of them was your former husband.'

'How do you mean?' Ms Fraser sounded hostile.

'None of the men was called Jeremy Fraser.'

'Um...' In the telephonic space between them, the silence hummed softly as Brigid dragged herself from her busy present to the magazine supplement she had read some time in the past. 'Oh yes: I remember now. I thought it was a bit odd, myself him calling himself by a different name – though it's obvious why he would when you think about it.'

'Was he still using Jeremy as a first name, because if so—'

'If I think hard enough, it'll come back.'

'It's all right: I've got the magazine in front of

me.' Cassie read out the names of the four men featured.

'Has the one called Phil Davies got hair with yellow streaks in it and a wife dressed like something out of *Oklahoma*?' Brigid asked.

'They've all got hair with streaks. The one with the wife in a red-and-white-checked dress with puff sleeves—'

'That's the one.'

'—is called Erroll Summers.'

'I think that's him,' said Brigid. 'The thing is, I was so staggered to see his face that I didn't read the words very carefully.' She gave a snort of laughter. 'Erroll, for God's sake!'

'Were you surprised that he was using a different name?'

'Not in the slightest, once I'd worked out why. I mean, he'd left here under something of a cloud – or a potential cloud. He probably adopted it to avoid any further encounters with the police, if they came looking for him.'

'Did you know that the police at Highbury did actually go out to Australia?'

'I didn't. Were they looking for him or for someone else?'

'They were after the man I mentioned before – Tony Spezzioli.'

'Oh yes.' There was a moment's pause and then Brigid said: 'I'm afraid I still haven't remembered where I heard the name.'

'Let me know if you do.'

The receiver replaced, Cassie looked again at the article. Erroll Summers was an attractive man, in a bullnecked, brick-red kind of way. He wore chinos and stood beside a horse, squinting into the sun, holding a wide-brimmed hat against his thigh. Cassie stared at him, devouring the image, assimilating set of shoulder, cut of jaw. Had this person murdered her father? Had those hands once held a knife which had killed an innocent man? Was he the one she sometimes saw in the half-waking nightmares which were currently plaguing her? And if it was, how would she prove it? How could she ensure that he paid for what he had done?

The sequence of events took shape in her mind. Jeremy Fraser, sailing too near the wind, doping a horse, fixing a race. Harry Swann finding out, threatening to inform the police or the Jockey Club, thus jeopardising Fraser's livelihood, perhaps even exposing him to the possibility of a term in jail. Maybe Fraser already knows Tony Spezzioli; maybe he simply cultivates him as part of his murder plan, offers a bribe to create a diversion, and when Harry Swann appears, as he almost certainly would, given the kind of man he was, stabs him. Swiftly in, and swiftly out.

She thought further. if she were to go to Australia, would she find Tony Spezzioli working on Fraser's land? If she had access to Old Ruby's bank or post office account, would she discover regular payments from Australia? And had Ruby died because somehow Fraser/ Summers had learned of Cassie's enquiries and been afraid she might give something away which could threaten his new security?

From the page, Fraser grinned lopsidedly at the camera. In the foreground his ginghamed wife sat in an old-fashioned wooden hay-cart, with her arm around a silver-blond boy of about ten, while another older child leaned against one of the big wooden wheels, holding a kite. Beneath the double-page spread, the text stated that fourteen years ago, Rosemary Summers had come out to stay with some cousins, had met her future husband at a local dance, and had only been back to England once since. She was quoted as saying that she loved it out there, the freedom, the scenery, the absence of pollution and traffic, it was a much healthier environment in which to bring up children. There was no mention of Summers himself being English, but if Brigid Fraser was right, he would obviously have tried to erase his origins. Cassie wondered why he would consent to appear in the supplement of a newspaper published in England: wasn't he afraid that someone would recognise him?

Her hands were a little less than steady. She could feel hatred boiling; looking at the two blond sons, she wondered whether she could do to them what their father had done to her.

For the moment, this was a question to which she did not want to find an answer.

Naomi was sitting alone in the communal lounge off Catherine Pepper ward. The décor was standard issue: battered magazines, low plastic-topped tables, a television set talking quietly to itself in a corner of the room. Above a fluffy blue dressing-gown with a spray of flowers machine-embroidered on the pocket, Naomi's face was brighter, her expression more cheerful than last time Cassie had seen her. Only her despairing eyes and the shadows round them betrayed her inner turmoil. Had she been a hurt child, Cassie would have put her arms around her and offered comfort. Instead, she produced the flowers she had brought and the expensive glossies purchased from the newsagent outside the hospital entrance.

'Magazines. That's kind,' Naomi said, her fingers stroking the silky paper, lingering on the face of Tom

Cruise, Roseanne Arnold. 'I can't read books at the
moment, I don't seem able to concentrate for more than
two minutes at a time.'

'That's not surprising, is it? People poking around
inside you, giving you drugs,' Cassie suggested. She
wished she had had the foresight to vet the magazines for
articles relating to childbirth, motherhood or pregnancy.

'It's not just that,' said Naomi, but she did not
elaborate.

A nurse passed the open door and put her head inside.
'Everyone all right in here?'

'Yes, thank you,' Naomi said, obediently

'You've got a visitor, Mrs Harris. That's nice,' the
woman said, with bright inanity. Addressing Cassie, she
added: 'You can get tea at the machine down the hall if
you want.' She moved on down the corridor, her skirt
neat over her backside.

'They'd say "That's nice", if you'd arrived wearing a
label saying you were a registered brothel keeper,' Naomi
murmured.

'They're all the same, aren't they,' Cassie sighed,
moving with spurious relevance into the real reason for
her visit.

'So how're things?'

'My dear,' Naomi said, lowering her voice, 'you can't
imagine the drama. The hospital's buzzing with it.
Apparently the gynaecologist who's – who *was* treating
me – Mr Ray – was murdered in London a couple of days
ago.'

'My God!'

'You must have read about it in the papers.'

'I vaguely remember,' lied Cassie.

'They think it was some druggie he surprised breaking
into his car.' Again Naomi's fingers slid across the surface

of the glossy magazines lying on her lap. With the self-absorption of the unwell, she added: 'I've been transferred to someone else.'

'Is that good or bad?'

'Good, I suppose. At least he doesn't keep pushing me to have a hysterectomy.

'You know how sorry 1 am about—'

'I don't want to discuss it,' Naomi said shortly. She began to cull the little fabric balls which fuzzed the front of her dressing gown. Then she said: Honestly, this place is worse than a brothel. You know that nurse who just poked her head in? She's supposed to be involved with one of the housemen, even though he only got married a couple of months ago.' She yawned suddenly, making no attempt to mask it, offering an extended view of an unhealthy tongue and the fillings in her back teeth. 'Gosh,' she said. 'I'm sorry. It's the drugs and stuff...'

'That's OK.' Cassie got to her feet. 'Look, I'll come and see you again – how much longer are you going to be in here?'

'I don't know.' Naomi too got out of her chair. 'I really do appreciate your coming, Cassie.' Even so, from her tone, the disengaged look in her eyes, Cassie realised that she probably preferred to be left alone. It was easy to understand how, once immersed in the hospital environment, among the tests and the charts, the routines and the in-gossip, visitors from the world outside could seem as alien as men from the moon.

'Give me a call some time,' she said, leaving it vague, and walked away along brown polished corridors which flowed like rivers towards the exit.

At Paddington, she took a tube to Knightsbridge. The florist shop which had received the original order for the wreath sent to the Rays was situated in a back street between a dry-cleaner's and a sandwich bar out of which a lunch-time queue was already trailing. Inside, among smells of moss and dampness, she waited until a teenaged girl in a pink overall appeared from behind tiers of green vases holding clashing red and yellow rosebuds.

'How can I help?' she asked, with a professional smile.

'I want to enquire about an order which was placed here.' Cassie gave the details while the girl found an order book on the shelf below the counter in the middle of the shop.

'Yes.' The assistant riffled through carboned pages and stopped at one. 'Was there something wrong? Didn't the flowers arrive in time?'

'I wanted to talk to the person who took the order.'

'That was me, as a matter of fact. What exactly did you want to know?'

'Basically, whether you remember anything at all about the customer who placed the order.'

The assistant frowned. 'We've already had a telephone query about this, I believe.'

'That's right.'

'I really don't remember anything at all about it. This is a very busy shop, as I'm sure you can appreciate. Private clinics all round us, people coming in all the time, embassies and consulates and so forth. Not to mention the usual reasons for buying or sending flowers.' She pinched a thick wodge of pages together. 'These are the orders for that day alone: you can see how many there were.'

'You remember nothing at all?'

'I've already explained—'

'Not even whether it was a man or a woman?'

The girl stared down at the copy receipt. 'I really

can't...' She shook her head. 'I have a vague feeling that it was a woman but I could be completely wrong. The only thing that stands out is that it was a funeral wreath and we don't get many of those ordered here. Flowers for the bereaved, yes, but not something as formal as this.'

'A cross,' Cassie said helpfully.

'That's right.'

'White roses.'

'Yes.' The girl looked more alert. 'The first couple of florists I called down in the area it was going to couldn't fill the order, didn't have enough white roses.'

'What did the customer do?'

A frown creased the girl's forehead. 'I remember ... she – it was definitely a she – walked over to the window and looked out into the street. Impatient, she was. Or reluctant. When the second place I contacted couldn't do it either, I almost thought she was going to drop the whole thing and walk out. There's not a lot of call for white roses.'

'Do you remember what she was wearing?'

'A white shirt, silk, 501 jeans,' the girl said, more confidently, as it came back to her. 'Quite attractive, really, considering she was old.'

'How old is old?'

'Thirty-five-ish,' said the girl, then, realising Cassie was pretty decrepit too, added: 'Not that that's old, of course, not really old, of course it's not, just ... not exactly young.'

'Was this woman Asian, by any chance?'

'Could have been. I hardly notice things like that, there's not many people coming in round here who're what you'd call plain up-and-down ... um ... Anglo-Saxon. Black hair, yes, I suppose she could have been, now you mention it. But I don't think she was.'

216

Cassie recognised that she'd probably got as much as she was going to get. She left her card, urging the girl to get in touch if she remembered anything else, anything at all.

On the Underground, making her way up to Islington, she reflected on the identity of the woman sending wreaths to the Rays. Not Lolly Hayden White, that much was certain. Not in 501s.

At Highbury, Cassie made her way to the police station. Behind a glass screen, a burly man sat watching a video monitor with its back turned to the public: he could have been reading the latest crime statistics or watching *Killer Bimbos of Copacabana* without anyone being the wiser. Beyond him, a woman sat slowly tapping a computer keyboard, while another was hunched over a ledger, running her finger down its columns. Cassie waited until the man came over to the screen.

'I'm looking for Sergeant Wilkinson,' she said.

'Friend of his, are you?'

'Would that get me in to see him?'

'It might.'

'I'm a friend,' said Cassie. She winked. 'A *close* friend. Know what I mean?'

The man raised his eyebrows and moved towards an internal telephone console. 'Name?'

'Cassandra Swann. Tell him it's about the Harry Swann murder.'

The man frowned, punching in numbers. 'Which one's that? Doesn't ring any bells. Sure you've got the right place?'

'It's an old case.'

'Len?' the man said into the receiver. 'Got a friend of yours down here, a *close* friend, name of Cassandra Swann. Something about a murder—' He put his hand over the receiver. To Cassie, he said: 'Harry Swann, was it?'

She nodded.

'Yes, Harry Swann, Len.' He listened for a while, then nodded. 'Right you are. I'll do that.' Replacing the receiver, he pressed a buzzer under the counter top and motioned towards a glass door leading into the business side of the building. 'He's in the canteen. Go through and he'll come and get you.'

'Thanks.'

'Very nice cuppa, up in the canteen,' he remarked, and went back to the screen he had been watching. Neither of the women looked up from their work.

Len Wilkinson was a man in his early forties, soft in the middle, balding on top. He came down an institutional staircase and shook hands with Cassie. 'Come about your dad again, have you?' He led the way upstairs and into a canteen which smelled of cigarettes and chips.

'That's right.'

'Well, looks like you're in luck.' He stopped. 'What did you call it, the other day: serendipity? Because old Jimmy Bright stopped in not ten minutes ago. We was just having a natter over a coffee.'

'That's fantastic,' Cassie said. 'I was hoping to get hold of him some time.'

She followed Wilkinson to a table and was introduced to a dapper man in his late fifties who had been contemplating a cup of something which might as easily have been paint water as coffee. He wore glasses, a brilliantly white shirt and a striped tie beneath a smart tweed jacket: he could not have been further from the decrepit image which Sergeant Wilkinson had conjured up for her in their previous telephone conversations.

While Wilkinson went over to the serving counter to get her a cup of tea, Jimmy Bright rose to his feet.

'Miss Swann,' he said briskly. 'Nice to meet you.'

Cassie murmured politely and sat down in the place he indicated.

'I had a phone call from Jill Lockhart – Davis, as she is now – the other day, saying you'd been in touch,' Bright said. 'I was very interested to hear what she had to say, your theories about your father's death and so on.'

He looked up as Wilkinson returned carrying two cups of tea. 'Look, Len, no offence, old mate, but this could get a bit sensitive, know what I mean?' He nodded at Cassie. 'Might be best if you...'

'Oh. Right.' Wilkinson looked disappointed. He slid a white cup and saucer towards Cassie. 'Right then. If you're sure...'

'I think it'd be best, Len.'

'I'll leave you to it, then.'

'I'll pop in before I go,' Bright said.

'Fine. Fine.'

Bright watched him go. 'Hope I wasn't out of order there, but old Len can go on a bit. Difficult to get a word in, sometimes. And he wasn't involved in the Swann case, wasn't even around at the time. Didn't know your dad like I did. He was a good bloke, was Harry, a decent bloke, and there's not many you can say that about. Anyway...' He leaned confidentially towards Cassie. 'Your theory is that it wasn't an accident, your dad being knifed, like?'

'That's right.' Cassie explained some of the circumstances which had led her to this conclusion while he nodded. He was so far from the old dodderer she had expected that she was still readjusting.

'Have you heard about what happened to Ruby Spezzioli?' Jimmy Bright said, when she had finished.

'Yes.'

'Any thoughts on that?'

'I don't have anything to go on, but it does seem rather coincidental that one week I'm asking about my father, and the next, she's killed.'

'That's what I thought. The thing is, I'm not on the force any more, but I do a spot of writing for the *Police Review*, got an occasional column in one of the nationals, and I do have unofficial access to the files. I don't know if Len said, but I'm putting together a small history of London murders, me and a friend. We're starting here, this area, where we're both based, hoping it'll expand if the first one is a success. Naturally, your father's death is of interest, since nobody's ever been charged.'

'I still find that odd.'

'So do I. I wasn't on the case myself, but I remember it. When I went back to the files, I found one or two pieces of information which don't seem to have been properly followed up.'

'Like what?'

'Like your father's lady friends. Bit of a lady-killer, was Harry Swann, and no one ever looked into them very closely. I wondered if we might not be looking at a *crime passionnel* here, some jealous husband or boyfriend.'

'Have you gone into any of it?'

'He covered his tracks remarkably carefully,' Bright said. 'Or else he was very, very discreet. Couldn't find a whisper.'

'If he was that discreet, how do you know he even had all these lady-friends?'

'Word got about. For instance, someone told me they'd seen Harry with a woman at the races. That it was a different woman from the one the same bloke had seen him with in one of the restaurants on Upper Street. Someone else saw him with another woman, once, walking in Epping Forest. Didn't match the description of either of the first two. And there were others.' He stared at Cassie's face and added gently: 'There's no law against it, my dear.'

Cassie chose not to hear this. 'What about Tony Spezzioli?'

'What about him?'

'I mean, he disappeared to Australia and the police went out there, but never found him.'

'That's right. They didn't. Which might have been because he wasn't there.'

'What?'

'Disinformation, I think they call it these days. Protecting your own.' He laughed suddenly. 'Know who Tony Spezzioli is today?'

'Who?'

'He's only Tino, of Tino's Trattoria.' Bright paused, waiting for Cassie to react but the name meant nothing to her.

'Italian restaurants. A chain of 'em. A couple in Soho, one in Hampstead, one down in Kensington – you must have seen them around the place.'

'I don't live in London,' said Cassie.

'Tony Spetz must be well on his way to his first million by now. If not his second.'

'I thought he went to Australia.'

'So did we. That's what we were meant to think.'

'Do you mean he never went, that he's been here all the time, and everyone knew about it?'

'Not everyone, sweetheart. Old Ruby did. One or two others. His sister, for instance. Took me a while to track him down, but I finally got there. Leaned on a couple of sources, called in a favour or two.' He laughed, showing a well-cared-for double set of false teeth. 'At one point we even had a round-the-clock surveillance on Old Ruby. And all the time, Tony was right under our noses.'

Cassie assimilated this information. 'Do you think he killed my father?'

'No, sweetheart. It's no more than a gut feeling but I'm absolutely sure he didn't. Wasn't much to write home about, but not a killer. No way.'

Cassie found this assurance fairly definitive. 'Is he the one who's been looking after Old Ruby?'

'Yes, indeed. The old girl was under strict orders to keep shtum about where the money came from, and had enough sense to see which side her bread was buttered.'

'Have you spoken to Tony – Tino – about the night my father died?'

'Dropped in the other day, didn't I? Made myself known. Told him I happened to be passing, not that he believed me. He swore blind he didn't know anything about it, didn't have anything to do with it. Put on a bit of weight, has Tony, gone legit. Wife and four kids down Leatherhead way, drives his Jaguar in every day. Swimming pool, posh school for the children, villa in Italy. Really got it made.'

'But if he's legitimate, why did he need to keep his whereabouts secret?'

'Now you're asking.' Jimmy Bright tapped the side of his nose in a clichéd gesture. 'Turns out you're absolutely right. Someone *did* pay him that night, handed over a fair amount of boodle for him to start that fight while whoever it was got on with whatever they wanted to do. He swears he had no idea it was murder. Says he was terrified when he realised. Didn't want to be involved in something like that. So he did his disappearing act, got old Ruby to give out that he'd gone to Oz. No reason for anyone not to believe her, old lady like that, crying her eyes out, telling everyone she didn't know how she was going to get along without him.' He laughed again, showing the law enforcer's grudging admiration for the ingenuity of the criminals he had to deal with. Cassie had seen it among the screws in the nick. 'I even bought the old bat a gin or two myself, felt that sorry for her.'

'And where was he?'

'Gone up to Newcastle, he's got cousins up there. That's where he got into the catering trade: the cousins run a small hotel out near Jesmond.'

'So who,' Cassie said, 'paid him?'

'Didn't want to tell me,' Jimmy Bright said. 'Had to twist his arm a bit, if you know what I mean.'

Cassie could guess. Threats of the new bogeymen: the VATman, the Inland Revenue, the Health Inspectors. Any one of them could cause untold trouble for a self-employed person in the catering trade. She nodded again, trying to conceal her impatience.

'Turns out it was some bloke from somewhere down Swindon way. Don't know how he picked on Spetzy to do his dirty work. Tony says he never knew what line of business he was in, nothing about him.'

'What sort of bloke was this?'

'Big chap, Tony said he was. Posh accent, red face, clothes a bit shabby but good quality. Country gent.'

Was this a description of Jeremy Fraser? From everything Cassie had heard, it fitted him closer than a wet suit. Except that there were thousands of other men to whom the same particulars also applied. 'Nothing that marked him out?' she asked lightly. 'Facial tics, or strawberry birthmarks, little finger missing, something like that,' trying to make a joke out of something which was deadly serious.

'He didn't say.'

'Did he have a name, this country gent?'

'If he did, he wasn't handing it out to all comers. Paid Tony in cash, no personal details. Seems to have had it all planned.'

'So I'm not really much further forward, am I?'

'Except you know for certain that it was a put-up job.'

'And it was definitely Harry Swann this chap was after?'

'That's right. Of course Spetzy swears blind he thought all they were going to do was duff Harry up. Didn't ask why, didn't want to know. He was dead scared when he realised what had happened.'

'They,' Cassie said.

'Pardon?'

'You said Tony Spezzioli thought *they* were going to beat up my father. Who was the other person? Or possibly persons?' Meacher had mentioned a youth in a cap. So had Jill Davis.

'No idea,' Bright said. 'Don't know whether the other person came along just on the night, or whether he'd been in on the planning.'

'Could you find out?'

'Will do, sweetheart.'

Cassie knew she was supposed to feel indignation at this patronising endearment which demeaned not just herself but all womankind. Hard to do: Jimmy was a nice old boy who intended no offence and would be mortified if challenged on it. Besides, Jimmy had known her father.

'And any description at all of the other person,' she added. 'Anything which could help identify either of them.' She opened her bag and pulled out the picture of

Brigid Fraser's former husband which she had cut from the article in the colour supplement. 'I'd really like to have this back,' she said. 'But if you're going to see Mr Spezzioli again, could you ask him if this might be the bloke?'

'Course I could.' Jimmy Bright looked at her curiously. 'But tell you what: why don't you do it yourself?' His eyes were bright behind his glasses. 'Pop in to Tino's, have a lasagne, glass of chianti, ask for the boss. Mention my name, if you like.'

Cassie looked at her watch. Nearly one o'clock. 'I could, I suppose. It's just about lunch-time ... Where is it?'

She took down directions, shook hands with Bright, thanked him profusely, promised to be in touch.

'Any more help you need, just ask,' he said. He twinkled at her. 'I'll want exclusive rights to the story, mind.'

'You've already got them.'

15

Tino's Trattoria, in Charlotte Street, proclaimed its gastronomic allegiance by flaunting a red-white-and-green striped awning. Beneath it, half a dozen tiny tables stood on a strip of pavement, trying to create the illusion of a sidewalk café in some town where eating outside was less of a hazard than here, among the traffic fumes and the pedestrians. Not being partial to pasta alla carbonara monoxide Cassie went inside. The place was cosy, intimate, with bench-seats set round the walls and more tables in the middle of the room. She gave the décor high marks for not featuring either Chianti bottles or fishing nets with starfish trapped in the mesh. Above dado level, the walls were covered in a mural which featured an indiscriminate selection of Italian culture, both ancient and modern: gondolas, beaches, busts of emperors, the Colosseum, ice-cream cornets, St Francis of Assissi, bunches of grapes, Botticelli's Venus.

A dimpled waiter came over and she ordered lasagne, a green salad and a glass of red wine. It seemed weeks since she had faced such substantial fare; she handled the guilt by pointing out to herself that she was engaged in primary research.

'Is Mr Spezzioli here?' she asked when the waiter returned with her order. At his uncomprehending look, she added: 'Tino?'

'*Ah, si.* You wish to speak?'

'If possible.'

'Who is, please?'

'Tell him I'm a friend of Jimmy Bright's.'

'No problem.'

She was half-way through her lasagne when a man approached the table and stood looking down at her. He was not enormous, but very solid. No one would want to be under any window he happened to fall out of. Any trace of the thin young man who had gone to the races with Harry Swann, twenty years ago, had long since been overlaid by years of good living. Most of the curls had fallen out.

'I'm Tino,' he said, his accent Italianate. 'You wanted to see me?'

'Please sit down, if you've got a few minutes.' Cassie indicated the seat opposite hers.

He hesitated, looking back towards the kitchens where pans were being banged about and exuberant Latin cries could be faintly heard. 'You said you were a friend of Sergeant Bright's,' he said, still standing. 'What's the problem?'

'My name's Cassandra Swann.'

He did not try to hide his acquaintance with the name. Alarm spread like oil across his face. Pulling out a chair, he sat down, leaning towards her. 'What you after?' he said, all pretence of continental Europe banished from his voice.

'You know who I am?' she said coolly.

'I can guess. Especially after the Sarge was down here just the other day. Harry's girl, right?'

'Got it in one, Tony.'

'Do you mind,' he said, looking round to see if they'd been overheard. 'The name's Tino, all right?

Has been for the past twenty years.'

'Look, Tino, I haven't come to cause trouble of any kind,' Cassie assured him. 'I want you to do two things for me, then I'll pay my bill and go.'

Spezzioli lost some of his tension. 'I already told Sergeant Bright everything I know.'

'Except that he didn't ask what I want to ask. Which is: first of all, is this ...' she fumbled with the clasp of her handbag, '... by any chance the man who paid you to start some kind of commotion the night my father was killed?'

Tino began to sweat. His forehead dripped with it: the cheeks of his ruddy moon-face shone as though he had been dipped in glycerine. 'I didn't know what they was going to do,' he said and she heard the street whine in his voice. 'I had sod all to do with it, wasn't nothing to do with me, what happened to Harry. If I'd of known—' He broke off. 'What've you come for, if not to stir up trouble?'

'This picture,' Cassie said, pushing forward the photograph she held cut out of the colour supplement. 'Is it the man you were working for?' She put it like that, intending to frighten Spezzioli further, hoping that he would try to shift the blame and in so doing, give something more away.

He looked down at Erroll Summers and Cassie could see recognition dawn as he looked again at the face of the man he had conspired with, all those years ago. 'Maybe,' he said reluctantly. 'Could be him, all right or his twin brother. Hasn't hardly changed in all this time.'

'I said there were two things I wanted from you: here's the other. The night my father was killed, this man didn't come alone. Can you tell me who he was with?'

'Some lad or other.' Spezzioli shrugged, his eyes still

absorbing details from the photograph. 'Looks as if he's doing all right for himself, doesn't he?'

'Just like you.'

The ruddy cheeks turned a deeper crimson. 'Hard work and good luck, that's how I've made my pile,' he said.

'Probably the same with this man, too. Whereas my father never had the chance, did he?'

'Come off it.' Again Spezzioli looked round the restaurant. 'Wasn't my fault he copped it.'

'Wasn't it? I know you were standing outside the pub, with some of your mates, waiting for this bloke to show up.' She tried to visualise it: the big etched window onto the street, the two swing doors into the Public Bar, the single door into the Saloon, and the gang of semi-louts outside, pushing each other, joking, waiting. 'And when you saw him walking towards you, him and this lad, you began to do what you'd been paid for. Started fighting, knocked the policewoman to the ground, kicked her, made a bit of a row. Isn't that what happened?'

Spezzioli gave it some thought, nodded. 'More or less,' he allowed. 'Except we wasn't right outside, we was on the other side of the street, opposite the Public. The bloke – this bloke –' his fingers lightly brushed the photograph on the table – 'was on the same side as we was.'

'So my father had to cross the road to come and see what was happening?'

'That's right. Not all that difficult, tiny little street off the Holloway Road. Well, you know that, same as I do. A bloke went by on a bicycle, but otherwise the road was clear. Like you said, we was mucking about with this – uh – this policewoman, and your dad come over, asked us

what was going on, and before you knew what was
what...' The unspoken words hung in the air like a wisp
of vanishing smoke.

'Someone had pulled out a knife.'

'That's right.'

'Who, Mr Spezzioli? Do you have any idea who it
was?'

'It wasn't one of us locals, that's for sure. There was
Looney Barnes and me, kind of shoving up against each
other. And Jase Meacher. The Maloney twins. Just
larking about really. Never realised what was going on
next to us.'

'Are you certain it wasn't anyone in your group?'

'Absolutely, cross my heart and hope to die.'

'Not even the Maloneys? Weren't they always being
put away for GBH and the like?'

'They wasn't carrying that night, swear to God. None
of us were.'

'If none of you had a knife, it must have been one of the
other two, then, mustn't it?'

'Dunno. But it definitely wasn't us.'

'Which means it was either the chap who was paying
you,' Cassie said, while Spezzioli winced. 'Or the other
person. The lad.'

He shrugged. 'How would I know? I didn't see
anything.'

'Describe him for me.'

'He was just a lad. What else can I tell you?'

'It was definitely a boy?'

Spezzioli seemed astonished. 'Course. Wasn't no bigger than a pint pot. I remember he had to run to keep up
with the other bloke.'

'Do you remember anything specific about him? Anything that would help to identify him?'

'Only saw him for a second or two. He had a cap on. White face, walked kind of hunched up – look, miss, don't get me wrong. I liked your dad, we all did. Dunno why I got talked into doing what I did but. Christ knows I never intended anything like . . .' Again the trail of words died slowly into nothingness. 'You got to understand, we had nothing in those days, no jobs, no prospects, no money, nothing. Just drifters, couldn't hardly read or write, some of us, no-hopers at school, nothing down the employment office, what else could we do but hang about, looking for something, for anything, that would make things different? I was lucky, I suppose you could say. That night, what happened . . . it changed my life, really. But I never intended . . . never once thought . . .'

'That's OK,' Cassie said, although it was not and never would be. She did not want to listen to the sour bubbles of Tony Spezzioli's conscience as it rose painfully to the surface. Whatever he had agreed to, twenty years ago, she could well believe that he had not expected it to be murder. 'I was talking to Jason Meacher the other day—'

'Jason, eh?' The suspicion was back in Spezzioli's eyes. 'Know him, do you?'

'No. And he didn't mention any of this. Did he know that it was all a set-up?'

Spezzioli shook his head. 'No. I was the only one. And the other bloke, of course. This one.' Again his hand rested on the picture taken out of the colour supplement. 'Dunno about the young chappie.'

'Well.' Cassie took a couple of deep breaths, dropped her shoulders, made an effort to relax. 'I'm sorry about your Aunt Ruby.'

He glared at her, looking for sarcasm or blame; she guessed that in his life he had been on the wrong end of a lot of both. 'Yeah, well,' he said. 'Poor old girl. What a way to go.' His mouth set thinly. 'I hope they get the bastard who did it.'

'You don't think there's any way that it could be connected with my father's death, do you?'

Stupid question. Tony Spezzioli wasn't the sort of man who made connections. Rather, he moved from one fixed point to the next, not looking back, nor even around.

His expression was inimical. 'Course not. Some shit, excuse my language, broke into the place and did the old girl in for her pension book and a couple of bits of jewellery worth sod all.' His eyes glistened. 'She was good to me, Old Ruby was. Always had faith in me when nobody else did, even when I didn't seem to be worth it. Always encouraged me. The best thing about all this...' his gesture encompassed the restaurant '...is that she was still around when it all started to go good. Told her often enough, I had her to thank for it.'

Cassie was surprised at the flood of empathy she felt. Gran had been the same, Gran had always had faith, always encouraged. The only difference was, she hadn't lived to see the results. And they certainly weren't anything like as spectacular as Tino Spezzioli's. 'I'm really sorry,' she said again. 'I met her once.' She finished the wine in her glass. 'What about women?'

'You what?'

'Did you ever see my father with any women?'

'Saw him chatting them up, from time to time. Never saw him with anyone in particular. There was a bird sometimes, at the races. And another he used to take out to dinner. Never saw her, mind, but one of the blokes down the pub saw him once, in one of them restaurants near the Angel. Fancy tart, he said, big boobs, but ladylike with it, know what I mean?'

'More or less.' Cassie ate the last piece of ciabatta

bread. 'Thank you for your help. And I've really enjoyed the food.' She looked around for the waiter with the dimples but Spezzioli shook his head.

'On the house, for Chrissake,' he said hoarsely. 'Least I could bloody do.'

16

'Cass?' The cautious voice was Natasha's.

Cassie rolled over in bed and squinted at her watch. Seven forty-five. Kind of early for a social call, wasn't it? Even on a working day. After her evening with Tim Gardiner, it had gone one o'clock before she got to bed and she felt she had not yet had her full complement of sleep. 'What?'

'Complications.'

'The Ray girls have fallen foul of the Christmas Pageant Committee.'

'No.'

'The Church Roof Fund lot? The Council for the Preservation of Rural England mob?'

'Slightly more bizarre than either. Have you seen today's papers?'

'No. What's the complication?'

'A woman,' said Natasha. 'Turns out Sammi had a mistress?'

'Only one?'

'This was a serious one. Is, I suppose. Turns out she's the reason he left the States and moved to England. I'm surprised you don't know about her.'

'Why do you say that?'

'Because she lives in the block of flats outside which Sammi Ray's car was found. Didn't Paul tell you?'

'And this woman's currently helping the police with their enquiries?' asked Cassie, evading the question.

'It's in the papers this morning, though your Paul told us, too,' Natasha said. 'Not you?'

Cassie wanted to scream, break glass, fling precious porcelain objects around and watch them smash against walls. 'I've been out a lot,' she said evenly. 'Expand a little.'

'Turns out Sammi met this woman when he and Vida were in Baltimore. She's married to an Englishman, a research scientist who was awarded a grant to set up a project at Johns Hopkins. She's admitted that she and Sammi fell madly in love and were in the middle of a passionate affair when the funds ran out and the husband came back to London. The wife went too, so Sammi followed shortly after, dragging a reluctant Vida, leaving his children at their universities in the States, generally causing all sorts of upheaval, just to be near the object of his desire.'

Somewhere inside Cassie something – was it her heart – hurt quite badly. Why wasn't Paul calling her? Why had he given Natasha all this information but not, in spite of her involvement both with him and the Rays, her? Whatever had happened to their relationship, it was obviously something pretty major.

'The research scientist found out about it,' Natasha continued, 'left the wife, who's now living in a flat in Cornwall Gardens or somewhere in that area. And it was outside her place that Sammi's body was found. The theory is that she killed Sammi in a jealous rage, perhaps because he wouldn't leave his wife for her.'

'Doesn't sound likely, does it? Quite apart from anything else, it'd be pretty stupid, if she'd killed him, to leave the body outside her home.'

'She says – again this is according to your Paul – that she hadn't seen him that night, wasn't expecting to see him, was as shocked and appalled as Vida at learning of the murder, has no idea how his car ended up outside her place, that anyway, why would she kill him if she loved him?'

'Is this what they call a turn-up for the book?'

'Sounds like it, doesn't it?'

'Why are you telling me all this?'

'I felt vaguely you ought to know before you read about it.'

'Very kind.'

'All right, Cass, I'll come clean. Is everything going well between you and Paul?'

'Since you ask, I don't think so.' Cassie was surprised at the steadiness with which she could say this.

'Why not?'

'I don't know.'

'I could tell, from the way he spoke, that something was wrong. Apart from anything else, he kept talking about his wife.'

'Oh, God.'

'Did you know about a wife?'

'I knew there'd been one.'

'Not had been. Is.'

'She's moved back?'

'That's what it sounded like.'

Cassie considered this. It would explain so much. Everything, really. Why hadn't Paul had the guts to tell her? 'Thanks, Tash.'

'I thought you'd want to know, if you didn't already. Not just about Paul's wife, but also about Sammi's mistress.'

'Has she been charged?'

'No. Paul intimated that there was only circumstantial evidence at the moment to connect her with the crime. Not even that, really.'

'How's Vida?'

'Walking wounded, really. She's about, but still on medication. As for the boy, Rashid, he's completely out of it, as far as I can tell.'

'What about the girls?'

'They've quietened down a bit. But I can't help feeling they're only biding their time.'

'Thanks, Natasha, for ringing.'

'I wish I could say any of it was my pleasure, but it's distinctly not.'

Cassie wrapped the pillows round her head and tried to pretend that nothing was wrong. It proved impossible. In the end, she turned over onto her back and stared at the low ceiling. If she was honest, everything was bloody awful. Paul had been avoiding her in the last few days, that much she knew. If his runaway wife had returned, she could see why, but where did that leave Cassie? High and dry. Out on a limb.

Adding to her deepening depression was the matter of Harry Swann's murder: perhaps she'd established to her satisfaction that the killer was almost certainly the man who'd approached Spezzioli, and that man was almost certainly Jeremy Fraser, but she was no further forward towards nailing him. There were the murders of Old Ruby and of Sammi Ray to depress her further. Not to mention what had happened last night.

God. Last night.

She had been sitting over coffee with Tim Gardiner, after a particularly pleasant evening – she had even managed to refuse a pud – when the door of the restaurant had crashed open and in had burst Charlie Quartermain, chucking himself about, patronising the head waiter at the top of his voice, knocking things over. She had hunched over her coffee cup, praying he would not notice her and was relieved when he sat down at the other side of the room with his back to her. What really chagrined her was the fact that the model-slim blonde who had come in behind him, was actually *with* him. Not only did she have a dress open to the navel, but she was drop-dead gorgeous. And twenty years younger than Charlie. Even more irritating was the way Charlie proceeded to converse with her in what, from Cassie's side of the room, sounded like perfect German. Somehow, that was the last straw.

'Call me petty,' she said aloud to the ceiling, and wondered if this was to be her fate, whether she would grow older and lonelier and battier, talking to herself, wearing lisle stockings rolled to the knee, wandering crazily along pavements with her hair held up with kirby grips, and plastic bags full of old newspapers in her hands. 'Call me petty...' Because she could not help the irrational feeling that Charlie had no right to be escorting stunning German girls to expensive restaurants. *Thin* girls. And if he did, then he bloody well shouldn't be able to talk to them fluently in their own language. Nor should he be able to walk past her table on his way to the loo, do an exaggerated double-take at the sight of her, swoop down and press a salmon-and-avocado mousse-on-a-bed-of-roquette-with-a-red-onion-coulis-flavoured kiss on her cheek and then proceed to talk in a familiar way about her to Tim Gardiner. 'It likes its food,' he'd said. *It*, for God's sake. 'But don't let it get too near the old Chablis or it'll start blubbering into its glass.'

'Shut up, Charles,' Cassie said furiously, and he went away, grinning.

Gardiner had seemed bemused. 'Friend of yours?' he'd said, with a quizzical jerk of the head at Quartermain's retreating back, and Cassie could only say sincerely: 'He's straight out of my worst nightmare.'

Quicksilver Quartermain, the Kid Who Never Quits, eh? Well, it had only taken a pretty face and a low-cut dress for him to quit *her*, despite all the declarations he'd made in the past few months. Not that she gave a damn; it was just very dispiriting to realise that you couldn't rely on anything any more.

She thought about the new factor in the Sammi Ray equation. The mistress. It was no surprise to learn that Sammi had one, but why would the police have brought her in for questioning? With the body found right outside her house, she ought to be almost the last person they would suspect. Even a *crime passionnel*, result of a lover's tiff, a sudden overwhelming rage or frustration, would have its immediate aftermath, with the body slumped to the floor, the panicked realisation that something would have to be done. No doubt the police would have searched the woman's flat for traces of blood, forensic evidence proving that Sammi had been there recently. If he had visited her that evening, instead of going home, they would find them, of course. Which would prove nothing. He had, presumably, been there before.

But if it was not the mistress, who was it? Were the police still working on the assumption of a disturbed car break-in, a druggie high on whatever powder it was that gave him those momentary illusions of splendour?

The phone rang again. Was it Paul? Please be Paul ... but it was Brigid Fraser. 'Sorry if I woke you,' she said in her brusque way. 'I've remembered where I met your Italian friend, Mr Spezzioli. It was with your father, once.

Harry used to organise outings to the races for the regulars at his pub – I'm sure you knew that – and he once introduced me to some of the people who'd come along. This chap, and a couple of others, twins, and a man with an Afro.'

'I see. Was this before your husband had left you?'

'A few months before, though he wasn't there that day. He was keeping a bit of a low profile, because of that business I told you about, with the doping and so on. The idiot. I can't even remember where it was – Market Rasen, maybe, or Folkestone. But I can remember Harry and his little group. And I recall thinking how much they all seemed to admire him.' Her voice softened. 'We were lucky, Cassandra, you and I.'

'Were we?'

'That he loved us, I mean.'

'I guess. Cassie was pretty certain she did not want to be part of a 'we' which included Ms Fraser.

'Anyway, I thought I'd let you know. Have you made any headway with your search?'

'Not really. Dead ends everywhere. Your former husband's sister, for instance. I rang her but the neighbour who was in watering the plants said she was away on holiday until the end of the week.' Cassie did not add that she had left her name, address and telephone number with the sister's neighbour, just in case.

'Bad luck. Though I don't know what help she could have given you: she and Jerry weren't exactly bosom pals.'

'So you said.'

'Don't forget. If you want to come and visit, let me know. I'd love to see you again. And I would so much like to talk to someone who knew Harry.'

'I'll keep in touch.' But Cassie knew she would not. She

admitted frankly that the reason was plain jealousy. She did not want to share her father with a stranger, she wanted to keep the memory of him to herself.

Once out of the shower, she looked at her watch. Nearly nine o'clock: what did that make it in Australia? With the help of her old school atlas and the telephone directory, she discovered that the Erroll Summers homestead was somewhere between eight and nine hours ahead of Honeysuckle Cottage. Which meant it was around supper time. She telephoned International Enquiries, gave the information she had garnered from the colour supplement and waited. It was only seconds before she had written down on a piece of paper the telephone number which would link her with Jeremy Fraser, alias Erroll Summers.

Now what? The paper lay in her hand. All she had to do was dial the numbers and she could be speaking to the man who had stabbed Harry Swann in the heart and left him dying in the street. This close to her quarry, she wondered what she would say to him. Not that that was important. Just to hear his voice would be enough. She thought of his two ash-blond sons and wished that the emotion she felt were something stronger than regret. She needed to feel hatred, surging anger, an overwhelming desire for revenge. But Harry Swann had been in his grave these twenty years and more; the damage done had long ago been assimilated, dealt with. This close, did it matter any longer who had killed her father, or why?

Yes.

It mattered. It had to.

Before she could register any more doubts, she dialled the number she had been given. If a woman answered ... but the voice at the other end of the line was indubitably masculine. 'Yeh?'

'Is that . . . is that Mr Erroll Summers?' Cassie said, her voice far from steady.

'Sure is. Who's this?'

'I'm trying to get in touch with Jeremy Fraser,' said Cassie.

'Never heard of him. This is the Summers residence.'

She should have thought this out before she telephoned, Cassie realised. There had been no guilty pause at the sound of the name, no sudden intake of breath – but then Erroll Summers was hardly likely to admit to a total stranger, phoning out of the blue, that he was Jeremy Fraser.

'The Jeremy Fraser I'm after used to breed and train horses in England.' she said, hoping she sounded more authoritative than she felt. 'He was married to a woman called Brigid Fraser until – until he—'

'What the sweet – Lizzie!' Erroll Summers suddenly roared. 'Come here, will you? There's some fruitcake on the line, looking for a geezer name of Jeremy Fraser.'

Distantly, a woman with a well-bred English accent answered: 'Jeremy Who?'

'Fraser,' shouted Summers, not bothering to place his hand over the receiver. 'Ever heard of him?'

'No.'

'Come and have a chinnie, willya? I got things to do.'

'Elizabeth Summers speaking,' someone said, a few seconds later. 'Who is that, please?'

'I think I must have been misinformed,' Cassie replied, striving for calm. 'I was told that your husband might know the whereabouts of someone called Jeremy Fraser.'

'I'm afraid I don't understand. Who is this person?'

'Flippin' horsebreeder,' Erroll Summers said in the background.

'And why would my husband know him?'

'Perhaps he met him when he was in England,' Cassie said, feeling increasingly stupid.

'Look, I don't know what you're after,' began Mrs Summers. 'But my husband has never been to England—'

'Too bloody right!' Summers said loudly behind her. 'Whingeing poms, warm beer, all that flippin' rain, give me a break.'

'—and, as you may have gathered, has very little intention of ever going.'

'Are you absolutely sure?'

'Of course I'm sure,' Mrs Summers said coldly. 'So is the rest of his family. Not to mention his friends. As a matter of fact, it's something of a family joke that he's never set foot outside Australia.'

'Not even before he met you, perhaps?'

'Never.' Mrs Summers was very firm about it.

At her end of the line there was a noise indicative of pillows beating the air and rushing mighty winds. A helicopter? 'Get off the ruddy phone, Lizzie, willya?' came Summers's voice. 'Tell the lady to sail down the Swannee, we got company.'

What now? It seemed fairly clear that Erroll Summers and Jeremy Fraser were not one and the same. Which led on to the reason why Brigid had thought they were. A physical likeness? A misidentification over the telephone? Or a deliberate attempt to mislead?

A shadow passed the kitchen window. Someone tapped at the back door. When she opened it, DS Walsh was standing outside. There had been a time like, oh, three days ago, when he would simply have come in, when he would have put his arms around her instead of grinning uneasily and saying, as he did now: 'Hello, Cass.'

'Come in.'

'Thanks.' He sat down at the kitchen table and began

playing with the coffee pot, moving the plunger up and down in the black liquid, looking utterly, she was glad to see, miserable.

'Coffee?' she said.

'Please.'

Fetching a mug, she told herself, fiercely, not to have a row, not to mention the wife, to be calm and womanly, to think Aunt Polly.

'Thought I'd update you on the Ray murder,' he said, not looking at her.

About bloody time. 'I'd be interested to know where you've got on it.'

'Not very far.' He outlined for her more or less what Natasha had already told her that morning. 'We're going to have to let the woman – she's called Jessica Tennant – go because we've got absolutely nothing to hold her on. No forensic evidence inside the flat, beyond fingerprints which would have been there anyway. We'd never even have known about her if it hadn't been for routine questioning of the occupants of the flats. When our man knocked on the door, she asked what it was all about and when he told her the name of the victim, she fainted.' For the first time, he looked at her; he smiled. 'I didn't know women did that any more.'

'Mostly they don't. Not since they got rid of their panty-girdles and their roll-ons.' She passed him a mug of coffee and pushed the milk jug towards him.

'Did *you* ever wear a roll-on?'

'Only once. When I was fifteen or so and hadn't yet realised you didn't have to conform if you didn't want to. Rebel without a corset, that's me.'

'And very nice, too, with *or* without. Ever gone in for stiletto heels and skin-tight latex, maybe a rhino whip?'

'Only for funerals.'

They both fell silent. Walsh sipped warily from the rim of his mug. 'Cassie...'

'What?'

'Cassie, I...'

'You don't take sugar, do you? How about a biscuit? Or a sandwich or something? Have you had breakfast?' she prattled, not wanting to hear whatever he had to say to her.

He looked defeated. He sighed. 'Anyway, this Jessica Tennant may have been his mistress, but she doesn't look like his murderer.'

'Presumably she's upset.'

'She seems to be absolutely devastated. I was up in London when they brought her in. She was white as a sheet, could hardly walk: might even have brought a tear to my eye if I wasn't a cynical old law officer, paid never to take things at face value.'

'What's the official view on the poison-pen letter writer? Could he or she be responsible? Or is that being treated as a side issue at the moment?'

'We've no way of telling whether the two are linked. If that stupid woman – sorry, the grieving widow – hadn't burned the damn letters...'

'It was the son's fault, not hers. She'd kept them. She knew she'd have to pass them on to you sometime or other, if they persisted.' Cassie fingered the pattern on the milk jug, trying not to meet Walsh's gaze. 'Do you have any theories at all?'

'As I said, it was either entirely random, in which case we may never catch up with the killer except by pure luck. Or else it was this letter writer, or someone with a particular motive for seeing off Dr Sammi Ray. In that case, chances are we'll get to him or her in the end. It's just a question of tracking them down.'

'What about Jessica Tennant's husband?'

Walsh<'s face closed down. 'Naturally we'll be talking to him. He's an obvious suspect.'

'But nothing, at the moment, points anywhere in particular.'

'That's right.'

'What about the funeral?'

'They've already released the body to the local under-taker here. We've established what we need from it: no point keeping everybody waiting I think it's planned for a couple of days from now. In Bellington. Cremation.' Walsh stood up. 'Cassie. I really have to explain something.'

'If it's about your wife, I don't want to know.'

'Who told you?'

'I kind of guessed. And then it was confirmed.'

'Oh, Cassie. I have to give it a try, whatever I feel about you. She and I – we've been together for years now, ever since we were at school. I can't throw all of it away if there's a chance it'll work. But don't think I'm not suffering.'

'Yeah, yeah, been there, done that, got the T-shirt, Cassie thought. 'I'm sure you are,' she said. 'I really do hope it works out for the two of you.'

'I don't think it will. But I have to give it a go.'

'Of course you do.'

'I can't believe you feel as calm as you sound.'

'But I do,' said Cassie.

When he'd gone, she was going to take all Robin's old aluminium saucepans into the garden and throw them against the wall of the outbuildings. Several times. And at the back of the kitchen cupboards there were several saucers upon which houseplants now deceased had once rested. She would smash them one by one. She would

probably scream at the same time. Loudly. She might
even shout obscenities. That's how calm she was.

And after that, she would probably drive in to Bellington
– or even Oxford, where there was more scope – and look
for some outrageously expensive item of clothing. A pure
silk teddy with real lace inserts, perhaps. A pair of those
fuck-me shoes with straps and peep toes and heels up to
the hip. A skirt made of jade-green leather. Something
like that. Something to persuade herself that she was still
feminine and lovable and worth bothering with. Anything,

just so long as she didn't have to sit staring into the empty
hearth and wishing Paul's wife were on another planet.

17

The following morning, Cassie drove over to Larton Easewood. The village was quiet today, the continuing heat imprisoning people in their homes. The normally bustling High Street was almost deserted apart from a mother or two standing outside the greengrocer's, prams to hand, a woman in a tweed skirt walking a dachsund, another almost identical woman peering in through the window of one of the antique shops, some OAPs milling round the door of the bakery. Where the street branched, Cassie turned off towards the green. Youths holding motor-cycle visors and beer cans lounged on the benches at the edge of the grass. Confetti lay thickly on the path leading between gravestones to the church door; she glimpsed Canon Granger pulling a giant weed from the wall which surrounded the churchyard. Beyond the green, there were more shops, a couple of pubs, a post office. Beyond that, the Sinclairs' Queen Anne house.

Natasha let her in without speaking. She seemed distracted as she led the way to the kitchen. 'Coffee?'

'Please.' Cassie dropped wearily into a chair. 'The workmen are driving me mad.'

'It's always the way,' Natasha said, with anodyne imprecision. She made a few passes at the pile of newspapers on one end of the table, and removed a baked clay mug which featured a grotesquely ugly face on one side and the word DAD on the other.

'I actually picked up their ghetto-blaster this morning before I left and walked towards the lily pond with it,' said Cassie. 'But I didn't have the balls to throw it in. So now they know they can flout my authority with impunity.'

'You've got to show them who's the boss.'

'I've already done that several times but they don't seem to take the point. Do you think Chris might have a word?'

'Chris? Can you imagine him getting stroppy with a workman? Or a workman taking him seriously, if he did?'

'With difficulty.'

'You should get that friend of yours – Charlie, is it? – to sort them out.'

'He already has once, but the effect seems to have worn off.' Thinking of Charlie Quartermain reminded her that next Sunday he was supposed to be bringing his father to lunch, though she still had not worked out quite how that had happened. She pulled a newspaper towards her. 'Is this today's?'

'I think so. I haven't had time to read it yet.' Natasha swiped with a J-cloth at the top of the stove where someone had over-enthusiastically been boiling milk.

Carrie glanced idly at the front page. Half-way down, a paragraph headline murmured MISTRESS IN MURDER CASE RELEASED. Beneath it, a picture showed a woman being helped into a car by two burly men. A woman called Jessica Tennant, who was, according to the paper, the thirty-six-year-old mystery woman at the centre of the murder a few days earlier of Dr Sammi Ray, distinguished gynaecologist, found dead in his car in Runald Gardens,

SW7. The woman had a hand up to her face but nonetheless gave an impression of the sort of lithe elegance which Cassie had hungered for all her life. She put back the flapjack she had taken from the plate which sat on the table.

'I know I'm here to talk about the business,' she said, still looking at the photograph, knowing that the woman was familiar though not sure why, 'but before we get started, is there any chance of bumping into – accidentally on purpose – Major Timson?'

'Would that be the same Major Timson who is captain of the local cricket team, a man known to have quarrelled with Sammi Ray?'

'Golly, you're quick.'

'Why do you want to bump into him?'

'To see if I can identify the man I saw coming out of the playing field behind the Rays' house.'

'Oh God. The Rays.' Natasha turned sharply, twisting the J-cloth in her hands. 'I'm not sure why, but they seem to have adopted me as den mother. Vida came over this morning to tell me that during the night someone had spray-painted something across the inside of the front wall.'

'And I'll bet it wasn't a message of condolence.'

'It was, in a way. The exact wording was: WOG R.I.P.'

'A kindly thought.' Cassie slouched against the slats of her chair. 'It makes you despair, doesn't it?'

'It makes me bloody murderous. Those poor women, as if they haven't had enough to put up with...' Natasha spoke through gritted teeth as she slapped the cloth into the kitchen sink. 'They're in bloody *mourning*, Cassie, and someone does this to them.' She shook angry shoulders. 'Anyway. Major Timson: I should think he'd be at the school, wouldn't he?'

'I rang St Christopher's. It's half-term.'

'I'd forgotten. In that case, Major Tim and his wife will have gone up to Scotland for a few days, hill-walking.'

'They always do that, do they?'

'Yes.'

'And half-term started the day before yesterday,' Cassie said reflectively. 'So last night's little graffiti job couldn't have been him. And on the assumption that the same person is responsible for the letters and the turds, etc., that's one more suspect eliminated.'

'Yes.'

'Which leaves Simon Bates the medical student—'

'Except he's in Edinburgh, visiting his girlfriend. I was talking to his mother yesterday while we were waiting outside the library van to change our books.'

'So we have one last suspect. Lolly Hayden White.'

'I was the one who thought of her. If I remember rightly, you were the one insisting that anyone who played bridge couldn't possibly be guilty of so much as a split infinitive, let alone of those letters.'

'Possibly I was wrong,' said Cassie. 'Anyway, her bridge game's gone off to such an extent you could hardly say she played any more.'

'So she now becomes eligible for the Writer of the Year Award, poison-pen category, does she?'

'Originally nominated by you, don't forget.'

'What a mess.'

'I know. And I can't really see Lolly creeping about with a can of spray paint, can you?'

'But I *can* imagine her writing those letters.'

'Seems to me,' Cassie said, 'that you're jolly lucky nobody sent you any when you first arrived. As you've pointed out, you're not exactly a WASP, are you?'

'Something I constantly offer up thanks for. But you're

right: if someone in the village has taken against the Rays on racial grounds, then logically they would have done the same to me.'

'Which brings us neatly back to Lolly, the true motive for the letters being her desire to get them out of the Old School House.'

'We don't *really* think it's her, do we?'

'She's got motive and opportunity. And she's certainly been playing off-form recently, possibly indicating a guilty conscience.'

'What about that wreath?'

'The daughter might have sent that,' said Cassie. 'The one she wants to come and live near. What's she like? Could she be in it with her mother?'

'A raven-haired beauty,' Natasha said. 'That's how the local newspaper described her when she got engaged.'

'So, given that the florist's assistant spoke of a black-haired woman, she could have been the customer who ordered the wreath.'

'No reason why not.'

'Could she have been the one to murder Sammi?'

'She could, I suppose.'

'Does this raven-haired beauty have a job?'

'She works in the dispensary at the General Hosp—' Natasha broke off. 'So she might even have known Sammi.'

'Or made it her business to know him. Or even had an affair with him, like various others. And having the affair, have discovered that he had another mistress up in London, and waited outside until he came out that night and killed him in a fit of jealousy and rage.'

'But the mistress in London says he didn't visit her that night.'

'Maybe she's lying. Or maybe the raven-haired beauty

killed him elsewhere and then drove his car to Runald Gardens in the hope of incriminating the other mistress, before making her escape on foot.'

'Cassie.'

'Or got him to drive her to Runald wardens and *then* killed him. The possibilities are endless. Or maybe she lured him—'

'Cassandra! There are police on the case at this very moment. Surely they'd have picked up on all of this stuff.'

'Would they really have got on to Lolly Hayden White? You can't beat local knowledge when it comes to crime solving.'

'Are you going to tell the police all this?'

'Not until there's a bit more hard evidence. But you've got to admit that it's a neat theory.'

'Too neat. I could just about imagine a senile Lolly – not that she is, but if she had suddenly become so – sending those letters, but the way you're bringing Serena Smith – that's her daughter – in on it, turning the poor woman into a murderer, is too much.'

'Then one has to look at other motives.' Cassie straightened. 'To business,' she said. 'After which, I shall visit the supermarket at Bellington and seek out the manager, keeping my eyes open for traces of paint about his person.'

'What about Serena?'

'It won't hurt to see where she was the day that wreath was ordered.'

'And if she was at work, and can therefore be eliminated, how about Lolly?'

'An open mind, dear Watson, must be kept.'

The supermarket manager was extremely helpful about the E numbers in the pots of yoghourt Cassie had consulted him about, listening patiently to her account of the type and severity of the skin allergies she suffered if she came within spitting distance of an additive, and offering good advice about having a word with her family doctor. He was not the man she had seen emerging from the cricket field at Larton Easewood.

Now, she walked slowly up the steps of the police station, only a few yards away from the supermarket. At the entrance desk, she asked to speak to Detective Sergeant Walsh, saying she had information to give him. When they tried to fob her off with someone else, she said that she would only speak to DS Walsh; when they asked her name, she said she was Natasha Sinclair, hoping that no one would ask for formal identification, afraid that Paul would refuse to see her if she gave her own name. Her stomach churned at the thought. How had her love affair so quickly been reduced to this?

He came half-running down the stairs, looking at his watch, smiling. When he saw her, the smile slipped and wavered. 'Cassie,' he said, coming close to her, taking her elbow.

'I came to talk about Sammi Ray,' she said, keeping her chin up, very cool, very Vicarage, though her heart felt as though someone were slowly tearing it into shreds. 'Not about anything else.' His hazel eyes, the way he brushed his hair to one side, were so familiar to her that seeing him was like looking into a mirror.

'Let's go in here,' he said, pushing open a grey-painted door and ushering her into an interview room which contained a long table with a shiny washable surface, and four dented wooden chairs.

'The thing is,' Cassie said, 'there are one or two things I ought to have told you. Or at least, which it would make me feel better to tell you.'

'Should I be recording this?'

'No.' Quickly, Cassie filled him in on the possibility that Sammi Ray had been a less than perfect husband. She spoke of the bruises on Vida's skin, and the cigarette burns. She told him about the dentist, about the cricket team, about Lolly Hayden White and her daughter, Serena Smith, also bringing in the funeral wreath dispatched via the Knightsbridge florist shop.

DS Walsh stopped her there. 'What you've said is very interesting,' he said, 'and we'll certainly check out the bits which we haven't so far uncovered for ourselves. But we already know who sent the wreath – we've had a formal identification from the assistant at the shop. Besides, the perpetrator has admitted it.'

'Who was it?'

'Jessica Tennant.'

'The mistress? Why on earth would she have sent Vida Ray a wreath? The other way about I could have understood, but—'

'Her claim is that Mrs Ray has been making nuisance telephone calls to her for months, dozens of them a day, and all through the night so she can't sleep.'

'Why doesn't she have her number changed?'

'Because she's involved with some kind of television production company, and says it would cost her literally hundreds of pounds to change all her letterhead and publicity material. She sent the wreath in what she now says she realises was an idiotic attempt to scare Vida Ray off.'

'Did it work?'

'The phone calls have stopped.'

'How did she know who it was? Did Vida identify herself?'

'She says she just knows. The same thing happened

right after she started her number with Sammi, while she and her husband were still in the States.'

'What did Sammi say about it? She must have told him.'

'According to Mrs Tennant, he just shrugged, said she couldn't really be sure it was Vida, and that anyway, if it was, Vida was like that, "highly-strung" was the phrase he used, and that she would eventually tire of it and turn to something else. Especially if she got the job she was after.'

'And does Jessica Tennant also admit to the anonymous letters?'

'Those she absolutely denies. Says they're nothing to do with her. Says it was hard enough sending the wreath and she'd never have gone through with it if she hadn't been at the end of her tether. Anyway, how could she have been responsible? They were hand-delivered.'

'It's not that long a drive from London.'

'Interesting,' Walsh said. 'Do you suppose she brought the dogshit with her, or did she count on there being some lying around when she got to Larton?'

'It's perfectly feasible that she did it. Otherwise, we have to believe that there were two different people persecuting the Rays.'

'The wreath was a one-off. She said she almost backed out when the shop assistant couldn't find a local place with the white roses. Almost walked out of the shop.'

'Does she have any theory about who might have killed Dr Ray?'

'No. She thinks he must have arrived to visit her, although they had previously arranged not to meet that evening, but she says he can't have been mugged while he was parking his car, not in that neighbourhood.'

'I wonder what he was planning to do that evening, if he wasn't going to see her. Where he was going to stay? Why he was even staying up in London when he'd planned to go down to Larton.'

'No idea. There wasn't a crisis on at his hospital or anything – that's been checked.'

'So he'd rung home to say he was staying up in London, but not the mistress, to say he was on his way.'

'A surprise for her, perhaps. That's the way lovers are, isn't it?' Walsh's voice changed gear from professional to tender. 'Oh, Cassie...' He put an arm round her shoulders and tried to pull her closer to him but she resisted. 'What's wrong?' he asked.

'What's wrong is that you're living with another woman, even if she is your ex-wife, and if you really want to make a go of things with her, you shouldn't be coming on to me.'

'It's not working out, her and me.'

'I'm not surprised, if you behave like this. How much of a chance are you giving it?'

'I want to be with you, not with her.'

'You and she've been together since your schooldays.' Cassie said remorselessly. She stood up. 'I wanted to give you the information, in case you didn't already have it. Now, I shall go.'

'I love you. Cassie.' His lovely mouth was sad.

She walked out of the room without saying anything, her head filling up with tears which she was determined not to shed. At least, until she was out of his sight. Being strong was not much fun.

Back at Honeysuckle Cottage, she telephoned Brigid Fraser again. 'Sorry to bother you, but the lad who left at around the same time as your husband – do you remember?'

'Yes.'

'What was his name? Do you have any idea where he went?'

'Why do you ask?'

'Because I'm wondering if he was the young man seen with your husband at the time my father was killed.'

'Who saw them?'

'There are half a dozen witnesses,' said Cassie.

'I didn't realise that – but it fits in, really.'

'How do you mean?'

'Because in stable parlance, a lad doesn't have to be a man. It can also be a girl. In fact, a great many stable lads are female. She was called Elizabeth Taylor, and was one of Jeremy's many conquests. I don't know why she stayed on after he left. In fact, she went only seconds before I dismissed her, if you really want to know.'

'If the lad with your husband that night was her, why would she have gone along with such a thing?'

'She might not have realised exactly what he intended. Or she may have been delighted at finding a way of getting back at me for sending her packing.'

'Did she know about your – liaison with my father?'

'I'm sure she did. As I said before, by then, we weren't making a particular secret of it.'

'Do you know where she went?'

'I haven't the faintest idea. I didn't give a damn, if you really must know, as long as she got away from me.' Remembered bitterness thickened the edges of Brigid's words.

'Something else,' Cassie said. 'Erroll Summers, the man you said was your husband, I spoke to him on the phone and he flatly denies being Jeremy Fraser.'

'Well, he would, wouldn't he?'

'He also said that he had never been to England in his life.'

'Again, if he's Jeremy, what else would he say?'

'His wife agrees, says he's never been out of Australia, that everybody knows that, including his family.'

'Oh.' Brigid breathed impatiently into the phone. 'Well, perhaps I was mistaken. All I can say is, he looks bloody like Jeremy.'

'As Jeremy was, perhaps, rather than as he is.' Cassie reminded herself that Tony Spezzioli had also identified him, though more tentatively than Brigid Fraser.

'Perhaps that's it,' Brigid said. 'After all, it's twenty years since I last saw the bastard.'

'Another dead end, then.'

'Looks like it. I'm really sorry if I've wasted your time.'

'That's OK.'

Cassie pressed the connection button and when the dialling tone returned, called the number Sergeant Jimmy Bright had given her. When he answered, she said: 'The lad who was with Jeremy Fraser that night—'

'Hang on,' he said. 'I don't think it's been established beyond all reasonable doubt that it *was* Fraser.'

'After talking to Tino Spezzioli, it has, as far as I'm concerned.'

'What about the lad, then?'

'It might have been a girl, called Elizabeth Taylor.'

'Elizabeth Taylor? Where've I heard that name?'

'I'm not talking about the one who married Richard Burton.'

'Neither am I.'

'This one worked for the Frasers and had an affair with Jeremy before his wife found out and sacked her.'

But Jimmy was not paying attention. 'Yes, I definitely remember the name – wasn't there a bit of a hue and cry, years ago?'

'I don't recall.'

'I'll check it and get back to you.'

'It probably won't make any difference. But I was thinking that if we could get hold of a photograph, maybe someone could identify her – Tony Spezzioli, or Jason Meacher or someone like that.'

'Leave it with me,' Sergeant Bright said. 'By the way, have you heard that they've got the bugger who did in Old Ruby?'

'No!'

'Layabout by the name of Alan Clark. He was caught trying to cash Ruby's pension, said it was for his bedridden mother. As if they wouldn't have recognised the name at Ruby's local post office. He admitted the whole thing when he was collared. Didn't seem to give a flying fu ... a damn about it, when we charged him. Makes you wonder what we're all coming to, doesn't it?'

'I've been wondering for years.' Cassie felt a weight lift from her. 'So Ruby's murder had nothing to do with my enquiries at the Boilermakers?'

'Nothing at all, sweetheart. That's one bit of the load you can let drop.'

'Load?' How could Jimmy Bright possibly know about the burden of unspecific guilt which sat between her shoulder blades, sometimes lighter, sometimes heavier, but always there?

'That's what I said.'

She smiled, knowing he would hear it in her voice. 'Thanks, Jimmy.'

'That's all right, Cassandra.'

Something woke her. What? She lay listening, hearing nothing at first but the murmur of the sleeping house. Plaster shifted softly between the old struts, mice rustled past wattle and daub, thatch settled. But then, above

these and the noises of the night outside, she heard
something else. Steps below, outside the deep-set windows of the sitting-room. A shuffle at the kitchen door.
The passing of someone who did not wish to be noted.

She got out of bed with infinite care and crept towards
the top of the boxed-in stairs. At the turn, a step creaked,
but there was nothing she could do about that; the risers
were too steep for her to take two at a time without the
serious risk of breaking her neck. Carefully, she pushed
open the door into the sitting – room. Did she imagine it,
or had a shadow passed the window? Furniture made
unfamiliar by darkness tried to snare her as she moved
across the room and peered outside, keeping out of sight
as far as she could. She could see the outbuildings, the
concrete mixer, grass spreading away towards the hedge
behind which lay her vegetable garden and the pond. To
one side, the apple tree leaned, each separate fruit
layered with dust from the conversion work. There was
nothing else to be seen, nothing that should not be there.

A dog. She needed a dog, a Rottweiler, for preference,
bred to kill and trained to like it. An animal which would
leap into the hostile night and rip the throat out of any
intruder. Failing that, what other weapon did she have?
In the kitchen, she inched her hand along the dresser and
found the pepper grinder and, next to it, the cut-glass salt
cellar. She picked it up. If necessary, she could fling the
contents into the intruder's eyes. Pepper would have been
better, but whoever was outside was hardly likely to stand
still while she tried to immobilise him with freshly ground
peppercorns. And without putting on the light, she
wouldn't be able to distinguish the ground pepper carton
in the wall cupboard from the *fines herbes de Provence*.
Somehow, she did not feel that a pinch of rosemary and
thyme was going to stop whoever was outside.

Again, something moved beyond the window. A human shape loomed close against the glass, peering in. She crowded back against the dresser, her heart thudding so loudly that she was not at first sure she had really heard the telephone when, almost beside her hand, it began to ring. The shape vanished as she snatched it up. A familiar voice spoke softly in her ear. 'Hello, Cassie, how's it going? Cold, are you? Boyfriend on duty tonight, is he? Want someone to come round and warm you up, do you, because I'm hot for it, Cass, hot for you, can't wait to get inside your knickers and give you a really good—' She heard the obscene suggestions roll one after the other from Steve's tongue – was he on cannabis, or something stronger? – and felt nothing but relief. If he was making dirty phone calls to her, then he could not be prowling around outside the cottage.

In that case, who was?

The knowledge that it was not Steve, armed with his Stanley knife, gave her the impetus she needed. For one mad second, she actually considered asking him to contact the police on her behalf, then common sense took over and she cut the connection. Out in the garden, insubstantial shadows glimmered in the pale darkness of a summer night; she knew it was too late, that the prowler had gone, but none the less dialled 999. The police operator who answered her call was reassuring. He told her to hang up, that there was a patrol car nearby, not to go outside but to lock herself into the most secure room and stay there until help arrived.

Which it did, sirening up the lane with lights flashing, ten minutes later. Six thousand seconds, during which Cassie died a million times. She had been mad to accept her godfather's suggestion that she move in here, a woman on her own, miles from anywhere, a prey to whichever passing maniac took a sudden fancy to a little light rape and murder. The insecurity was too high a price to pay even for escaping from the twins. But if she hadn't taken up Robin's offer, she'd probably have killed herself by now, goaded to death by *nouvelle cuisine* and homunculae in size three shoes.

As she suspected, the police found no one. No cars had been sighted leaving Back Lane, there were no identifiable tyre tracks, no lipsticked cigarette ends or incriminating buttons had been dropped outside the gate. 'Whoever was out there,' one of the young police constables said, trying to sound as though he firmly believed someone had been, 'it's a pity they didn't leave any evidence for us to find.'

'I'm sorry to call you over here again.' Cassie. said, 'but someone was definitely out there.' As she thought about it, the vague shadow she had seen through the windows took firmer shape. 'And it's the second time this week.'

From his expression, she knew he saw her as a premenopausal old bat who lived in the delightfully fearful expectation of wicked men hiding behind every bush. 'Then they must have come across the fields at the back and through the wicket gate at the end of your property.'

'I've lived here for more than five years,' said Cassie. 'And I've never called you out before the other day. It's not just me imagining things. I definitely saw someone.' The shape grew in her mind, clothes attached to it: jeans, weren't they? A hooded anorak thing. A woolly cap. Anonymous clothes, intended to maintain anonymity. She dismissed the hideously rolling eyes, the vampire teeth, the hole where the nose should have been as no more than the product of a terrified imagination.

* * *

She slept badly after that. Despite the heat, she had shut and locked the windows and slid the newly installed bolt across the bedroom door, so that the room was stifling. Who was out there and what did they want? And how would she cope if – when – they came back? Next time, she would he more prepared – but how? She needed a weapon, but what? There was a knobkerrie downstairs by the front door, which used to belong to Robin's old nanny. It was better than nothing but not as good as, for instance, a gun. Once, somewhere, she had held a gun: she could still remember the heavy wickedness of it in her hand, the smell it gave off of oil and steel and deadly destruction. A gun was meant to kill; if she had one, she doubted, were the moment ever to arrive, whether she would even be able to point it at someone, let alone pull the trigger, knowing what the result might be.

18

There was a woman striding up the path. A formidable woman of a certain age, the sort who fills her days by chairing committees and organising jumble sales, who heads up local council planning authorities and, when really incensed, padlocks herself to trees to save them from the chainsaws of developers.

Was she looking for bridge lessons? Did she want Cassie to sign a petition about aircraft noise? Was she the new PPC for the Liberal Democrats?

'Nancy Sutton,' she announced, when Cassie opened the door. 'By the way, did you know your thatch needs doing? Leave it much longer and it'll be useless by the time winter comes.'

'I've had my name down with the thatcher for months,' said Cassie. 'There only seems to be one in the whole of the south of England and he's booked up until 1996. I don't know where I figure on the list but I must be coming up near the top.'

'It's the same in East Anglia,' the woman said, following Cassie into the sitting-room. 'Incidentally, you should never invite strangers into your home without asking for some form of identification.'

'But I know who you are. I recognised the name.'

'How do you know I'm who I say I am?'

Cassie turned and faced her. 'Mrs Sutton,' she

said firmly. 'Are you or are you not Jeremy Fraser's sister?'

'Of course I am.'

'But can you prove it?'

'Actually, no. So I can see my proposition falls flat on its nose,' Nancy Sutton said cheerfully. She poked a finger into the soil of the Goose Foot plant on the window seat. 'You've really let this poor plant dry out, haven't you?'

'You obviously got the message I left at your home.'

'My neighbour passed it on. I was holidaying down near Taunton with some old chums – best friends at school, still are after all this time – but things broke up earlier than planned because Monica got one of those tummy bugs and decided to go home. It wasn't the same without her. So I thought I might as well drop in on my way back, since you'd told Mrs Hegarty – that's my neighbour – that it was in connection with my brother.' The impression Mrs Sutton gave of a woman who would have had no trouble beating off hostile natives and slavering tigers with nothing more than an umbrella suddenly vanished. 'Do you really know where he is?'

'Well, as a matter of fact – I was ringing you in the hope that you did,' Cassie said.

Nancy's shoulders slumped. 'I thought it was too good to be true.'

'Aren't you in touch with him?'

'Not for the past twenty years. What one never realises is that as one gets older one so desperately wants to set things right. I can't say I had much time for him when we were younger: quite frankly, he could he a bit of a swine.'

'That's what his wife said.'

'As it happens, it was over his wife that we quarrelled. But I'd so much like to set things straight between us, before it's too late. So when I got your message...'

'I'm sorry if I gave the wrong impression. It was his former wife who gave me your name and phone number.'

'I haven't seen Biddy for years.' Nancy Sutton pulled a book off the shelves, peered at it, blew along its top edge and replaced it. 'You can damage your books, you know, if you don't dust them regularly.'

'These old houses,' Cassie said. 'It's impossible to keep them clean.'

'Which is why I opted for modern when the old boy – my husband, I mean – finally turned up his toes. Sold off the idyllic farmhouse with its beams and inglenooks and bought something on an estate. No upkeep to speak of, right-angled corners, none of these crevices and hidy-holes full of spiders. I hate spiders. There's a big cobweb in the angle of the ceiling up there – don't know if you'd noticed.'

'Do you have any idea where your brother might be?' Cassie asked, realising that the only way to cope with Nancy was to ignore her.

'None at all. Last I heard, he was in Australia. Could be dead, for all I know, but I hope not.'

'You said you quarrelled over Mrs Fraser. How, exactly?'

'I told him it would be a disaster if he married her, that she was too wild to make him, or anyone else, a good wife. He told me to mind my own bloody business.'

'Wild?'

'Too much imagination. And, frankly, a little too inclined to exaggeration.'

'A liar, in other words.'

'Yes. And I was right. She brought out the worst in

Jerry, you see. Egged him on to do things he would never otherwise have done. They got up to some really terrible things when they were engaged.'

'She told me he beat her up.'

'I'd have done the same,' Mrs Sutton said in emphatic tones. 'Knocked some sense into her. It's what she needed.' She uttered a derisive bray of laughter. 'Beat her up, my foot. He might have put her over his knee occasionally, but nothing more than that. He doted on her, actually.'

'Before they were married, you mean?'

'I didn't see much of them afterwards. Jerry wouldn't allow us to visit – probably on her instructions. I always thought she must have done something really drastic to make him leave her. Mind you, she's quietened down a lot, I understand. Runs that establishment of hers very efficiently, makes a decent living.' She sighed. 'Pity there weren't any children.'

Cassie found the picture she'd cut from the colour supplement and showed Mrs Sutton the photo of Erroll Summers. 'Mrs Fraser thought this was him.'

Nancy took one vigorous look. 'It's nothing like him,' she declared. 'Same colouring, and the way he stands is rather like Jeremy used to look sometimes. But you couldn't possibly mistake this man for my brother.'

'Even after twenty years?'

'Absolutely not.'

'I showed it to someone else who also thought it could be him.'

'It's nothing more than the most superficial likeness.'

'Why would his former wife make such a mistake?'

'I can't imagine. Unless she's spent so long trying to forget him that she doesn't even remember what he looked like.'

'And you have no idea at all where he might have gone?'

'None, I'm afraid.' Mrs Sutton shook her head. 'Oh dear. What a disappointment. I really hoped that you knew something.'

'Perhaps he's feeling the same way as you do,' Cassie said. 'That old quarrels ought to be made up, that it would be nice to get in touch with his family again after all this time.'

'I'd like to think you were right. I really would.'

On the way out, Mrs Sutton tapped the oak panelling which lined one wall of the sitting-room. 'I should have that checked, my dear. You can't be too careful, with death-watch beetle on the increase, so I read recently, not to mention woodworm.'

'I will,' lied Cassie. If the place had stood solidly for four hundred years, a little woodworm wasn't going to bring it crashing to the ground. As Mrs Sutton's car drove efficiently sway, she wondered if she herself would be spending holidays with her best chums from school when she was the same age as Nancy Sutton. Not that she'd made any. Or, worse still, that she would be so much in need of companionship that she was reduced to staying with Primula and Derek rather than face another day alone. The prospect was horrific but counterbalanced by the realisation that she could never, *ever*, be that desperate. She often had to point out to herself that one of the many compensations for living alone was that there was no partner who would one day die, leaving all the rest of a life to be filled with worthy works.

Runald Gardens, SW7, was a rectangle of iron-fenced green, round which rose, on three sides, solid blocks of apartments fashioned from liver-coloured brick. Jessica Tennant's building was not hard to find; Cassie just followed the gawkers. Getting inside was more difficult, but she represented herself over the intercom as a local friend of Sammi Ray's, perhaps implying that she knew him better than was in fact the case.

Mourning may have become Electra but it certainly didn't suit Jessica Tennant. Last time Cassie had seen her, she had seemed younger than her age: grief had aged her by ten years. Yet Cassie envied her now as she had envied her before, despite the deep shadows beneath her eyes, the expensively-cut dark hair which looked as though it had not been brushed for days, a disorder about the dress which was far from sweet. Beneath the dishevelment, Ms Tennant was a beautiful woman, not much older than Cassie and infinitely more elegant, though elegance was not a quality Cassie had ever aspired to, nor, indeed, believed herself capable of. She followed Sammi Ray's mistress into a high-ceilinged drawing-room and refused coffee. Floor-to-ceiling windows over-looked a communal garden to the rear; a plane tree growing immediately outside flooded the room with a light as delicately green as a lettuce leaf.

'What do you want to tell me?' Jessica Tennant said. Her voice was slightly husky. She raised her hand to brush hair back from her forehead.

'Not tell so much, as ask.'

'Do you have any kind of official capacity?'

'None at all, I'm afraid. But I did meet the Rays on various occasions and there seemed to be something very odd between them. It' not the kind of thing you can tell the police, because it's so vague, but I wondered if you could add any information. Because I can't help feeling that whatever happened to Dr Ray – and I'm so very sorry, Mrs Tennant – must be connected in some way with his personal life.'

'They weren't exactly a put-together couple, were they?'

'It was something more than that. A kind of jarring space between the two of them. I found it very disturbing.'

'So did Sammi.' Ms Tennant looked out at the plane tree for a moment, then walked over to one of the sofas which stood here and there in the big room and sat down. She said: 'The police seem to think that he was the victim of a mugging that went wrong.'

Cassie took an armchair opposite her. 'Do you?'

'Frankly, no.' Animation glowed briefly in Jessica's face, as she leaned towards Cassie to emphasise her point. 'I told them it was virtually impossible, in an area like this, that anyone would even try to murder someone outside in the street. Let alone that they'd get away with it. There are far too many people around. Have you ever been around Gloucester Road at eleven o'clock at night. It's like Oxford Street during the sales.' Jessica grimaced, reached for a rectangular crystal box on the coffee table and took out a cigarette. 'Sammi hated me to smoke,' she said. 'He didn't himself and he hated being round anyone who did, so I stopped. But it's been a life-saver since he died.' Lighting it, she took a couple of deep drags and blew smoke up at the ceiling, showing the long lines of her throat.

'Why do you think he rang his wife to say he couldn't come home that night?'

'I don't know. He'd already told me he was going down to Larton. I can't see why he would have changed his mind, unless he simply didn't get away early enough to make it worthwhile going home. But then he'd have come here. Or at least rung me.'

'So what do you think happened?'

'I think he was killed somewhere else and his car was driven here. Not to try and incriminate me, but to show me. Just to show me.'

'Show you what?'

But Ms Tennant was suddenly weeping, bending, hair falling across the hands in which she had buried her face. 'Oh God,' she said. 'Oh, Sammi.' Her body shook with distress.

Cassie got up and sat down on the sofa beside her. She took the cigarette away before it set Jessica's hair on fire and put an arm round the woman's shoulders. The delicate shape of her spine curved like a bow under her grubby shirt.

After a while, when the wild tears had subsided a little, she asked again: 'Show you what?'

'That – that Sammi didn't b-belong to me. That I'd never h-have him. That even though we loved each other, w-we couldn't ever be together.'

Cassie thought about this. Then she said: 'You're specifically accusing someone, are you?'

'Of course.'

'In other words, Dr Vida Ray.'

'*What*?' Jessica Tennant's look made it clear that she thought Cassie had gone mad. She reached for the cigarette which had been stubbed out in a heavy glass ashtray and relit it, shaking hair away from her face, smearing her wet cheeks with the back of her hand. 'Vida? For God's sake. Listen, it suits Vida down to the ground to have something to hang over Sammi's head. She can play the injured wife to her heart's content, make him suffer, make him feel guilt. The last thing she'd want

is him dead. In fact, if anyone was going to kill someone,
it would make more sense for Sammi to have murdered
her.'

'If she didn't do it, who did?'

'Rashid, of course. That conceited sleazy no-talent
little mother's boy. That ... *jerk*.'

'I can see you really like him.'

'Like him? Jeee-sus.' Ms Tennant shook her head and
stared towards the windows, slow tears forming in her
eyes again and running heavily down her face.

'Did you tell the police this?' Cassie was confused.
Last time – the only other time – she had seen Jessica
Tennant had been in Blackwell's book shop, in Oxford.
She and Rashid had seemed to be getting along fine
then. Yet, if she replayed the scene, she had to admit
that it was the young man who had done the hugging,
Jessica who had seemed not to care for it over-much.
Perhaps she had simply misread the entire encounter.

'Of course not. I may not like the little prick. but I'm
not going, to shop him without proof, am I?'

'It might help their enquiries if they considered him as a
suspect.'

'I'm sure they will. Do.'

'Even though he was down at his parents' house,
spending the night with his mother?'

'Easy enough to slip out when she's asleep – and there's
a witch, if you've ever seen one – drive up here and ... do
wh-whatever he did to Sammi.' Jessica's lips began to
tremble and she pulled hard on her cigarette, at the same
time reaching for another which she lit from the one
already in her mouth.

'What would be his motive?'

'Dislike of his father. Wounded ego because I wouldn't
sleep with him. Desire to show what a man he is.

Or a combination of all three. Who really knows?'

Cassie said: 'I have in fact seen you once before.'

'After all the newspaper photographs, I feel as if the whole world's seen me,' Jessica remarked bitterly. 'It's as if I've become public property, to be pointed at and picked on by anyone who wants.'

'I saw you in Blackwell's, in Oxford, not very long ago. And you were with Rashid Ray. In fact, you seemed quite friendly.'

'Blackwell's? Oh, you mean that big bookshop?'

'Yes.'

Jessica Tennant sighed heavily. 'He'd been nagging and pushing and begging me to help him. Perhaps I ought to explain I'm one of the directors of a small television production company. Rashid was convinced that the only reason I wouldn't get him the starring role in some gigantic mega-production to be put out by the BBC in ninety-seven parts, was sheer bloody-mindedness. That, and the fact that I'm – I was – his father's lover, and his father, so he believes, hates him.'

'So what were you doing together in Oxford?'

'I was up there talking to one of the college bursars about using a college garden as a location for a project my company's involved in. And I agreed to meet Rashid for a drink. That's all. That is absolutely all. I had nothing to offer him – and if I had, I wouldn't. This is a guy who couldn't act his way out of a paper bag, believe me, despite what his mother chooses to think.'

'And there's nothing else between you?'

'Jee-sus. I'd have to be pretty desperate to want Rashid Ray. Those cheap looks. That dreadful cologne he wears. Sammi was a hundred times better looking than Rashid could ever be. But he kept coming on to me, despite my giving him an absolutely unequivocal no, despite my making it clear that I not only disliked the little turd but I despised him too.'

Was this what had triggered Sammi Ray's murder, assuming that Jessica Tennant's theory was correct, and Rashid Ray was responsible for it? And was she was going to have to wonder for the rest of her life whether, if she had given Rashid the job he wanted, if she had not made her contempt so clear, if she had responded to his overtures, Sammi might not have died?

'You sent Dr Vida Ray a funeral wreath,' Cassie said.

'Don't remind me. I'm really ashamed of that.'

'There must have been a reason.'

'Listen, if you'll had to put with the phone ringing constantly, night and day ... and I had to pick it up because it might have been business. I shouted at her, told her to leave me alone. I can't tell you how unnerving it is when there's no response from the other end. I even threatened her. That's why I thought writing "Heed the warning" might have some effect. And it did.'

'She stopped the phone calls?'

'Looking back, it seems such a stupidly melodramatic thing to have done. But I was at the end of my tether. Falling apart.'

Driving home from the station, Cassie felt unaccountably depressed. Heat, dense as cheese, hung over Bellington as she came down the High Street and crossed the river towards the road out of town. Swans drifted among polystyrene cups and floating popsicle sticks, people sprawled under the trees along the bank, the generator of an icecream van spewed black fumes into the faces of the children queuing to buy cornets and iced lollies. The rain-starved grass was yellow; from the trees, leaves hung lankly, like unwashed hair. Out in the wider countryside, the fields of rich corn were sheened with poppies and rabbits skittered across pasture where cows endured. The sky was full of swallows hunting for insects.

Cassie made herself a Pimms and sat outside on the bench set against the whitewashed wall. Sweat lay along her arms. She got up and walked down the garden to look at the pond. Sombre among the reeds, the piece of slate which Charlie Quartermain had carved for her stood reflected in the water. She counted a dozen goldfish lurking under the waterlily pads. It was quiet tonight. She could not hear even the distant sound of traffic.

Only on the way back to the house did she realise what was different. The concrete mixer had gone. She pulled aside the heavy piece of plastic which hung over the entrance into the outbuildings and was amazed to see how completed they seemed. The windows were still unglazed, there was no door, the floor was patchily damp. But it was possible to see how it would look when everything was completed. And it looked good.

Rashid Ray. Getting ready for bed, she considered the idea. In bed, with the light out, she went over it again. The more she thought about it, the more she realised that Jessica Tennant's theory had to be the right one. How easy it would have been for the young man to wait until his mother was asleep, then drive fast along the motorway to London, locate his father and kill him, before driving Sammi's car to Runald Gardens and leaving it there. Easy enough to walk back to where he'd left his own car and be back in Larton Easewood, all within three or four hours, at the most. Perhaps he even set up an appointment with Sammi, excusing the lateness of the hour by saying it was the only time he was free, that he simply had to talk to his father, it was about a matter which couldn't wait.

Two things were absolutely clear in Cassie's mind. One was that she never wanted to have anything to do with DS Walsh ever again. The other was, that she would do anything to talk to him, now, tomorrow, as soon as possible. If she contacted him about this information, would he already have worked out the hypothetical scenario for himself? Would he think that she was simply trying to get back together with him? And if he did, what did that matter?

Trying to answer this question satisfactorily, she dozed off...

...only to be woken by the telephone. Nearly midnight. Too early for Steve. She snatched up the receiver, thinking – hoping – it might be Paul Walsh.

A voice said: 'Those socks haven't turned up, have they?'

Not Paul. ''Fraid not, Robin,' she said. 'try to imagine my despair.'

'This is something I could really do without. 'You can't imagine what it's been like here for the past couple of weeks.'

'All that sun, that cheap wine, the food, the swimming pool—'

'*Please*. Don't talk to me about swimming pools.'

'If I did, it would be a short conversation.'

'One of the problems has been that the man who's supposed to clean mine hasn't shown up for five days.'

'Oh my *Gaahd*,' shrilled Cassie. 'Not *leaves* floating in your pool. Not dead *flies* lying about on the surface with their legs in the air. How dis*gust*ing.'

'I'll ignore your sarcasm for the sheer delight of telling you more.'

'Do I need a doctor to hear this?'

'Madame Joubert, the cleaning woman, left one of the shutters unfastened and it's banged itself right off one hinge. I can't tell you the difficulty we have round here, finding someone to repair things like that. And then the other day I bought a plastic barrel of the local red, intending to bottle it, and there was a loose bung or something and the whole lot leaked away.'

'No!'

'*In* the back of the car, if you can imagine.'

'All too easily.'

'And then, to cap it all, two days ago I drove to the airport to meet Bob and Tich—'

'Bob and who?'

'Tich. You remember them: Bob teaches English up in Cumberland and Tich writes serious fiction.'

'You mean, novels which not even his mother will read?'

'I mean works of high literary merit.'

Cassie smiled to herself. 'Is Tich the name he writes under?'

'Cassandra, you must curb this urge towards frivolity. Can you imagine an author being taken seriously if he used the name Tich? Anyway, you know perfectly well what name he writes under. But that's not the point. The point is, I drove all the way to the airport in the sweltering heat and waited for four hours for the delayed flight from Gatwick, only to discover that they weren't in fact arriving until the following day.'

'Their mistake or yours?'

'And when I got back, it was to find I'd driven over my favourite panama hat which for some reason was lying in the courtyard, and absolutely ruined it.'

'How terrible for you.'

'Anyway, knowing you were bound to let me down,

I've done some hideously expensive telephoning and discovered that I can get new socks in Oxford. So all you have to do now is find my Leander blazer and take it to the cleaners before I arrive next week.'

'Next week?'

'I told you, ages ago, that we're going to Henley.'

'We?'

'You and I. Cassandra. Me in my freshly drycleaned blazer and new socks, you in a frock which covers your knees. A hat would be a bonus, but I don't insist on it.'

'Right. I'm looking forward to it.'

'Me too.'

'Robin.'

'What?'

'Do you know anything about my father's death? Anything I ought to be told about?'

There was a pause, which lengthened into a silence. Finally, Robin said carefully: 'What else do you want to know? You're already aware that he was stabbed in a street brawl outside his pub. Probably by one of his regulars, though they denied it.'

'Do you really believe that?'

'Is there any reason why I shouldn't?'

'Because I think someone deliberately killed him. It wasn't an accident. And I think I know who.'

'Oh, Cassie.'

'I simply need to prove it.'

Apparently going off at a tangent, Robin said: 'What I chiefly remember about Harry was that he was a man of integrity. Very left-wing, very anti-privilege. He hated injustice, he hated indifference, he hated people who ignored the suffering of others.'

'And?'

'I made it my business, for Sarah's sake, and for yours –

despite your disrespectful attitude, you're my god-
daughter, after all – to drop in on him every now and then.
The last time I went was only a couple of days before he
died. And I know he was very upset about something.'

'Any clues as to what it was?'

'He didn't say anything specific but I gathered that he'd
discovered some kind of scam, some kind of dishonesty
which he felt he ought to do something about. But it
wasn't that which bothered him, it was the fact that
whatever it was, he knew the people involved.'

It was Cassie's turn to say nothing while she mulled it
over. Then she said: 'Was it to do with horse racing?
Some kind of race-fixing?'

'I don't know.'

'But you think it might have been the people involved
in it who killed him?'

'I don't know, Cassie. As I said, I've always thought it
was an accident.'

'But he was definitely upset about something?'

'Yes. He spoke at some length about fraud, and
swindlers and how wrong it was to cheat people out of
their money when they had so little of it to start with.'

'I see.'

'The problem is. Cassie, that nobody really saw what
happened. Those louts hanging around, kicking the
policewoman, they didn't see anything – the police
established that quite clearly – and it wasn't any of them
who stabbed Harry, though I remember one of them was
supposed to have fled to Australia. But the police went
out there and never found any trace. There were some
other people around at the time, but their never came
forward to eliminate themselves from the police enquiry,
so we don't know what they saw, if anything. I'm afraid
I'm not being very helpful.'

'You've told me something I hadn't heard before, which is that something was bothering him.'

'No witness, that was the trouble. Or if there was, he or she has never come forward. In spite of all the people around at the time, nobody saw what really happened.'

Cassie remembered Jill Davis saying that the only person who really knew what had happened was Harry Swann himself. But that wasn't true. There was someone else. There was the person who killed him.

19

Another uneasy night. Around four o'clock, Cassie got up and went down to the kitchen for a glass of iced water from the fridge. How much longer would the heatwave persist? Opening the back door on its new chain, she breathed in the leaf-scented oppressive air. There had been no rain for weeks. She would have walked about the garden had it not been for the possibility of prowlers lurking. Plus the fact that the dry grass was still heavily impregnated with plaster dust which would track all over the house.

Back in bed, she read a couple of chapters of *Dead Bawd*, another of Tim Gardiner's works. It was not very gripping and after a while she began to nod off, but instead of sleep came images she did not want to see. She was aware that she only had to open her eyes to stop them, but her lids seemed welded shut and again she was forced to watch the young woman on the ground, booted feet lifting, a bicyclist riding past, his bell ringing. *Wake up. Wake up.* But she couldn't and now two people were walking along the pavement opposite her, a big man and a small one, the latter half-running in order to keep up with his companion. *Don't look, turn away.* Light spills from the doorway below, someone crosses the road, a shadow going in front, other shadows coming behind. Walking into danger. My comfort, my safety. *Please, no. Please stop*. Feelings, not thoughts. Light on the studs set into bootsoles, light making a halo of a beer can's end, light on the small man's throat and the knife in his hand as he lunges towards the shadow now stopped in the middle of the road ('What're *you* doing here?') and then blood on the roadway, blood black in the light from the street lamps, and a white face looking up at her, *no witness, that was the trouble*, two shadows slipping around the corner and away, people screaming, feet running, shouts, as all her safety, all her comfort dies beneath her gaze. And all the time, the drumbeat of her heart ... *wit*-ness, *wit*-ess ... the terror racing along her body.

Stop!

Cassie pushed back the bed covers and sat up. She was sweating heavily, perspiration shining at her wrists and beneath her breasts. The back of her neck was wet with it, and she lifted her hair away from her skin with a hand that trembled. God. What was her subconscious telling her? That she should not have probed into what was better left alone? Having so recklessly tried to disinter the past, were these dreams, vivid as memories, except that they had never happened, going to victimise her for the rest of her life?

Down in the kitchen, comforting herself with the routines of making tea, toasting bread, she found the details would not leave her, particularly the image of her father's white face lying, flat and pale as a winter moon, the gutter.

In an effort to clear her mind, she thought again about Jessica Tennant. Could Rashid Ray really have garrotted his own father? In the cold light of day, the motivation seemed a lot less secure than it had last night. But there might be another one, more primitive and much simpler.

Money.

Money: why you need it, hove you spend it, what you'll do to get it. The love of money is the root of all evil. How much more so is the lack of it? Lack of it impoverishes, not just in the physical sense but spiritually and intellectually as well. The person without it never stops thinking about it, concentrates on little else but an increase in the amount personally available. Because money empowers.

A quick trip to London. There was an exhibition at the Hayward she wanted to see but because of the heat, she decided to leave it for another day. Walking through Soho, she stopped in at a print shop and had a couple of copies of a photograph run off. It was early enough that when she arrived at Tino's restaurant, the waiters were still putting the little café tables out on the pavement, beneath the awning. When she asked for Tino himself, she was told he wouldn't be there before ten, so she waited at a place further down the road, drinking coffee and reading the paper, making a few pencilled alterations to the copied photos. Dust rose in little puffs along the gutter and skittered on down the street. There were window boxes hanging from some of the tall houses, trails of lobelia and ivy, pelargoniums bright in the hazed sunshine. Just after ten, she returned to the restaurant; Tino himself came forward at she walked into the cool interior.

'What?' he said. 'Thought you told me you wasn't going to bother me again.'

'I wasn't. But then I had an idea.'

'Hope it didn't hurt.'

'Now, now, Spetzy.' Cassie showed him a photograph. 'Take a look at this.'

He stared down at it. 'OK. So I took a look. Now what?'

'Does it seem in any way familiar? Do you recognise it?'

'No.'

'How about this, then?'

He studied the new photograph. Slowly, he said: 'I see what you're on about. But I couldn't be sure. Not in a court of law, I couldn't.'

'But between ourselves? Because that's all I need. No one's ever going to be had up, no one's going to pay for it. It's just for me. I need to know.' Suddenly, her eyes were wet. 'Mr Spezzioli, I simply have to know. You can understand, I'm sure, after what happened to your Aunt Ruby.'

He breathed in and out several times, shallowly, like a lizard, then reaches out a hand and clumsily touched her shoulder. She suspected that had one been part of his own more demonstrative culture, he would have put his arms around her until the tears had dried. 'Yeah, OK,' he said gruffly. 'I'll stick my neck out. I'd say you're right.'

From Bellington station, she rang Natasha. In the course of the conversation she learned that the Rays had gone to London that day to visit their solicitors. Right. Fate had taken a hand and Cassie was prepared to join the bidding. With any luck, she might even make a contract.

On her way to Larton Easewood, she again stopped at the police station. Pushing open the glass doors, she saw that the reception counter was manned by the same cop as before. 'Ah,' he said. 'Detective Sergeant Walsh's close friend.'

'That's right. Is he in?'

'I'll call him down.'

Buzzed through the inner doors, Cassie walked. Be cool, she warned herself. She took several connected breaths. Be calm. When Walsh appeared, before he could make any comment, she said: 'Have you any idea of the contents of Sammi Ray's will?'

'Of course.' He could see from her expression the pointlessness of moving closer to her.

'And?'

'Apart from a substantial legacy to Mrs Tennant, and small interim bequests to his children, it all – and there's a surprising amount of it goes to Vida.'

'Does she need it?'

'Not really. But why am I telling you this?'

'I'll respect your confidentiality. Do I take it that Vida's money is tied up in some way?'

'Trusts and investment funds, mostly. Not that she's short of a bob or two.'

'How about a quid or two?'

'What?' He frowned briefly. 'Oh. I see what you mean. A quid or two might be more difficult to come by.'

'But she's comfortably off, even without Sammi's money.'

'By my standards, most certainly. Why are you asking?'

She told him. She said: 'Thank's, Paul.' She turned to leave him.

'Cassie,' he said softly. When she didn't answer he went on: 'If I came back, would you have me?'

She stopped, stood still, conscious of air blowing past her, wondering if it was the sound of his heart swooping like a swallow to join hers. 'You haven't given it long enough.'

'Both Di and I know it isn't going to work. She's moving out, going to stay with her sister. At least we're friends, this time.'

'I'm not going through this again.'

'You won't have to, I promise.'

'Commitment?'

'Longterm.'

'Babies?'

'If you want them.'

'What if I don't?'

'We can talk about it.'

'Later,' said Cassie, and continued walking out of the station and got into her car. She sat for a moment in the overheated interiors windows rolled down and the fan on full. Babies. Had she really said that? *Babies*, for God's sake. Then she turned the key in the ignition and drove on.

At Larton Easewood, she did not stop at Natasha's house but continued on past it, to where the Old School House stood alone at the edge of the village. In the lane beyond, she pulled in close to the hedge. From here, it would be easy to start a car without anyone hearing, even in the quiet that falls over a rural community after ten o'clock. Even with the windows open on a summer's night. And anyone who did hear would find it difficult to pinpoint the exact direction the sound was coming from.

Drugged coffee would have been the easiest way, she decided. Then up the motorway to London, park the car somewhere convenient to the private hospital near Knightsbridge, waylay Sammi as he got into his car, preparatory to driving home, or even get in with him, kill him and drive his body to Runald Gardens. And home again to Larton, a good night's sleep and a simulated shock! horror! discomposure the next day. A cinch for an actor. Even a bad one.

She climbed the gate into the cricket field and walked along the hedge until she came to what she expected to find: a place where the bushes grew sparse and had clearly been recently pushed aside. She found herself at the back of the Ray house, behind the garage. She moved cautiously towards the porch. On the wing wall, someone had evidently been at work with paint remover because there was no sign of the most recent message from the anonymous letter writer. She rang the front-door bell, rung it again, waited. Although a car stood on the bricked forecourt nobody answered. She rang once more, waited. Nobody came.

Trying the garage up-and-over door, she found, as she had expected, that although it was pulled down, it was not locked. Tugging it up until there was a big enough gap, she ducked inside. It was a large garage, with space for at least two cars. There were patches of oil on the floor and a couple of bikes leaning against a wall. As she had thought, the place was used as a storage space and workshop. Shelves across one wall held a variety of odds and ends: bottles of methylated spirit, a power tool in a plastic case, jars of screws end nails, a tool-box, a spray can of paint, some paintbrushes, a plastic carton of putty. From the wall hung a saw, a garden broom, folding canvas chairs, a lightweight lawn-mower. Most of it had probably been left behind by the previous owner.

She picked up the spray can and shook it, listening to the beads rattle around inside. It seemed almost full.

Behind her, a voice said. 'What are you doing?'

She turned. Rashid Ray, pale and sick-looking, his crumpled shirt hanging lopsided over unbuttoned jeans, his feet bare and his hair sticking up in a bedroom rumple, was standing against the half-open garage door.

'I know how it all happened,' Cassie said.

'Oh God.' He closed eyes which were sunk in purple-brown sockets. He did not look in the least dangerous. 'What am I going to do?'

'You really don't have a choice, Rash.'

291

'The police, do you mean?'

'I'm afraid so.'

He groaned, his chest shaking under his shirt. 'Can you imagine how terrible this is?'

'I can come some of the way. My father was murdered, too.'

'It's not just that. And my sisters have no idea. What am I going to do?'

'I've already said.' Cassie found it hard to feel any sympathy. 'You can't keep it quiet.' Rashid Ray seemed the classic cliché: handsome but weak, the spoiled mother's darling, the pet of the family. Who could have guessed that Sammi Ray's failure to join the fan club would lead eventually to his death?

'I suppose not.'

'And in any case, if you don't go to the police voluntarily, I shall tell them myself.'

She moved towards him, meaning to duck beneath the angled door. He pressed himself up against the wall, as though unwilling to touch or be touched by her, and at that moment, outside in the forecourt, a car pulled in between the brick pillars and parked in front of the garage. She and Rashid listened as car doors slammed and one of the Ray girls said: 'I'll do it, Mammi.' Footsteps came towards the door. They could see a sharp shadow on the laid brick, then a pair of delicate feet, varnished toenails, strappy sandals. A tiny puff of breath as someone bent to the lower edge of the door, then it was heaved right up and slid with a grating noise into the mechanism attached to the garage ceiling.

Cassie had no idea whether the young woman facing them, her face changing from surprise to concern as she stepped to one side to allow access to the garage, was Rita or Dina or Shula. Nor did it matter. Her attention was

focused on the woman behind the wheel of the car who,
even as she watched, suddenly slipped it into gear and
drove it hard at Cassie.

In the back of the car, the mouths of Rashid's other
sisters hung open in their bespectacled faces. There war
scarcely time for them to register either shock or terror.
In the driver's seat, Vida Ray's expression was stony as
she deliberately tried to run Cassie down.

Rashid and his third sister screamed as Cassie plunged
to one side, falling heavily onto her hip, knocking Rashid
hard against the wall, catching the girl a blow across the
body. She had half expected this. That fact and the
inability of Vida to get up much speed in the space and
time available were the two things which saved her.

'Don't let her out of the car,' she snapped to Rashid.
And, as he hesitated: 'You've got no choice.'

'What is this all about?' his sister – Dina, Cassie
decided – said. 'What's going on?'

Rashid started to cry. He stood on the oily concrete and
wept, knuckling his eyes like a little boy. 'It was Mammi,'
he said.

Cassie flung herself against the driver' side of the car.
'Don't let her out,' she said again. The two daughters in
the back were scrambling about, reaching for the door
handles, trying to extricate their limbs from the hampering folds of their saris. One of them wound down the
window. 'Don't let your mother out,' Cassie said urgently,
but it was too late, for Vida had whipped her body across
the passenger seat and opened the door on the other side
of the car.

'Bad mistake, Vida,' Cassie said, hoping she sounded
in control. 'Trying to run me down in front of witnesses.
Tut tut.'

If only the retaining wall were not there, they might be

seen from the lane, the police could be summoned. As it was, they were all stuck here, the women in the back of the car, Rashid and Dina behind Cassie, Vida herself standing silently on the other side of the garage, holding the passenger door, glaring like a vulture. By now she must have realised the futility of what she had done, the pointlessness of taking off, trying to get away. There was nowhere she could go, no way to escape the consequences of her actions. On the other hand, the six of them might stay here for hours unless relief arrived.

Keep them talking, Cassie thought to herself, and maybe something will sort itself out.

'We should have thought more about why you didn't want to show your husband those anonymous letters,' she said.

There was a fluttering from the back of the car. 'Anonymous letters, Mammi?'

'We should have realised that we only had your word for any of it: the dog-turds, the petrol-soaked rag set on fire and pushed through the letter-box, the graffiti.'

'Turds?'

'Fire, Mammi?'

'In fact, I looked at the wall just now and there was absolutely no sign that anyone had ever sprayed anything on it.'

Vida continued to regard her, unblinking.

'Natasha and I believed you because we had absolutely no reason not to,' Carrie continued. She could not keep talking indefinitely. Someone was going let have to call in the cavalry. Rashid was the only one likely to do so but, like Dina, he seemed to be rooted to the garage floor. 'It was only when I started to wonder why Natasha herself had not been targeted by this supposed racial bigot that it occurred to me that perhaps he didn't exist.'

'Bigot?' said Dina, behind Cassie. 'Mammi, what does she mean?'

'Those scars across the wrist which we couldn't help seeing every time you clanked your bracelets around,' Cassie said. 'How genuine were those?'

'Say something, Mammi.'

'Scars?'

Behind Cassie, Rashid whimpered softly. 'Oh God,' he said.

'Did Rashid really tell you to burn those fake letters or did you decide to get rid of them before anyone gave them a closer inspection than Natasha and I?' asked Cassie.

'I never saw any letters,' moaned Rashid. 'I didn't even know about them.'

'Jessica Tennant told me that Sammi didn't smoke himself and hated to be around those who did, and I realised those burn marks on your hands had to be self-inflicted. Like the bruises round the neck, the black eyes and so on. Intended to make people feel sorry for you, intended to establish Sammi as the bad guy.'

'Oh, Mammi. Mammi.' The two daughters in the car were wailing now, like unhappy children.

'What the hell have you done this time?' Dina said. Her voice was very cold and clear.

'This time, she murdered your father.' Cassie said, willing to forgo the sympathy vote, wondering what other acts of violence Vida might have perpetrated. Judging by Dina's voice, the expression on the faces of her sisters Rashid's tears, they there upset but not surprised by what was being said. And if she was wrong about this one, Vida would surely say something. If she was not, it might stir someone into action.

'All those letters,' Cassie said. 'You wrote them yourself, didn't you? And when Jessica Tennant, goaded beyond endurance, sent you that wreath, you suddenly saw how to turn it to your advantage.'

Vida moved for the first time since she had got out of the car. Slowly, she shook her head.

'You told Rashid that his father wasn't coming down that night, after all, didn't you, although he'd never had any intention of coming in the first place, as you knew?' said Cassie, relentlessly.

'She put something in my coffee,' Rashid said. 'Something to make me sleep. But it tasted so horrible that I didn't drink it. I could tell she was up to something – in our family, we all know the signs – so I pretended to fall asleep. This was about eight o'clock. She went out of the front door and drove off in my new car, the one she'd just bought me.'

'She bought you a car?' Dina said. 'Where did she get the money?'

'I don't know. But she'd already told me to park it further up the lane, so that it wouldn't offend Daddy's eyes if he should see it. And when I got in the house, she told me he had rung to say he wouldn't be coming down that night.'

To Vida, Cassie said: 'So, with Rashid supposedly asleep, you drove up to London, lay in wait for Sammi – I imagine you'd arranged to meet him – and then killed him. Garrotted him.' She looked round at Vida's children and saw not just horror but resignation, as if they had been waiting for this moment all their lives.

'You finally fucking did it,' Dina said.

'I don't know if driving Sammi's car to Runald Gardens was in your original plan, but you probably thought it was an extra bit of trouble you could cause Jessica Tennant,' said Cassie.

'Rashid.' Dina said crisply. 'Go and call the police, and

then go and find someone who can help us. A strong man, preferably.' To her sisters, she said: 'Get out of the car and hold on to Mammi. This time, she's finally flipped.'

Her voice intimated many previous problems over the years; Cassie wondered what they might have been. The younger sisters looked frightened as they clambered out of the car and went to stand near, but not too near, their mother. As Rashid hesitated, Vida suddenly spoke.

'I did it for you,' she said. Today she wore a peacock-blue sari scattered with silver stars, with a silver border. A small blue star was stuck to her forehead, between her fine brows, and matched the silvery blue of her eyeshadow. 'For you, my son. While these ... girls...' the contempt in her voice made even Cassie flinch, '...had whatever they wanted from their father, you had nothing. Nothing. He always despised you, he always treated you wrongly.'

'Be quiet.' Dina commanded. 'What you say is lies.'

'I killed him because that way you should have some money, and I should have more. And with money, I could help your career,' Vida said.

'What career?' said Dina. She came forward so that she was standing beside Cassie. On the other side of the car, Rita and Shula blocked off Vida's escape route, were she minded to take it. 'You know, we know, even Rashid knows that he can't act to save his life. *Go*, Rash.'

'That is not true,' insisted Vida. Her head tremored slightly. Her eyes opened wider and wider. 'That is simply not true. He will be a big star one day, you will see.'

'As big a star as he was at tennis?' Dina said. Her tone was scornful; her accent markedly more American than it had been. She looked across the car roof at her sisters. 'Remember the tennis era, girls? When she moved down

297

to Florida with him? Remember that? Was it before or after she tried to turn him into Asia's answer to Jean-Claude Killy? When we all had to go to Aspen and watch poor Rash falling down in the snow?'

'He would have made a very fine skier,' Vida said, 'once he had conquered the problem of balance.'

'Balance?' cried Dina. 'That's what skiing's all about you stupid woman. Keeping your balance while hurtling down snowy hills at a hundred and fifty miles an hour. Rash isn't an athlete, any more than he's an actor.'

'What is he, then?' asked Cassie, drawn into this family inferno despite herself.

'A very ordinary guy,' said Dina, 'who's never been allowed to be just that. We, my sisters and I, were ... *girls*, so none of it mattered, we were allowed to grow the way we wanted. Make our own lives, develop our own potential. But poor Rashid, the *boy*, had all his mother's ambitions resting on what, I'm afraid, were his very inadequate shoulders.'

'And because my father,' one of the others – Shula? – said, 'would not give her money every time she decided on a new plan for Rashid, she hated him.'

'It was his fault,' Vida said. The tremor had worsened: her head had begun to shake violently from side to said. 'Sammi's fault. If he had not been such a miser, if he had paid for proper coaching, Rashid, my son, would have been able to do anything he wanted. But no. It was all lavished on you three: clothes and summer camps—'

'To get us away from you,' said Rita.

'—and piano lessens and college fees. Nothing was left for my son.'

'You're talking crap, Vida.' said Dina. Hatred was in her voice. The lines of her body were stiff with dislike. Her sisters' expressions mirrored hers. Loathing filled the garage like poison gas. Cassie did need to have much more of a rundown to understand some of the cross-currents which must have fissured the home life of the Ray family. No wonder Sammi had turned to Jessica Tennant. Was Vida clinically mad, she wondered? Her daughters had evidently seen her like this before since they gazed dispassionately at the twitching, shaking thing their mother had suddenly become.

'Poor Daddy,' Shula said.

'Poor Daddy,' echoed her sister.

'These notes,' Dina said to Cassie 'What were they?'

'Your parents were supposedly the victim of a poison-pen letter writer,' said Cassie. 'She took them to a friend of mine who lives in the village. I think she was trying to establish an ill-wisher so that when your father was killed, everyone would think this mythical person was responsible and start looking for him. Or her.'

Vida began to scream. Still holding onto the open car door, she pounded the roof of the vehicle while the screams mounted in intensity. Dina moved forward. 'The only thing to do when she gets hysterical like this is to knock her out,' she said briskly. 'I want you to know that as far as I'm concerned, this time it will be a real pleasure.' She went around the back of the car and swiftly punched her mother hard in the face. Vida staggered backwards, blood spurting from her nose and running down into her mouth. She did not let go of the car door. Dina hit her again. This time Vida sagged. A third punch, against the side of the jaw, and she fell to the floor, her sari catching on the frame of the door, a wisp of peacock-blue silk.

'Jesus,' whispered Cassie. The violence behind those three blows was startling.

'It may look brutal,' Dina said. 'But we've discovered that it's the only way to shut her up.'

'We did not wish to hate her,' Rita said to Cassie. 'We learned.'

'Daddy always said eve must be very kind to her.' said Shula.

'Daddy would have done better to have had her committed,' said Dina. 'Daddy was too soft for his own good. Daddy tried to sit on the fence. And now see what's happened.' She gazed down at her mother with an expression of loathing. 'Daddy is dead.'

What was going to happen to a young woman with such a talent for hatred, Cassie wondered? How could you function normally when your whole life had been abnormal?

'She did once slit her wrists,' Dina was saying. 'But only after making sure someone would be around to save her. I wish – we all wish – she'd succeeded. If I'd found her, I'd have left her to die.'

'Dina, Dina,' her sister murmured gently.

'It's true,' Dina said, her face beginning to break up into grief. 'You feel the same.'

'The self-abuse,' Shula said. 'It's part of the insanity. She must have started originally in a bid to make people sympathise with her for being married to my father.'

'We certainly did,' said Cassie.

'And then it became an end in itself.'

'But my father was a kind man.'

'A very kind man,' said Rita. She began to snuffle softly and Shula put an arm around her waist.

'Not a perfect one,' said Dina sharply, as Cassie thought about Jessica Tennant. 'But then who is perfect?'

'Who indeed?' said Cassie. Somewhere in the distance a police siren sounded. She wished she felt more triumphant.

20

She had arrived home last night, to find a message on her machine asking her to call Jimmy Bright, but she had not felt like talking to him or to anyone else. Vida Ray's mental deterioration had been an unedifying spectacle. A defiling one, too. Watching her collapse, Cassie was reminded of the way burning logs can retain their original shape long after they are reduced to ash; only when tapped with a poker do the seemingly solid structures show themselves to be as insubstantial as air. And looking at the faces of Vida's children, she felt strongly that in this particular dysfunctional family, the victims were those left to carry their burdens with them into the future, rather than this woman, or the man she had killed. Yet it should not be forgotten that Vida, too, was a victim.

Cassie dialled the number of the Highbury police station and asked for Jimmy Bright.

'That girl you were enquiring about,' he said, when she was put through. 'Elizabeth Taylor?'

'What about her?'

'I remembered where I heard the name. Looked back through the files and, like I thought, she went missing twenty odd years ago, and nobody's ever found her. Disappeared off the face of the earth. They found her Morris Minor abandoned at the edge of the cliffs near

Seton, not too far from her home, but if she chucked herself over, her body never showed up.'

'Another dead end, then.'

'Or possibly not.'

'How do you mean?'

'Doesn't it strike you as odd, all these disappearances connected to your father's death?'

'Unless they're as fake as Tony Spezzioli's was.'

'Not in Elizabeth Taylor's case. She came from a very close family in Devon, telephoned home twice a week, never missed. She was due to go on holiday with one of her brothers and his wife, a couple of weeks after she disappeared. Very excited, she was, first trip abroad.'

'Doesn't it seem likely that she and Jeremy Fraser went off together, just started a new life, leaving all the hassles behind?' Cassie remembered Erroll Summers's wife: he'd called her Lizzie, hadn't he? Though since he wasn't Jeremy Fraser, that fact became irrelevant.

'It might make sense for him. But not for her. Her family swore she wasn't the kind of girl who wouldn't keep in touch, who'd let them worry about her all this time.'

'Families always say that. It's so difficult to believe that your nearest and dearest are not what you think they are.'

'True.'

'Perhaps she found she was pregnant by Jeremy and killed herself out of shame. Having an illegitimate child was more of a stigma back then, wasn't it?'

'It's possible. We also checked out the known sexual offenders in the area, but they all came up clean. As for her car, nobody saw it arrive—'

'Which implies it was parked there late at night, doesn't it?'

'—nor was anyone unaccounted for seen in the area at the time. It looked like a straight vanishing act.'

'Or murder.'

'Right. Single women are so vulnerable. There's this builder chap at the moment, isn't there? Kitchen walls full of dead women. Same sort of area, too. It's the only explanation that makes any sense.'

'If she was the one with Fraser when he stabbed my dad—'

'I've told you before that you have no proof that he did. There weren't any witnesses.'

'Perhaps we'll find one.'

'After all this time?'

'But if she was the one with Fraser, perhaps he killed her, so that she wouldn't blow the whistle on him.'

'Oh yes?'

'I've been thinking about it,' Cassie said. 'If you planned it ahead, you'd kill the girl and dispose of the body somewhere. Then you'd drive your car somewhere near a station along the line to Devon, leave it there, maybe in the station car-park where it wouldn't be noticed, and then take a train back home. Then you'd drive the girl's car to Seton, abandon it on the cliffs and walk away. Maybe stop in a youth hostel or a pub, and the next day, take a train and get off near where you'd parked your own car, and drive home, nobody the wiser.'

'You've got it all worked out, haven't you?'

'I even know where you might try looking for her.'

'Where would that be?'

Cassie told him.

'Do you have any basis for saying that?' Bright asked.

'Only a gut-feeling.'

'Cassandra.'

'Yes, Jimmy?'

'I don't know what you're up to, but you be careful.'

'I will.'

Cassie went outside. On the bricked area which ran across the back of the cottage lay several sheets of newspaper, weighted down with stones. Lifting one, she peered underneath. A woodlouse scuttled across the white footprints which the newspaper was protecting. There were some below the kitchen window, more of them outside the sitting-room windows. Her night-time prowler had not been aware that the lawn was impregnated with plaster dust, or that he – or she – would leave this evidence behind. Until the previous morning, Cassie had not consciously registered the significance of the fact. The footprints might be useful as a means of identification, although without the corresponding footwear they proved nothing.

The phone rang inside the house. When she got back and lifted the receiver, she heard Charlie Quartermain's voice. ''Ello, darlin'.'

'Good morning, Charles.'

'Two things I wanted to say. First of all, the old geezer's none too well.'

'You refer to your father, do you?'

'Yeah.'

'I'm very sorry to hear that.'

'He'll pull round. Done it before, do it again. But looks like Sunday's off.'

'What a pity.'

'But I had another idea.'

'What's that?'

'I was looking through the racing pages today and saw that your favourite horse is running this afternoon.

Handsome Harry III. Wondered if you'd like me to pick you up, have lunch somewhere, make a day of it.'

Cassie thought quickly. Despite the drawbacks inherent in a day spent in Quartermain's company – the assumption of romantic significance, the risk of being seen with him by someone whose opinion she valued, the irritation that sooner or later he always set up in her – she was delighted at his suggestion. It provided cover for something she had already known she would have to do.

'Good idea, Charlie.' Her voice was genuinely pleased.

'So you'll come?'

'Yes.'

'Great.'

'Unless,' Cassie added tartly, 'you change your mind and decide to take the Fräulein with the tits.' She could have bitten her tongue out as soon as she said the words. What had possessed her to imply that she was in any way – which she absolutely was *not* – jealous?

'You talking about Heidi?' Charlie said.

'I do *not* believe she's called Heidi.'

'Something like that. Anyway, she's just a bit of fluff. Not like you, solid, know what I mean?'

'I do hope I don't, Charles.'

Handsome Harry III placed third in the fourth race but Cassie was more interested in the owners than in the runners. One owner in particular. Today, Brigid Fraser wore her spotted dress under a light navy jacket; watching her through Charlie Quartermain's binoculars, Cassie could see the good-luck charm round her throat.

Quartermain tugged at her skirt. 'Stand there much longer and I'll get out my chisel,' he said. 'You look like you've been turned to stone.'

'I've been watching Brigid Fraser,' said Cassie.

'Let's have a look.' He took the glasses away from Cassie and peered through them. 'Where is she?'

'Over there by that blue-and-white-striped tent. Just to the right of the entrance.'

'Oh yuss.' He focused the binoculars, breathing heavily. Today he looked somewhat smarter than usual, in a linen jacket and pressed slacks. For once, his shirt was not straining at its buttons. Under the brim of his panama, the big face seemed less obtrusive.

'Found her?'

'Yes. See, what did I say? She always wears that dress to race-meetings.'

'It didn't bring her much luck today, I'm afraid.'

'Third? It's not last, is it?'

'It's not first, either.'

'True.'

'She can't have changed much over the past twenty years,' Cassie said.

'How d'you mean?'

'If she can still get into that dress. Unless she's had it altered.'

'Shouldn't think she has. She's still petite – if you'll pardon my French. She always was a little thing. Used to make me laugh, seeing them together, the way she had to run to keep up with her hubby.'

'Did she?' Cassie sat down suddenly. . . . *He had to run to keep up with the other bloke*, Tony Spezzioli had told her. Was this how it had been for Paul on the road to Damascus, this feeling of having been slammed round the face with a sockful of scrap iron? Was this how Newton felt when the apple landed on his head?

Why hadn't she realised? Why hadn't she seen it all before? Why hadn't she realised that she *had* seen it all before. That there *had* been a witness to Harry Swann's murder?

It came back to her now, all the details she had blocked from her memory for more than twenty years because they were too terrible for her to hold onto. 'Charlie,' she said, and could hear the way the word fluttered from her like a dying moth.

'Yuss, darlin'.'

'I want to go over and talk to her. Will you come with me?' For once she did not feel inclined to tell him to stop calling her darling.

'Are you all right, Cass? You look a bit funny.'

'I feel a bit funny, now you mention it.'

The two of them walked together towards the tent. As they approached, the man who had been talking to Brigid Fraser walked bow-leggedly away and she looked round. Seeing Cassie, she frowned briefly before her face cleared. 'What're you doing here?'

Just what Harry Swann had said, surprised at seeing someone he knew in another context outside his pub.

Cassie indicated Charlie. 'Do you remember Mr Quartermain?'

'Of course.' Brigid smiled. 'The most Unforgettable Character I Ever Met.'

'Unlike your husband,' Cassie said.

'How do you mean?'

'According to your former sister-in-law, the man in that colour-supplement article doesn't resemble Jeremy Fraser in the least.'

Brigid Fraser frowned again. 'She's talking bollocks. There's a strong likeness. Though when I went and looked at it again, I could see that of course it wasn't Jerry. It was only in passing that I thought it was. Why are you making such a thing of it, anyway?'

'Elizabeth Taylor,' said Cassie.

'Whoorr!' said Charlie. 'Where?' He turned his head this way and that.

Brigid Fraser's eyes did not leave Cassie's. 'What about her?' She did not pretend not to know to whom Cassie referred.

'Any theories as to where she might have gone?'

'None at all. Why should I have? As far as I'm concerned, find Jeremy and you might find her. Otherwise, I haven't set eyes on her since the day she drove away in that funny little Morris Minor.'

'How did you get back to your place from the cliffs at Seton?' Cassie said.

'What?'

'You heard.'

'I don't know what you're talki—'

'You probably wore walking boots and a kagoule,' Cassie said. 'Just like all the other hikers. Nobody would have noticed you, despite the police enquiries.'

Brigid Fraser looked up at Quartermain. 'Is she all right?'

'Looks OK to me,' said Charlie, disingenuous as hell. 'And she's pretty clever. Got a college degree and all that.'

'As it happens,' Cassie said, 'I told the police this morning where I thought she might be buried. Along with your husband. I imagine a team of them are on their way to your cottage near Ross-on-Wye even as we speak.'

'What?' The word came out as a shriek of outrage. 'You *what*?'

'You see,' Cassie said, moving closer to Charlie, glad of his bulk beside her, 'I've never come across a compulsive liar before. Someone who lies about everything, automatically, even if there's no need to. I've met people who

lie for a purpose . . .' the image of Vida as she had last seen
her, flashed across her inner eye, '. . . but never someone
who makes up things for the sheer fun of watching other
people believe what are complete falsehoods. Someone
who gets a kick out of starting from some totally untrue
premise and then adding a sentence here, a word there, a
piece of description here, another embroidery there, each
one wilder than the last, and watching the structure grow
more and more fantastical until it finally collapses.'
Anger and grief were catching up with Cassie; she
stumbled over her words, feeling them emerge from her
mouth in spasms, not flowing freely.

'Is she drunk?' Brigid said coldly.

'Might be,' conceded Charlie. She felt his hand circle
her arm reassuringly and knew it was said to keep Brigid
Fraser off guard.

'Let me give you a for-instance,' Cassie said. 'The
Erroll Summers thing. You thought vaguely, as you red
it, that it reminded you of your husband as he once was,
nothing more than that. Then, when I came along, you
couldn't resist telling me about it, never dreaming that I'd
delve into it as deeply as I did, or that I might contact the
man mentioned in the article. It was all lies.' She reached
out a hand and was glad when Brigid's nostrils flared with
sudden fear. 'Like this,' she said, touching the charm
which lay against the other woman's neck.

'What about it?'

'I don't believe my father gave it to you at all.'

'Why wouldn't he?'

'Any more than I believe your husband beat you up.'
Again, the image of Vida Ray came into her mind. Men
had such a poor press, these days, it wasn't difficult to
convince people that there was abuse when in fact there
was none. 'His sister said you were the leader in that

partnership, and that he adored you, he would never have hit you.'

'Mr Quartermain, do you think she ought to go to the first aid tent?'

'Yer,' Charlie said. 'In a minute.'

'I think it was you who was responsible for the horse-doping or race-fixing or whatever exactly it was that you did. And when my father found out, he decided he couldn't go along with it. I think he told you he would go to the police. Maybe be even said he was ending your relationship – if, indeed, you ever had one, which I somehow doubt.'

'You're mad. You don't—'

'I think you then persuaded your husband to go along with you in eliminating him – after all, he was only a man who ran a pub, Not Your Sort, Dear, not One Of Us. And he had the impudence, as well, to threaten your precious stables ... Oh, I don't suppose,' Cassie said, beginning to shake with rage and grief, 'that Jeremy realised you intended to kill Harry. I'm sure you didn't sell the idea to him as murder or he would never have agreed. So once he'd set up the diversion, Tony Spezzioli and his mates, and Harry was dead, you killed him too.'

'You can't be serious.' Brigid was looking round, as though for help in dealing with the crazed lunatic who confronted her.

'I should imagine,' continued Cassie, 'that poor Elizabeth Taylor was just insurance, in case anyone remembered the big man and the lad who came with him. By disposing of them before anyone had identified them, by giving out the story that Jeremy had left you some weeks before, implying that the two of them had gone off together, you must have thought you were pretty safe. Until I came blundering along.'

If Cassie had had any doubts about her thesis before, they were completely dispelled by the anger and fear which flashed briefly across Brigid Fraser's face.

'Even supposing,' Brigid said contemptuously, 'that what you said were true – which it's not – how could you possibly prove such an extraordinary story?'

'I won't have to. Not if the police discover the bodies near your cottage. The one where you were supposed to have such wonderful weekends with my father.' Regret and sorrow diminished her. 'He was a *good* man, Mrs Fraser. He probably only wanted to help you, until he realised exactly what you were up to.' A sudden fragility flooded through her; what she wanted most of all was to crawl into bed and pull the covers over her head, blot out the world.

Charlie put an arm round her shoulders. His touch was reassuring. 'and in case it's of interest to you,' she continued, 'I've preserved the footprints of whoever it is who's been lurking around outside my cottage recently – I'm sure the police will find a match. I suppose you decided you'd have to get rid of me, too, before I discovered too much. How you must have regretted all those casual lies.'

'Footprints prove nothing.'

'Not on their own, they don't. But not only have I found someone who might identify you as being on the scene when my father was stabbed, I've also found a witness to the killing.'

'There weren't any,' said Brigid, adding hastily: 'at least, according to the papers.'

'There was one.'

'Where?'

'In the flat above the pub. She was eleven years old, a child called Cassandra Swann, who woke up one night and went into the front bedroom, her gran's bedroom, to see what all the noise was outside in the street. And saw a small man, no more than a lad, stick a knife into her adored father's heart. Except it wasn't a man, it was a woman wearing a charm on a silver chain around her neck, a chain which caught the light, a charm exactly like this one. In fact, I wouldn't be surprised if it *was* this one.'

She had expected Brigid to snarl and snap, to try to run, anything but what she did. Which was simply to close her eyes and say quietly: 'Even after all this time, I suppose I never really thought I'd get away with it.' She hesitated. 'I did love him,' she said. 'I really did. But he was going to go to the police and then I would have lost my horses. I couldn't let him do that. I just couldn't. I didn't really have any choice – I had to kill him.'

She turned and walked away from them. Quartermain made a move to follow her but Cassie stopped him. Another victim, she thought. Another of life's casualties. She supposed that when she had time and peace, she would more easily be able to come to terms with the demons which had for so long beset her, with the answers to what had been the central puzzle of her life. For the moment, she could only watch Brigid Fraser's retreating back and wonder at the fact that a demon should prove so ordinary, so banal. 'Let her go,' she said.

'But—'

'The police will pick her up.' She turned to Charlie. 'I'm tired,' she said, as though she were a child again. Unabashedly, she began to cry, arms by her sides, not impeding the tears which slid down her cheeks. There was grief in them, she knew, but at the same time, a feeling of tremendous relief, even elation, as though she had safely crossed to the other side of some raging torrent and could not continue her journey.

'Here, girl,' Charlie said. 'It'll be all right. I promise you.' He opened his arms wide and she moved into them to stand against his broad chest. It was as though she had gone back twenty years and Harry Swann, her father, was there; her father, her safety and her comfort, the big generous man she had loved so much and would never stop missing.

'Charlie,' she said, her voice muffled, and felt his big hand softly stroke her hair.